She remembers standing at her locker, hearing the whispers. Whispers about her. And about Luke. She remembers turning and seeing Dani and Lynn with a group of girls they knew from Yearbook. She remembers not understanding right away. And then Dani stared her down, eyes narrowed to slits. When Hallelujah dropped her gaze, she heard Lynn's peal of laughter. "So anyway," Lynn went on, "Luke said . . ."

By winter break, Dani was dating Luke. The rumors about Hallelujah had circulated and changed and circulated again. Still, on the first day of the new semester, she mustered up the courage to say something. Dani laughed in her face. Called her jealous. It was like they'd never been friends at all.

ALSO BY KATHRYN HOLMES

*How It Feels to Fly*

# the
# distance
# between
# lost and
# found

KATHRYN HOLMES

An Imprint of HarperCollinsPublishers

HarperTeen is an imprint of HarperCollins Publishers.

The Distance Between Lost and Found
Copyright © 2015 by Kathryn Holmes

Library of Congress Cataloging-in-Publication Data

Holmes, Kathryn, date
     The distance between lost and found / Kathryn Holmes. — 1st ed.
          pages     cm
     Summary: Sophomore Hallie Calhoun, her former friend Jonah, and new friend Rachel
leave a church youth group hike in the Great Smoky Mountains and become lost for five days,
struggling to survive as Hallie finally speaks about the incident that made her a social pariah and
Jonah admits why it hurt him so much.
     ISBN 978-0-06-231727-8
     [1. Survival—Fiction.   2. Lost children—Fiction.   3. Interpersonal relations—
Fiction.   4. Conduct of life—Fiction.   5. Faith—Fiction.   6. Great Smoky Mountains (N.C.
and Tenn.)—Fiction.]   I. Title.
PZ7.H7358Dis   2015                                          2014005863
[Fic]—dc23                                                        CIP
                                                                   AC

Typography by Carla Weise
16 17 18 19 20   PC/RRDH   10 9 8 7 6 5 4 3 2 1
❖
First paperback edition, 2016

For my parents, who never stopped believing

She's alone. More alone than she's ever been. It's just her and the trees closing in and the sun beating down. The branches block her path, holding her back. The birds are laughing at her. The ground drops out from under her with no warning, and she stumbles. There's no one to catch her. She falls hard. She lies still for a moment, gasping, feeling pain and fear and hunger and panic roll across her in waves. Then she uses the nearest tree to pull herself back to her feet. She has to keep moving. No one else can help her do this. It's all up to her.

Everything is different. The five days she's been out here are a lifetime. Before is a memory. Before that—barely a dream. Now, there's only ahead. One foot in front of the other. This trail will lead somewhere. It has to.

She used to think alone was the answer. Alone would stop the whispers and the taunts. Alone couldn't get her into any more trouble. Alone meant not getting hurt. Now, she'd give anything to see another human being. To hear someone call her name.

the
# first
day

# 1

THE LAUGHTER STARTS AS A LOW MURMUR. HALLELUJAH might not have even noticed it if it wasn't coming from a few seats down. From where he's sitting. But she hears the laughs, hears them spreading, and she knows. She's not surprised. She expects this. Still, she feels anxiety blossom.

She just wants to be invisible. He can't even let her have that.

And so she folds in on herself. She stares at the fire pit. She watches the embers glow and the sparks float up with the smoke through the opening in the gazebo ceiling. She inhales the burnt air.

She waits.

And then something hits the side of her head. It bounces off her shoulder and lands on the wooden bench next to her. She glances down. A tiny twig.

A few seconds pass, and then another twig hits her. This time, on her cheek. She ignores the muffled laughter.

Refuses to look over. Tries not to react. Because that's what Luke wants.

Directly across the fire pit, their youth group director, Rich, is oblivious. He's leading campfire songs, strumming an acoustic guitar, eyes closed.

The next twig bounces off the top of Hallelujah's head. The one after that gets stuck in her hair, right by her forehead. She thinks about which is worse: brushing it away or leaving it. Then she pulls the twig loose and drops it on the ground. Her cheeks burn.

She knows she shouldn't let Luke get to her. But flicking twigs at her is just the beginning. Luke's got the other kids' attention. Next: the rumors spread. The real mocking starts. It's a chain of events he's been repeating for almost six months, a chain she doesn't know how to break.

So she does the only thing she knows how to do: she sets her face to stone and keeps her eyes on the fire.

The group keeps singing. Campfire standards. A few hymns. They all blur together in her ears, just notes and notes and notes. Singing used to be her life. She would stand in the choir room at school, in the church auditorium during Sunday services, in her backyard, in her shower, and let her pure soprano sail up to the highest notes. Music used to burst from her. She couldn't contain it.

She doesn't sing anymore. She can barely stand to listen.

When she's pretty sure Luke is done launching twigs at her, she lifts her eyes and lets her gaze travel around the circle, wooden bench to wooden bench. There are kids from her church. Kids from other churches who she knows from past youth group events, or from school. Kids she's never met before. They're all clapping. Singing. Smiling. She doesn't join in. She can't.

She doesn't want to be here, anyway. She doesn't belong here.

She closes her eyes and sees herself the way she used to be. She sees herself a year ago, on a retreat just like this one, except on a college campus instead of in the Smoky Mountains. She sees herself sitting with a group of friends. Singing every song. Cracking jokes. And then she opens her eyes, and she's back in this new version of her life, where she's alone and silent, and where she is the joke.

Rich and his guitar are replaced by the director of Hiking with Him, a clean-cut thirtysomething in cargo shorts and Tevas named Jesse. Jesse starts talking about the week ahead: daily hikes, nightly campfire circles, life lessons to be learned.

Hallelujah tunes him out. She looks up at the wooden gazebo ceiling. Knotholes. Spiderwebs. Some kind of nest in one corner. She stares at it, at all of the individual bits of brush that make up the whole, an uneven, bristly mass wedged into the eave.

She feels uneven and bristly. All the time.

She thinks about being somewhere else, anywhere else. Anywhere Luke isn't. Anywhere she doesn't have to keep reliving what happened.

And then she hears Luke's voice. She can't tune him out,

no matter how much she wants to. His voice is in her head.

"Hallie! Hurry it up!" He whistles at her. Like she's a golden retriever.

She looks around. She's sitting alone. Everyone else has left. Left her sitting there. No one said her name, touched her shoulder to let her know. Or maybe someone did, and she didn't hear it, didn't feel it. Now it's only her and the dying fire.

Luke, Brad, and Jonah are standing outside the wooden gazebo. The three musketeers. When she turns her head their way, Luke says, "It's like there's no one in there, under all that hair." He adds, speaking slowly, "Curfew. Remember? You don't want to be late." He's so smug it hurts to look at him. Hallelujah can't believe she ever thought he was cute, with his stupid tan and his stupid shaggy brown hair and his stupid chocolate-brown eyes.

"Sorry," she mutters, getting to her feet. It's the only word she says. She follows the musketeers back to the lodge, a few steps behind. Always a few steps behind.

2

HALLELUJAH STARES AT HERSELF IN THE BATHROOM MIR-ror. Frizzy brown hair. Dark circles under her blue eyes. An angry zit on her chin. Absolutely nothing to "hallelujah" about.

She's steeling herself to go back down the hall to the girls' side of the dorm, telling herself that being ignored won't kill her, and neither will having a few more people laugh at her, no matter how much it hurts, when a voice startles her:

"So what was all that?"

Hallelujah spins around to see a girl coming out of a toilet stall. She doesn't know this girl, but she saw her at the campfire earlier.

"What was all what?" Hallelujah knows the answer. Of course she knows. Luke. What else could it be?

And sure enough, the girl says, "The twig thing. That looked kind of annoying."

*Annoying.* One way to put it. "It's fine. It's nothing."

The girl approaches the sink, turns the faucet, splashes her hands in the water. She doesn't use soap. She dries her hands on her jeans. "I'm Rachel."

Hallelujah doesn't answer right away. Why should she trust this girl? With anything? Even her name? But then she decides she's being paranoid. Clearly, Luke's grapevine hasn't reached Rachel yet. "I'm Hallelujah."

"Your name is Hallelujah? Seriously?"

"Seriously."

"Huh. Are you super-religious or something?"

"No. But my parents are. And they couldn't have kids for a long time, so when I showed up, they named me Hallelujah." She shuts her mouth abruptly. Too much information.

"So, Hallelujah—"

"Everyone calls me Hallie."

"Do they?" Rachel's eyes sparkle, even in the fluorescent bathroom light. She has an easy smile. For an instant, she reminds Hallelujah of Sarah—quick to laugh, to talk to someone new, to put herself out there. And the missing hits, sudden and deep. Hallelujah had a best friend, before Sarah moved to Georgia last summer and got new friends and a new life. Before Luke.

Rachel says, "I'm gonna call you Hal. If that's okay." The last sentence is an afterthought, like asking to come into a room when you're already inside.

Surprised, Hallelujah says, "Sure." She rolls the name around in her brain. Hal. *Hal.* It sounds kind of edgy, kind of cool.

Hallelujah is not cool. She was pretty popular at her private Christian middle school, but when she started public high school, that popularity faded, leaving her solidly middle-of-the-pack. A side effect of being the polite, rule-following girl everyone's parents loved. And of being blessed with the name Hallelujah.

Still, until everything happened with Luke in the fall, she had a social life. She had friends. Sarah, before she moved away, and Dani and Lynn, and Jonah, and her choir classmates. She was happy. That girl wouldn't recognize her now.

"So, Hal." Rachel links her arm through Hallelujah's. Another thing Sarah used to do. It makes Hallelujah want to squirm away and hold tighter, all at once. "I heard something about a party tonight? Behind the lodge, in the woods?

I heard that guy Luke's kind of the ringleader. You go to the same church, right? Where his dad's the preacher? If that twig thing really wasn't a big deal . . ." Rachel pauses, like she's giving Hallelujah a chance to take her earlier words back. Hallelujah stays quiet, so Rachel goes on, "Maybe you can show me where the party is? We can make a break for it after lights-out? I bet we could slip out this window and no one would even notice."

Hallelujah *did* hear Luke and Brad talking about sneaking out tonight. They were going over their plan in the backseat of the church van this afternoon. Right under Rich and the other chaperones' noses.

She knows where the party is. Or at least which way to head after getting past the parking lot.

But she can't sneak out. She can't—

"I'm not here with a group. I'm by myself," Rachel says. "I was really hoping to meet some cool people this week. Please?"

"I—I don't usually go to those things. Parties," Hallelujah croaks. Even as she says it, a scene flashes into her mind. Dani's family's lake house, back in September. Their whole extended friend group spread out on the back porch. Lynn's boyfriend playing the guitar while Hallelujah and Jonah and a few other kids took turns singing. Drinks appearing. One being pressed into Hallelujah's hand, a beer she didn't actually drink but that she felt cooler just holding. And at the end of the night, Luke convincing all the guys to jump in the lake, the girls cheering them on.

"C'mon." Rachel smiles winningly, making eye contact with Hallelujah in the mirror. "It'll be fun. You'll see."

It won't be. She knows it won't be.

But as she clings to Rachel's arm linked through hers, and as she remembers that warm night on Dani's back porch, Hallelujah is tempted. She should say no. For so many reasons. But she kind of wants to say yes.

Rachel is inviting her out. Hallelujah had almost given up on being invited anywhere ever again. And if Rachel came here alone, maybe she's lonely too. Maybe she needs a friend. Maybe they could be that for each other.

Maybe. If Hallelujah doesn't ruin it.

She smiles. It feels strange on her face. And she says, channeling Hal, feeling daring and even a little bit excited, "Okay."

# 3

THE PARKING AREA BEHIND THE MAIN LODGE IS DARK. They run from van to van, pausing to listen for signs of being followed, footsteps in the gravel. But there's nothing. Just the night sounds. Cicadas. An owl.

Beyond the church vans, it's about a ten-second sprint into the woods. They duck behind a massive tree.

"Where to?" Rachel whispers.

Hallelujah looks over her shoulder at the lodge. The

building is a hulking shadow. The two dorm wings that extend out from either side of the common area look like arms reaching toward her. Beckoning for her to come back where it's safe.

She takes a deep breath and ignores her gut. "That way." She points off on the diagonal, following the line of the boys' dorm. "I don't know exactly where."

"That's okay. They can't be far. We'll just look for a campfire, right?" Rachel starts walking into the woods.

"Right," Hallelujah echoes. She takes one last peek at the lodge, then follows Rachel.

For a few minutes, their only communication is the snapping of twigs beneath their feet: *I'm still ahead of you. I'm still behind you.* Hallelujah uses the glow from her phone to scan the area, looking for signs that someone came this way before they did. She wonders if she should do something to mark their path. Breadcrumbs. But Rachel is forging ahead. Rachel is confident. And so Hallelujah tamps down the urge to rip a strip from her shirt and tie it to a tree branch.

And then she hears voices. Not far. They made it.

As they draw nearer, Hallelujah finds herself slowing down. Through the trees, she can see a group of people sitting on logs in a circle around a campfire. She spots Luke immediately. He's facing away from her. His laughter echoes in the air.

She can still go back. It's not too late to turn back.

"Come on, Hal!" Rachel says. She walks out into the clearing.

Hallelujah ducks behind a tree. This was a bad idea. She shouldn't be here. And what if—what if Rachel knows? What if Rachel set her up? What if Luke did?

She sticks her head out, trying to see without being seen. Feeling ridiculous as she does it. And anxious. Ready to run away at a moment's notice. Ashamed by her fear.

Luke turns around. He looks Rachel up and down. "Who are you?"

"I'm Rachel Jackson. From Bristol." Rachel holds out a hand.

Smirking, Luke leaves her hanging. "And who said you could be here?"

Hallelujah can't see Rachel's face. She does see Rachel's extended hand fall to her side. For the first time since they met in the bathroom, Rachel doesn't look so sure of herself. She calls out, "Hal? A little help?"

"Someone else out there?" Luke squints in Hallelujah's direction. He stands. He steps over his log bench and pushes past Rachel. Hallelujah can't move, can't breathe, and in four more steps, Luke has her by the arm. He's marching her into the light.

When he sees who it is, he drops her arm quickly, looking disgusted. "Hallie. You've gotta be kidding me."

Behind him, Brad's on his feet. "Well, glory, Hallelujah!" he whoops. The girl next to him shushes him, and he lowers his voice. But he keeps talking, giving his words a preacher-at-a-revival ebb and flow. "I never thought, Hallelujah, I'd see the day, Hallelujah, where you'd have the guts to show up here, Hallelujah, praise Jesus—"

"Give it a rest," Luke says.

"What, it's only funny when you do it?"

"Nah, she's always funny," Luke says, looking back at Hallelujah, dismissing her with a roll of his eyes. "You just aren't. You never do that joke right." He walks back to his seat. He glances at Rachel. "Turns out, there's a seat for you right here, next to me." He pats the unclaimed bit of log to his right.

Rachel walks over and sits. "Thanks. It's Luke, right?"

"Luke Willis. This is Brad"—a nod of his head to the left—"and Jonah"—a nod to the right, to where Jonah is sitting off to one side, poking at the fire with a long stick.

Brad says, all smiles, "Hey." Jonah says nothing.

Hallelujah feels frozen on the edge of the circle, like there's some kind of force field keeping her back. She's not sure if they put it up, or if she did. And she doesn't know whether to stay or to go. Which option is more humiliating.

She stands there while Luke gives Rachel a beer, while he casually drapes his arm across her shoulders. She stands there while the rest of the group does introductions. Besides Luke, Jonah, and Brad, there are two guys and a girl from Chattanooga and three girls from Knoxville. Hallelujah met the Knoxville girls at last year's youth group retreat. They all have perky, cute names—Brittany and Madison and Kelsey—and the bouncy hair and stylish clothes to match. They're the kind of girls that always swarm around Luke, moths to a flame. Rachel fits right in: petite, blond, pretty, outgoing.

Still, they're looking at Rachel with expressions somewhere between curiosity and jealousy. Hallelujah bets it has something to do with Luke's hand sliding up and down Rachel's arm. With the way he checked her out before telling her to sit by him. Hallelujah has seen the Knoxville girls' expressions before. On other faces.

She watches Luke lean across Rachel, his arm still around her, to get a beer from a backpack near Rachel's feet. She watches him hand the beer to one of the Chattanooga guys and then set his free hand on Rachel's knee. She watches, and she remembers how amazing it felt when it was her, and suddenly she's a little sick.

She tells herself that warning Rachel about Luke is not her job. Rachel seems nice, but they just met. Rachel could turn on her. And whether she knew what she was doing or not, Rachel convinced her to come out tonight. Being here, feeling like this—it's partly Rachel's fault.

"Hal—come sit!" Rachel is looking back. She motions toward a sliver of space between Jonah and Madison. "There's room."

"No. There's not." Luke says it without even turning around. "How do you and Hallie know each other, anyway?"

"We met in the bathroom. Earlier tonight. She seems cool." Rachel smiles at Hallelujah. Hallelujah can't bring herself to smile back.

"Sure, if you like the strong, silent type. I don't. No

offense." Luke laughs, and Brad laughs, and the girls from Knoxville take that as their cue to laugh too. Like it was actually funny.

Rachel doesn't laugh. She's still smiling, but now it's like she's not sure whether she should be. "Come on, Hal," she says. "We'll make room."

But Luke's shaking his head. "Sorry. Guess I'm not being clear. There might be room for someone. But there's not room for Hallie. *Hal.* Whatever you wanna call her. Besides. She has to get back. Curfew."

Rachel looks from Luke to Hallelujah, confused. "We're all breaking curfew."

"Yeah, but it's Hallie's fault we have early curfew in the first place. And it's her fault we have so many chaperones to deal with." Luke's counting on his fingers, holding them in the air. "Plus, they'll probably be checking up on her. So she can't stay."

"How is all of that her fault?" Rachel asks. "What'd she do?"

"Yeah, Luke. What'd she do?" It's Jonah. Hallelujah is kind of shocked to hear his voice. It's low, with a dark undercurrent that's unfamiliar to her. Then again, it's been months since they talked. And a lot has changed. "If I remember it right," Jonah goes on, still staring into the fire, "she wasn't the only one."

Luke looks over at him. "What's that supposed to mean?"

"Nothing," Jonah says. "Just making an observation."

"An observation," Luke repeats.

"Yeah."

There's a moment of silence. It's uncomfortable. Hallelujah feels like the night sounds get louder to compensate. The wind rustling tree branches. The hum of cicadas. Birdcalls. They're suffocating her.

Then Luke shakes his head and laughs. "Whatever. Hallie still has to go." He swings around to look at her directly. "What are you waiting for?"

Hallelujah blinks, wishing that small movement could make her vanish. Everyone in the circle is staring. Waiting for her to leave. Their eyes cut into her. She takes two steps backward, tears clouding her vision.

*Don't cry. Don't cry.*

She turns and starts walking away. Walking, not running. She doesn't want to give Luke that satisfaction.

And then she sees a flash of light in the woods. She squints into the dark, rubbing her eyes. "Someone's coming," she calls back to the group. She's not sure why she warns them, other than to make it clear that she isn't responsible. She didn't rat them out. Or maybe she did, unintentionally. Maybe Luke's right—the adults were watching her. To see what she'd do.

Either way, no one answers. There are now two lights shining through the trees. Big beams. Serious flashlights. The kind chaperones might grab when they find empty beds in the lodge after curfew. Hallelujah hesitates. She takes a few steps back toward the clearing and says, louder, "Someone's coming."

Luke's on his feet in an instant. "Where?" He looks past Hallelujah, seeing the lights. He curses. "Everyone up! Let's go!" When people don't move immediately, he barks it again: "Up! Now!" Then he shrugs. "Your funeral." He turns and runs into the woods.

Chaos erupts. The girls are squealing, the boys shushing them. Beers are chugged, the cans thrown into the dirt. Then the group scatters. Rachel races past Hallelujah. There's a shout from the darkness ahead: "Hey! Stop!"

Hallelujah's legs won't run. Her lungs won't breathe. It's happening again. She's about to be caught in the act. And this time, there's no one to blame but herself. She's so stupid. She's—

"Hallie, come on!" Jonah is scooping up empty beer cans and shoving them into his bag. He grabs Hallelujah's arm, and the touch is like a jolt from a defibrillator. She can move again. She looks at him. They make eye contact for the first time in ages.

They run.

# 4

THE TREES JUMP OUT AT HER FROM ALL SIDES, APPEARing in an instant where before there was only darkness. She can't see her feet. She's running blind, hoping she won't trip, won't run into anything, is going the right direction.

She can hear Jonah behind her. He crashes through the leaves and brush like a bear. If anyone is chasing them, they'll have no trouble staying on their trail.

But for all she knows, she's that loud too. Her gasping breath and her feet hitting the ground and her pulse pounding.

He didn't leave her behind. He's with her now, even though he could probably run faster without her. He stays. She doesn't know why.

There's no time to think about it. She sees the lodge up ahead, blocked by fewer and fewer trees as they get closer.

They reach the parking lot and pause on the edge, looking. No chaperones. But they can hear shouts behind them.

"C'mon," Jonah whispers, touching her arm again. He leads her out onto the gravel. They weave from van to van, staying out of sight of the lodge windows. Facing the woods, they're completely exposed. The shouts are getting closer.

They reach the van parked closest to the boys' dorm wing. Jonah peers around the side. He mutters something.

Hallelujah inches closer to him. "What?" she whispers. Her lungs are gripped in a vise. Her heart is straining.

"Window's closed." He points to the one they must've used to sneak out earlier. "How did y'all get out?"

"Girls' bathroom." She looks, points. That window, at the end of the girls' wing, is still cracked open. A miracle. She can breathe again.

"Okay. Let's do it."

They run to crouch beneath the window. Jonah looks in

all directions, then slowly, silently slides the window up. He unfolds from his crouch and his upper half disappears into the bathroom. He pauses. Hallelujah can see his body tense. Fight or flight. His hands grip the sill. He lifts up onto the balls of his feet, and his calves tighten.

An excruciating few seconds pass before a whisper floats down: "All clear."

Jonah pulls himself inside in one smooth motion. Then he reaches out a hand.

Hallelujah takes it. She grasps his forearm and he grasps hers and she is pulled up to sit on the sill so much faster than she could have climbed. It takes her breath. She swings her legs inside and lands on her feet.

The dark bathroom is ghostly, filled with shadows. There's a little bit of mud on the floor that wasn't there earlier tonight; they aren't the first ones in this way. Through the window, they watch as a figure runs out of the woods into the parking lot. One of the flashlights is hot on his heels. Another figure appears at the opposite end of the lot, then turns and ducks back into the woods.

Jonah slides the window down until it's only cracked—helping the others while covering his own tracks. Then he opens the bathroom door and checks the hall.

"Looks safe," he says, "but move fast." He glances back over his shoulder at Hallelujah. He reaches out, pulls a twig from her hair, and hands it to her. Then he's out the door.

"Thanks," she says to his back. She wonders how long that twig was in her hair. If it's one Luke flicked at her earlier. If anyone was going to tell her.

She drops it into the trash can next to the sink.

She hovers in the doorway, psyching herself up. And then, heart pounding, she tiptoes down the dark hall to the large shared bedroom. Moonlight is streaming through the windows. It illuminates her single bed, her duffel bag tucked under the blanket. It catches the faces of the three Knoxville girls at the other end of the room. They all look her way, wide-eyed. When they see it's just her, they turn their backs, whispering.

Hallelujah is changing quickly, silently, into sweatpants and a T-shirt, when she sees that the girl in the next bed is staring at her. For a second, Hallelujah is sure she's going to call out. Bring the adults running. But she just rolls her eyes.

"Go to bed. Before you get us all in trouble," the girl mutters. She flops over onto her other side, turning her back to Hallelujah.

Shaking a little, Hallelujah slips under the covers. She feels her body settle into a groove in the mattress that hundreds have settled into before. There's a spring digging into one hip, and she shifts and turns, trying to get comfortable, until her adrenaline fades and she can sleep.

*She remembers standing at her locker, hearing the whispers. Whispers about her. And about Luke. She remembers turning and seeing Dani and Lynn with a group of girls they knew from Yearbook. She remembers not understanding right away. And then Dani stared her down, eyes narrowed to slits. When Hallelujah dropped her gaze, she heard Lynn's peal of laughter. "So anyway," Lynn went on, "Luke said . . ."*

*She remembers the note, in English class. "You knew I liked him." Dani's clean cursive. Hallelujah stared at her friend's back. Dani didn't turn around. And she didn't respond to calls or emails in the weeks that followed.*

*By winter break, Dani was dating Luke. The rumors about Hallelujah had circulated and changed and circulated again. Still, on the first day of the new semester, she mustered up the courage to say something. To warn her former friend about who Luke really was. Dani laughed in her face. Called her jealous. Luke dumped Dani in February. Dani and Lynn still refused to speak to Hallelujah. It was like they'd never been friends at all.*

the
second
day

# 1

THE LIGHT FLIPPING ON IS BRIGHT AND SUDDEN AND painful.

Hallelujah groans and rolls over, burying her face in her pillow. The pillowcase smells like cheap detergent. She finds a wet spot. She was drooling.

She sits up. Yawns. Stretches. And remembers what she was dreaming about.

Hanging out with Jonah. Movie night at his house. Sometimes they watched movies that were really good, but this time he'd picked action over substance: things blowing up and people driving cars off buildings, shooting at each other out the windows as they fell. Jonah loved stuff like that. Hallelujah didn't, but that didn't stop Jonah from pushing her to watch something with Bruce Willis or the Rock at least once a month.

Hallelujah smiles. For a second, she can't wait to tease Jonah about his bad taste in movies affecting her dreams.

And then her smile fades, because of course she can't tell him. They aren't friends anymore. Him speaking to her last night for the first time in months doesn't change that. And anyway, in the bright light of morning, last night doesn't feel real. It feels as much like a dream as being back on Jonah's couch.

She tries to shake away her sudden sadness by going through the morning motions. She brushes her teeth. She showers, welcoming the feeling of the hot water cascading over her body and watching soap and shampoo swirl around the drain. She covers a few zits and yanks her wet hair back into a ponytail. She dresses: soft, worn jeans, a tank top, a long-sleeved shirt over that, cotton socks, hiking boots laced tight. She stuffs a jacket, an extra shirt, and extra socks into her backpack.

Alongside the water bottle, energy bars, swimsuit, T-shirt, and shorts she was told to bring, just in case, the extra clothes make her backpack heavy and awkward. She can't imagine carrying it for ten miles. But she follows instructions. Better safe than sorry.

She manages to finish getting ready for the day without saying a word to anyone. She keeps her head down. She tries to move through the room like a ghost. To be unseen.

At breakfast—slimy powdered eggs, soggy bacon, and dry toast—Hallelujah sits alone at the end of a long cafeteria table in the common room, staring at her plate. The eggs are already congealing, which turns her stomach a little. She's no gourmet chef, but she cooks a couple times a week, and she's getting better. She likes cooking. It's one of the only things she likes these days, now that she's not singing and has no friends.

Even when she completely fails at a new recipe, it doesn't look as bad as this. Still, she knows she'll be starving later if she doesn't eat now. She takes a bite. And another. She tries not to taste too much.

As she's finishing her meal, Luke and Brad walk past, Brittany and Madison and Kelsey right behind them. And Rachel. The four girls are practically wearing matching outfits: short-shorts and spaghetti-strap tank tops, jackets tied around their waists. Messy ponytails that probably took half an hour to get *just right*.

Luke looks back at Hallelujah and smirks. The Knoxville girls follow his gaze, see her sitting alone, and laugh. Whispers are exchanged. They know she's watching. They're counting on it. And it hurts. It does. But she tells herself she can handle it. As she washes down her last bite of toast with a swig of orange juice, avoiding the stares, she repeats it to herself: *You can handle this week. You can.*

She hears Rachel's voice. "I'll be right there, okay?" A moment later, the chair to Hallelujah's right slides out. "Hey, Hal," Rachel says, plopping down.

Hallelujah looks over. "Hey," she says warily.

"You make it back okay last night?" Rachel asks.

Hallelujah flashes back to her moment of frozen panic, when the lights were coming closer and Jonah took her arm. "Yeah."

"I thought you were right behind me. Then you weren't."

A shout from the front of the room: "Ladies and gentlemen! Focus over here!"

Hallelujah spins to see hike director Jesse standing in the doorway, arms crossed. In his plaid fleece pullover, frowning, he looks like a grouchy lumberjack.

"It was brought to my attention that some of y'all were out in the woods after curfew last night," Jesse announces. His words are met by a low rumble of conversation, a rumble he stops by lifting one hand. "Not only is that against the rules, it's not safe. And it will not be tolerated." He scans the room. "We have a good idea who was involved. So you can save yourself some trouble by going ahead and coming forward." He pauses, like he expects someone just to walk up and confess.

"Phew," Rachel murmurs. "We're in the clear."

"What do you mean?" Hallelujah whispers back.

"'We have a good idea' means 'We don't actually know,'" Rachel says. "He's trying to lay a guilt trip on us."

Hallelujah peeks toward the others who were out last night. They're all together, minus Jonah, at a table in the back corner. None of them looks particularly guilt-ridden. Luke's actually nodding, his face solemn and thoughtful like he agrees wholeheartedly with everything that's being said. It's his preacher's-kid face. The one that has all the grown-ups fooled. Including his dad. *Especially* his dad.

"But how can they not know who it was?" Hallelujah asks.

Rachel shrugs. "Someone screwed up. Don't question it."

Hallelujah still feels uneasy. She'll be the first person the chaperones talk to. She's sure of it. Any hint of trouble comes back to her now. She has that reputation.

It's not fair.

After waiting another few seconds, Jesse coughs. "Well, know that this is your last warning." He starts to walk away, then adds, "Be outside in fifteen minutes."

The buzz of conversation starts back up. A lot of people look at Luke. A few sets of eyes find Hallelujah. They stare, even though she's not nearly popular enough to get invited to sneak out. Not anymore.

Rachel was a fluke. Rachel only needed her to find the party.

So why is Rachel sitting here now?

"Anyway, back to last night—" Rachel starts.

"I don't want to talk about it," Hallelujah says automatically.

"You could've told me there was something up between you and Luke. Before I dragged you out there. I asked you what was up, and you said nothing. But it clearly wasn't nothing."

"Like you honestly care." The words are out before Hallelujah even realizes what she's saying. It's not until she sees Rachel sit back in her chair, a stung expression on her face, that she realizes how harsh she sounds.

"Ouch," Rachel murmurs. "You don't even know me.

You don't know what I care about."

"Rachel!" Luke's voice. Rising above the din.

Hallelujah feels like every head in the room swivels toward Luke, and then toward her and Rachel.

"One sec!" Rachel shouts back. She lowers her voice. "Hal. I'm trying to apologize. For putting you on the spot last night. I didn't know. Okay?"

Hallelujah thinks of Luke's arm around Rachel's shoulders. She says nothing.

"You don't still like him," Rachel goes on. "Do you?"

Now Hallelujah pushes her chair back. "Who told you I liked him?"

"Luke said—"

Hallelujah doesn't wait to hear what Luke said. She grabs her backpack and her paper plate covered in powdered-egg slime and runs for the trash can, and the hallway, and the front door.

# 2

She sits on the porch steps. She leans against the wooden railing. The gnarled limbs are worn and polished from the touch of hands. She is shaking a little, and she hates it.

She's cold. That's all it is. It may be April over in Knoxville and down in Chattanooga, but up here in the mountains, at 8:00 a.m., it feels like February. The grass on either side of the gravel path in front of the lodge is crisp with frozen dew. The clouds are low and wispy-wet.

Hallelujah is thankful for her long-sleeved shirt and jeans. She thinks about Rachel, still inside the lodge, wearing shorts and a tank top. She wonders if she should tell her to grab some layers. She decides to go back and tell her.

She changes her mind.

In the fuzzy early light, Hallelujah can see that their lodge sits on top of a high ridge. She can see for miles: trees of different greens, blue water, brown log homes sending out spirals of smoke from redbrick chimneys.

She sits there, alone, looking out, listening to the morning birds chirping and the wind rustling the trees' vibrant green leaves. She breathes in the wet pine and wet grass and wet air and feels less choked.

She thinks, *What did he tell her?*

It doesn't matter. Because nothing's going to change. But it does matter. Because with Rachel, for a few minutes last night, she let herself think something might.

She should have known better. It's been this way since October, since Luke told that first lie about what happened between them. Since he trashed her reputation. Made her into a joke. Since he transformed her into someone her parents don't trust. Someone with no friends and no voice.

He's more popular than ever, while she dreams of disappearing.

She hasn't been to a youth group activity since it

happened. Until now. At first, she wasn't allowed to go. It was part of her punishment. Her parents grounded her—no social activities. Meanwhile, Rich put her on youth group probation, because she'd violated the code of conduct they'd all signed at the start of the year.

Despite everything, she didn't really mind being punished. Not like that. The last thing she wanted was to spend extra time with Luke and Jonah and everyone else who was making her life miserable. Home, alone, was so much safer.

But three weeks ago, Rich met with her parents. He told them he'd spoken with Luke's dad and they both thought Hallelujah had been absent from the youth group long enough. She needed to be brought back into the fold. Being with her youth group peers, under Rich's supervision, would be good for her. It would help her move past the incident.

The *incident*. That's what Rich called it. Like everything that had happened and was happening with Luke could be boiled down into that one sanitized word.

Hallelujah hates thinking about it. Everyone discussing what to do with her. And anyway, she could have told her parents that being here wouldn't help. She would have, if they'd asked her. If she'd thought they'd listen.

Or maybe she wouldn't have brought it up after all. She hasn't tried talking to her parents about everything since that long drive home. When they asked for her side of the story and she couldn't find the right words. When her dad finally threw his hands up and told her to stop making excuses, to take responsibility for her choices, and her mom kept repeating, *We'll talk about this later.* And then later didn't come, because after the lectures, after the disappointment, the humiliation of telling them the truth was just too much, and Hallelujah stayed silent.

She'd been sure that was the best choice. She'd thought, then, that things would get better. But they didn't. And now it's too late to make it right.

She hears Luke now. His voice rising above others, getting closer. It must be almost time to leave.

Hallelujah checks her backpack. She has everything she needs.

She's ready.

## 3

THE VANS DROP THEM OFF AT THE TRAIL HEAD BY ABRAMS Creek Campground. Kids pour out, backpacks on, and assemble next to the trail marker. They're the only group there, but with more than twenty-five of them, plus about ten chaperones, their chatter is a roar.

Hallelujah isn't talking to anyone. No one tries to talk to her. She stands on the edge of the group as Jesse and one of the other chaperones count heads. She watches.

The Knoxville girls are flirting with Brad, all teeth and eyelashes and hair-flipping. Rachel is talking to one of the girls from Chattanooga, but her eyes dart over toward

Hallelujah. Hallelujah looks away quickly.

She finds herself scanning the group for Jonah. He wasn't at breakfast. Which is weird. She's never known him to skip a meal. He's a bottomless pit. Or at least he used to be.

And then she spots him. With Luke. Arguing. Jonah's hands are clenched into fists. Luke's face is twisted into a sneer. She only has a second to wonder what they're fighting about before Jesse calls for the group's attention.

"Gather round, hikers," he shouts. "As you know, today we're hiking up to Abrams Falls. Who's been there before?"

A few hands go up.

"Well, if you haven't, you're in for a treat. It's about six and a half miles up to the falls, the way we're going. When we get there, we'll eat lunch and swim a little, if the weather cooperates. Do a devotional. Then we'll head back, taking a different trail. As we hike, I encourage you to be aware of your surroundings—the majesty of these mountains, the detail of each leaf and bud, the vast scope of the entire forest. And, of course, have fun!"

Jesse pauses. Ahems at Jonah and Luke, who finally break apart. Luke walks over to Brad and the Knoxville girls, laughing like nothing's wrong. Jonah goes to the opposite side of the group. He stands alone.

"And now," Jesse goes on, "the moment you've all been waiting for: hand over your cell phones."

Groans. From all directions.

"You'll get them back at the end of the hike. Trust me,

you don't need them out here. Talk to each other. Look at the view. You won't regret it." He pauses, watching chaperones circulate, backpacks open. Hallelujah drops her phone into Rich's bag without hesitation. She wouldn't have anyone to call or text or email, anyway.

"I know you've all had safety rules drilled into your brains. I know you don't want to hear it anymore. So all I'll say now is: For most of this hike we'll be single file. There are a lot of us to keep track of. Learn who's in front of you and behind you. Memorize names and faces. We'll count heads every time we stop, but you'll have to help us out. The flock watches out for its own sheep. Got it?"

Nods. Mm-hmms. An overzealous "Yes, sir!" from Hallelujah's left.

"Then let's get moving!"

Jesse starts up the trail first, his plaid jacket a bright contrast to the trees. Jonah is right behind him. Hallelujah wonders how it's possible to have known Jonah well enough and long enough to be able to tell, just from the stiff set of his shoulders, that he's angry, and yet to not really know him at all. He's the same person who was her friend. Before. But he's also not that person anymore. Sometimes she feels like she made that guy up.

She shifts her pack on her shoulders. She lets Rich herd her into the line between a Knoxville boy and a Chattanooga girl, neither of whom acknowledge her. She focuses on the sensation of her hiking boots on the damp earth.

# 4

THE SUNLIGHT HITS THE GROUND DAPPLED, FILLED WITH tree-branch shadows. The light patches shift and slide as the wind moves the trees. Birds call out to each other overhead. And there are other sounds—insects, maybe, or tree frogs. Sounds she can't name.

Despite growing up not too far from the mountains, Hallelujah hasn't done a lot of hiking. Now, she's realizing she likes it. The way the mountains make her feel like a tiny part of something much bigger. And the way she could take a few steps off the path and feel completely alone and apart.

They cross a narrow log bridge over Abrams Creek, and she stops for a second to take it all in. The creek rushing by just a few feet below. The trees lining the banks on both sides, their branches arcing over the water. The way the log bridge vibrates with the others' steps, leaving her slightly off-balance, clutching the railing.

"Pick up the pace, Hal." It's Rachel. Right behind her. How long has she been there? Why is she there at all?

Rachel shrugs, answering the questions Hallelujah didn't ask out loud. "I caught up. I wanted to talk to you." She gestures around. "Single file. On a bridge. You can't run away, unless you swim. So can we talk?"

"I guess," Hallelujah mutters. She starts walking. Down

to the bank. Up a small hill. Over a fallen tree branch. Around a series of deep, old roots.

"You used to like Luke," Rachel states.

"Used to."

"But you don't anymore."

"Don't anymore." Hallelujah feels like a parrot.

"So what'd he do to you? Did you used to date? Did he dump you?"

Hallelujah snorts. If only it were that simple. "Ask him. You two seemed cozy enough last night."

"I don't want to ask him. I'm asking you."

"Why do you care? Why are you even talking to me?"

"Because—" Rachel takes in a deep breath. She lowers her voice. "Because the way you're acting has me kind of freaked out. If he did something really bad . . ."

Hallelujah turns to look directly at her. "Look. He didn't rape me, if that's what you're worried about." She says it low. To make sure no one else hears. And to keep her voice from shaking. "Beyond that—I don't want to talk about it."

"But—"

"I don't. Want. To talk about it."

Rachel blinks. "Fine. Whatever." She pushes past Hallelujah, up the trail.

They hike until they reach a crossroads. They turn left. They keep hiking. They take a short break, count heads, and start walking again.

Hallelujah waits for Rich to usher her into line near the back of the pack. This time, Jonah ends up behind her. His heavy footfalls remind her of the sound of him running last night, in the dark. She remembers him half in the girls' bathroom window. His muscular legs, his hand reaching down to pull her inside. Their eyes meeting.

She thinks again about their friendship. The bond they used to have. And how it came up almost out of nowhere. They'd known each other since fourth grade, since Jonah's family moved from Virginia and joined Hallelujah's church. But even after seeing each other in Sunday school every week, joining the youth group at the same time, and sharing a few academic classes, they'd never really talked.

Until ninth-grade choir at school. That first day, she'd walked in and been surprised to see him sitting at the back of the room. He'd lifted a hand and said, *Hey*. She'd said *Hey* back. After an awkward pause, she'd added, *I didn't know you sang*. He'd shrugged. Said, *I do. Kind of. Anyway, I had to pick an Arts elective*.

The next day, they started comparing musical tastes. Hallelujah liked passionate indie-pop. Singer-songwriters wailing and whispering with acoustic guitars and keyboards. Jonah liked old-school country. Cowboy hats and pickup trucks and broken hearts. Also, classic rock. Within weeks, they were trading songs, albums, artists. Ingrid Michaelson for Johnny Cash. The soundtrack to *Once* for the Eagles' greatest hits. They made an agreement early on: they didn't have to like everything, but they had to listen to everything.

And then they were sharing more than just music. Hallelujah convinced Jonah to read the Harry Potter books for the first time. Jonah launched an action movie marathon that continued until Hallelujah couldn't watch one more Fast and Furious rip-off and countered with *Sleepless in Seattle* and *Love Actually*. They watched old episodes of *Whose Line Is It Anyway?* on Jonah's computer, because he couldn't believe Hallelujah had never seen it. Then she made him sit through her new favorite show, a musical drama about a girl moving to New York City to try to make it on Broadway.

They didn't go deeper than that. No hopes, no fears, no dreams. Definitely no talk about who liked who. She never mentioned how hard she was crushing on Luke. If Jonah liked anyone, he never told her. Because of that, their friendship was easy. Uncomplicated by personal drama.

Which is why his silence after what happened with Luke hurt so much. She'd been sure that what Jonah had seen wouldn't change what they shared. That he'd give her a chance to explain. Instead, their friendship was as done as everything else in her life.

Hallelujah is pulled out of her thoughts by the sound of moving water. She turns the corner to see the group standing beside a creek. People are drinking from canteens and stripping off outer layers. Laughing. Catching their breath.

"There you are!" Rich strides over, looking relieved. He puts one hand on Hallelujah's shoulder and the other on Jonah's. "Luke noticed you two had fallen behind. That's what we mean about keeping an eye out for each other!"

Luke joins them, smiling like a proud dad. It's gross. "Glad to help, Rich," he says. Then he turns to Hallelujah.

"Looks like you have a new sidekick."

He means Jonah. Jonah, whose face is growing more cloudy by the second.

"Were y'all having fun back there?" Luke asks. His tone of voice is innocent, but Hallelujah knows exactly what he's getting at.

Jesse's voice rings out: "All right, everyone! Time to cross the creek. If you stay on these rocks, you'll be fine. And if you fall in—well, it's not deep, but it is wet. So be careful. We'll take a quick break on the other side before we move on." He starts lining people up. "Brad, why don't you take Madison and Kelsey across first."

Brad bows and Madison giggles and Kelsey pouts, looking back toward Luke like she wishes it was him, and Hallelujah wants to throw up.

They cross a few at a time, Jesse calling out names and waving his lumberjack-plaid arms around like he's conducting a symphony. Hallelujah sits on the ground and waits. She watches Rachel stumble on a wobbly, slick rock, fight for balance, save it, and strike a triumphant gymnast pose complete with cheerful smile. And then she hears it:

"Luke and Hallelujah, you're up!"

No. No way. She can't. She won't.

But Jesse is waiting. Rich is waiting. Luke is waiting. Everyone is watching. After hesitating a second longer, Hallelujah gets up, slings her backpack on, and walks over.

Luke extends his hand, a wordless *After you*.

She takes a tentative step forward onto the first rock. It

shifts and slides a little under her foot. When she's steady, she takes another step. And another. She feels Luke behind her. His shadow drapes over her, casts itself on the rocks ahead.

And then she steps on a rock that doesn't stay still. It shifts down suddenly, and her other foot slides, and her arms are flailing, and her backpack is so heavy, and she's falling, and Luke is looking down at her, smiling, shaking his head, and someone is squealing, and she realizes, with a splash, that it's her.

She is sitting, chest-deep, in the creek.

A crashing and splashing to her right. A hand reaching down. Jonah. He pulls Hallelujah to her feet, and she wobbles but stays up.

Jonah turns to Luke. "What the *heck*, man?" Jonah says "heck" like someone else might say a real curse word. Barbed. Spat out.

"I tried to catch her," Luke says, loud enough for the group to hear. He shrugs. "Guess I missed. You okay, Hallie?"

"Fine," Hallelujah chokes out. She wades the rest of the way across, feeling the heat of everyone's eyes, wanting to cry from frustration.

Rachel meets her at the bank. Hallelujah brushes by. Rachel follows her. "Hal, are you okay?"

Hallelujah spins and growls, "Why?"

Rachel looks confused. And wary. "Why what?"

"Why are you helping me?" Hallelujah's voice is rising, but she can't control it. "We don't know each other, and even if you didn't get it last night, you have to get now that

I'm not exactly popular. I can't help you get close to Luke. Not that you seem to need any help on that front. And I don't need your pity, either. So there's no reason for us to be friends. Okay?"

Rachel has gone still. For a second, Hallelujah thinks she's not going to say anything. But then she speaks. Her voice is soft, but it holds a lot of emotion, barely contained. "Wow, Hal. Message received."

"Everything all right?" Rich appears between the two of them, looking concerned. "Do you need to talk about anything? That's why I'm here, Hallelujah. I'm here for you."

She feels her anger drain away, like the water dripping from her ponytail. What's left is exhaustion. She's so, so tired. Of all of this. "No, sir," she says. "I just got upset when I fell. That's all."

Rich pats her awkwardly on the back. "Well, you're okay now."

"Sure," Hallelujah murmurs. She looks past him, wanting to say something to Rachel but not sure what to say or how to say it. Rachel is already walking away.

# 5

WHEN JESSE ANNOUNCES THAT IT'S TIME TO GET BACK ON the trail, Hallelujah watches Rachel approach Brittany, Madison, and Kelsey. She can't hear what Rachel says, but she sees the Knoxville girls' wide, condescending grins in response. Hallelujah takes a step closer, suddenly anxious.

"So you have a fight with your girlfriend, and now you want to hang out with us again?" Madison drawls. She looks over Rachel's shoulder at Hallelujah.

Rachel follows Madison's gaze. "Hal? Don't worry. We're not friends."

"Whatever you say." Kelsey rolls her eyes.

"Anyway, have a good week!" Brittany says brightly. The three of them turn and start up the trail, leaving Rachel standing by herself.

Rachel's shoulders slump. Then she straightens up. After a moment, she walks back toward the creek.

"What's she doing?" Jonah is standing next to Hallelujah.

"I don't know." Hallelujah tells herself she doesn't want to know. That she doesn't care. But she does. What just happened to Rachel is her fault. She's causing collateral damage just by being here. Never mind how she lashed out at the only person who has tried to be nice to her in ages.

Rachel stops at the bank. "I know you're still there," she says without turning around. Her voice is soft, barely audible over the running water.

Hallelujah takes a few steps closer. "Where are you going?"

Now Rachel whirls around. "Not that you deserve an answer, but I'm going home. This trip sucks." She looks past them, at the trail the group just took. Hallelujah turns and looks too. Everyone is gone. She can hear laughter, but she can't see anybody through the trees.

"You can't just go off by yourself," Jonah says. "You'll get in trouble."

"I'm counting on it," Rachel answers. She stares them down, turns, and wades right into the creek, heading back the way they just came. "Like I said: I want to go home. If I have to get in trouble in order for them to send me home, so be it. At least I won't have to deal with you anymore. Any of you! You all deserve each other."

"Okay," Jonah says. "You want to go home. Fine. You still can't hike off alone."

"She won't be alone. I'm going too." Hallelujah is a little surprised to hear herself say those words. But she doesn't regret them. Being sent home *does* sound better than staying here. And she's used to being in trouble. It might as well be for something she actually did. She might as well go in with her eyes open.

She walks into the creek. Jonah follows. "Me too," he says.

"You don't have to," Rachel says, hands on hips. "I can find my way back."

"We're coming." The more Hallelujah says it, the more right it feels. She doesn't know why it feels so right, since the rational thing would be to drag Rachel back to the group, to follow the rules, to keep flying under the radar. But this is what she wants to do.

They reach the other side. They look at each other.

Hallelujah is the first to speak. "Well?"

"Well," Jonah echoes. He's looking at Hallelujah like he's never seen her before. "Let's go."

# 6

THEY WALK. HALLELUJAH DOESN'T KNOW WHAT RACHEL and Jonah are thinking, but inside her head, she's arguing with herself. Second-guessing.

She's doing something she shouldn't be—this is like last night's sneaking out, multiplied exponentially. It won't end well. It can't. But she feels a weight lifted.

Rachel let Hallelujah come with her. After Hallelujah yelled at her and pushed her away. And sure, maybe they'll go their separate ways after today. Maybe they'll never talk again. But maybe, just maybe, this is the start of something new.

Jonah chose to follow them. He could've gone with the group, back to Luke, back to his life, away from Hallelujah. Again. But he didn't. He's here.

She's not alone, despite Luke's best efforts. Despite her own.

She feels hope well up. She isn't sure what to do with it. Hope is scary. Expecting the worst is easier.

And then, Rachel speaks. "I came to this thing by myself, and I hate coming to things like this by myself. But I honestly thought I might make some friends." She doesn't stop moving, doesn't turn around. "That's why I started talking to you. Plus, you looked like maybe you could use someone to talk to. But you—"

Hallelujah braces herself. It could be anything. She's boring. She's lame. She's ugly. She's too angry. She's too sad. She's too quiet. She tries too hard and she doesn't try hard enough. She only cares about herself and she doesn't deserve friends.

"You don't make it easy," Rachel finishes quietly.

Hallelujah takes in a sharp breath. Of all the things Rachel could have said. It's her fight with Sarah all over again.

It was Thanksgiving, only a month after Luke happened. Hallelujah had sent yet another email to Sarah in Georgia about what was going on. Her side of the story. How unfair it was. The latest awful thing she'd heard about herself at school. How much she missed Sarah, wished she was there. And Sarah had come online and messaged her directly: *I don't want to be mean . . . but you have to stop complaining and do something. Make Dani listen*, Sarah typed. *Make Jonah talk to you. Make Luke shut up. Stand up for yourself.* A pause, during which Hallelujah had gaped at the screen, hands frozen. Then: *You're my friend, but I don't know how much more whining I can take. I'm sorry.*

White-hot anger. That's what Hallelujah remembers. Sarah didn't understand anything. She wasn't there. She was always too busy to talk. She didn't get how much Hallelujah was hurting. And everything Hallelujah had been holding inside came out.

She'd called Sarah selfish. And shallow. Said she obviously didn't care about their friendship. Said she wouldn't bother her with her problems anymore. Sarah could move on with her life, like she clearly wanted, leaving Hallelujah behind.

After another pause, Sarah wrote, *Nothing is ever easy with you. You make things so hard.* And she signed off. That was the last time they spoke. Five months ago. Each waiting, Hallelujah assumes, for the other to apologize first.

Now, to Rachel, she says what she should've said to Sarah: "I'm sorry."

Rachel doesn't answer, but she nods. It's not much, but it's more than Hallelujah feels like she deserves.

Half an hour down the trail, they stop to eat lunch. Identical PB&Js with apples—two of each for Jonah—handed out by the chaperones after breakfast. Washed down with gulps of cool water. Hallelujah feels the lump of peanut butter and bread settle in her stomach. She sits back, enjoying the sun on her face and listening to the wind in the trees and the birds calling.

"Well," Jonah says after a while. "We should probably get going."

"Yeah. Guess so." Rachel stands, grabs her backpack, and starts walking. Hallelujah and Jonah follow.

They reach the crossroads from earlier. Rachel strides right through, but something makes Hallelujah pause. "Didn't we come from that way?" She points down the trail to their right.

Jonah looks thoughtful. "I wasn't really paying attention," he says. "Maybe?"

"No, we definitely went straight through here." Rachel reads the sign. "Hannah Mountain Trail. We were on that from the beginning. I'm sure of it."

Hallelujah studies both trails. Trees. Dirt. Leaves. They look the same.

"You're sure?" she asks Rachel.

"Yes." Rachel nods. "And if I'm wrong, we can always go back, right?"

"Yeah. Retrace our steps." Jonah still seems uncertain, but like he's being pulled in Rachel's direction.

So Hallelujah gives in. It's not like she remembers this morning perfectly, anyway. "Fine. Okay. Let's go."

# 7

THEY HIKE IN SILENCE FOR A WHILE. AND DESPITE HER jeans still being damp from sitting in and wading through the creek, and despite her backpack straps digging into her shoulders, Hallelujah gets a second wind. She feels like she could keep hiking forever.

There are no other people in sight. It's quiet. Until Rachel starts singing in time to her footsteps, an off-key rendition of "I've Got a Lovely Bunch of Coconuts." Out of everything she could have chosen. Jonah snorts and shoots his eyes back toward Hallelujah like, *Are you hearing this?* But he's smiling, and the fact that he shared that smile and that glance with Hallelujah makes her smile too.

Just like that, the tension is gone. They are a fizzled-out cartoon bomb, a balloon popped with a pin, helium-headed. They are going to get in so much trouble when they get back to the campgrounds, and not one of them cares.

Rachel keeps singing. She knows all the words. When she stops for breath, Jonah says, "Coconuts are tropical. This is a temperate zone!" in a terrible British accent. Rachel bursts out laughing. She stops and holds her knees, chest heaving. When she turns around to look at them, eyes streaming, Jonah says, amused, "It wasn't that funny."

That sets Rachel off all over again. She sits on the ground and laughs and laughs, and when Hallelujah admits, "I don't get it," Rachel laughs even harder.

"Monty Python," Jonah says.

Hallelujah shrugs. "Okay?"

"Old British comedy guys? From, like, the seventies? *The Quest for the Holy Grail*? Coconuts?" Jonah claps his hands together a few times, galloping in place like he's riding an imaginary horse.

Hallelujah stares. Rachel wheezes.

Jonah stops, looking embarrassed. "I could've sworn we watched that one last year." When Hallelujah shakes her head, he says, "Oh. Well, we should." He looks away like he hasn't just essentially invited Hallelujah over to his house for movie night. Like that isn't an extremely big deal after six months of radio silence.

Rachel's laughs have turned to hiccups. She gasps, "You guys aren't . . . so bad."

The scene feels surreal, with Rachel sitting in the dirt in the middle of the trail and Jonah leaning back against a tree and the afternoon sunlight coming in at strange angles. If another hiker were to come along, if someone were to take a picture of this moment, they'd probably assume: friends. Since childhood. Easy together.

But since no one appears with a camera to document it, the moment passes.

Jonah says, "We should be close now. We've been hiking long enough."

"Good," Hallelujah says. "Let's get this over with." The rest of the hike. Whatever punishment awaits them at the lodge. And after. She's ready to face it. At the same time, she doesn't mean that she wants this day to end. Not entirely.

She helps Rachel to her feet. Their eyes meet, and Rachel nods, and Hallelujah knows she is forgiven. She doesn't know why, but an olive branch has been offered. She's grateful for it.

They walk. Up small hills and down others, along straight trail and winding curves, over roots and through soft dirt and under low-hanging tree boughs.

The light changes.

As the light changes, so does the mood. Their silence goes from comfortable to tense, charged. Their breath comes in puffs. Their feet hit the ground, heavy.

Hallelujah thinks, but does not say, *We should be there. We should have been there an hour ago.* She's afraid to say it. Afraid saying it will make it real.

They walk faster, the sun slipping away from them. There's a sense of urgency now. They all feel it. They all create it.

No one will say it.

Not until they reach the top of a ridge and look out over a valley and see the sun dropping closer to the mountain-tops. Jonah squints into the light, drops his pack off his back and says, simply, "We screwed up."

Rachel nods, looking miserable. "No kidding. I'm sorry." Small words, but Hallelujah is glad to hear them from the person who insisted they take this trail.

Hallelujah sits down, suddenly exhausted. She slides her backpack off her back, rolling her shoulders to work out the kinks. She's got two sweat-stripes where the straps sat. "How long do you think we have before the sun sets?" she asks, trying to sound less anxious than she feels.

Jonah looks at his watch, worry creasing his face. "I don't think we'll make it back before dark. Either of you two bring a flashlight? All I have is this." He flashes the blue light on his watch screen.

Hallelujah shakes her head. Rachel shakes her head. They were supposed to be back in the vans by now.

"What do we do?" Rachel asks.

"We shouldn't keep walking after sunset," Jonah says. "Too dangerous. Who knows where we'd end up. I'd say our best bet is to start back, and when the sun goes down we find a place to camp for the night." He looks from Hallelujah to Rachel. "At this point, they know we're gone. So they're already looking for us. We might not even have to spend the whole night out here."

"Right. And we have some food," Hallelujah says. "Enough for tonight and tomorrow morning. I mean, we won't starve." She heaves herself to her feet. "I think there was a clearing, not too far back. Just off the trail. Maybe we can sleep there."

"Good, Hallie." Jonah nods.

They backtrack about half an hour. Hallelujah wishes they could just keep backtracking, rewind the film. She wishes she'd been louder at the crossroads, pushed her opinion, made herself heard. But she isn't used to making people listen to her, or even wanting to, and if she's honest with herself, she wasn't 100 percent sure she was right. And then she would have been the one leading them astray, not Rachel.

Rachel, who pulled them away from the group in the first place. Rachel, who picked the wrong path. Rachel, who—

Hallelujah forces herself to stop. Blaming Rachel won't help. And anyway, everything will be okay. They'll spend the night out here, and in the morning they'll start walking again—the right way—and they'll be at the campgrounds by lunchtime. And surely there will be someone from their group waiting for them, or someone alerted by their group, like a park ranger. And they'll be taken back to the lodge to clean up and eat and get yelled at. And then they'll get sent home. Like they all wanted.

"You know what would be useful right about now?" Rachel raises her voice to a shout. "Cell phones!"

Jonah snorts. "No kidding. But reception's probably bad out here."

"Still. We could've tried." Rachel kicks at a clod of dirt on the trail. It goes skittering past Hallelujah's feet. "They should've let us be prepared for this."

"Yeah, but we were supposed to stay with the group. . . ." Hallelujah fades off, seeing the clearing to her left. Down from the trail, a spot maybe six feet square with no trees, just soft grass. "Over there," she says, and points.

"Nice." Jonah heads down, long limbs crashing through the bushes. He looks around, nodding. "This'll do. I can make a fire over here"—he gestures to one corner of the clearing—"and we can put our bags up in that tree."

"You can make a fire?" Hallelujah asks.

"Put our bags in the tree?" Rachel says at the same time.

"I was a Boy Scout," Jonah says. "And we put our bags in the tree to keep our food away from bears."

"Bears?" Rachel squeaks. "Seriously?"

Hallelujah wants to lay down more blame: *You were a Boy Scout, and you didn't know we were going the wrong way?* But she bites back the words and follows Jonah's trampled path to the clearing.

The sun is low. The air is cooler without the light to warm it. Hallelujah pulls on the extra layers she'd shed earlier in the day: long-sleeved shirt, jacket, another pair of socks. Rachel puts on her own jacket, shivering a little. Her bare legs look thin and pale in the twilight.

And then they sit, feeling the temperature drop and watching the sun slip away.

Jonah has his back to them. He's crouched over a pile of wood, striking at a piece of steel with an attached flint. Watching him, listening to stone hit metal, Hallelujah wonders if the flint is a relic from Jonah's Boy Scout days. Or if it's some new thing, if Jonah has gone all *Man vs. Wild* since they stopped talking. She doesn't ask him.

Just as the sun drops below the horizon completely, it happens. A spark. A spark that Jonah fans into flames. Small flames. Beautiful flames.

"There," Jonah says, looking pleased.

They huddle around, as close as they dare to get without being *in* the fire. Jonah pulls on his jacket and rubs his hands up and down his shins and calves, trying to warm his skin. "You're the smart one," he says to Hallelujah after a few seconds.

"Me? Why?"

Jonah gestures at Rachel's bare legs, and at his own worn cargo shorts. "You're gonna be a lot warmer than us. Since you wore jeans."

"Oh. Right." Hallelujah thinks back to that moment this morning when she thought about telling Rachel how chilly it was. When she changed her mind. One more thing to feel guilty about.

"At least it's only for tonight," Rachel says. She's pulled

her knees up toward her chest and is trying to zip her jacket over her shins. The zipper doesn't quite reach, even with her knees right under her chin. "Just tonight," she repeats.

"Yup." Jonah pokes at the fire with a stick. Sparks float up. He rubs at his legs a few more times, and then starts popping his knuckles. Hallelujah watches his hands. He always pops his knuckles in this particular way. When he's thinking hard. Or nervous. He pops each finger, pinky to thumb, on his left hand, and then repeats the sequence on the right. Then he shakes his hands out like he's loosening the joints back up.

"Gross," Rachel says, and Jonah looks up, startled, like he didn't realize what he was doing.

"Sorry," he says. "So—should we eat? We should eat. Let's eat."

They take inventory. Jonah has one more peanut butter and jelly sandwich. Hallelujah has an orange juice from breakfast and the twelve-pack of energy bars she brought for the week. Rachel has a banana, two energy bars, and a can of Diet Coke.

"Wish I didn't eat two sandwiches earlier," Jonah mutters, staring at their small pile of supplies.

"Well, you did skip breakfast," Hallelujah answers.

He blinks at her, like he's surprised she noticed, and Hallelujah feels her face grow hot. She's glad it's dark. She's even more glad Jonah doesn't say anything else.

They split the sandwich three ways and each have an energy bar. And though they're all still hungry, they agree to put the rest of the food away. Just in case. If they're lucky, they won't need it.

Jonah shows them how to rig their bags so they're tucked up in the nearest tree. Then they gather back around the fire. It's only eight thirty, but in the dark, in the cold, it feels later. With the woods looming on all sides, it's like the fire is the only thing keeping the trees and the darkness from swallowing them whole.

# 8

THEY SIT. HALLELUJAH STARES INTO THE FIRE, watching Jonah's gently coaxed flames. And she looks at Jonah's and Rachel's faces. In the firelight and shadows, they look drawn. Gaunt. When Rachel catches Hallelujah looking, she smiles, and the effect is less reassuring than haunting. Hallelujah shivers.

"So what do we do now?" Rachel asks.

"Well, unless y'all want to tell ghost stories," Jonah says, "we go to bed. The light'll wake us up in the morning. And the earlier we get up and start walking, the earlier we get home. Right?"

"Right," Hallelujah echoes. It does sound right, but it also sounds hollow, like something you say to keep up the troops' morale. Not necessarily a bad thing. She tries a joke of her own: "So, who wants what side of the bed?"

Jonah lets out a "Heh" and Hallelujah feels a spark of pleasure: she made him laugh.

"Can I sleep in the middle?" Rachel asks. "I'm really cold. And I—I have to, um—" A deep breath. A quick murmur: "I have to go to the bathroom."

Just like that, Hallelujah has to go too. Badly. They've gone in the woods before. Earlier today, in fact. But that was daylight.

"I'll go with you," she tells Rachel. "And then you can stay with me while I—"

"Great."

They move away from the fire, out of the clearing. Each step feels colder and more vulnerable. No way to judge what they're about to step on. Just big tree-shapes in the darkness ahead and the occasional shiny leaf catching the moonlight.

Behind them, Jonah starts singing. To himself, while he tends the fire. Or to them, to remind them they're not alone. His voice is reassuring. Human, in this wildness.

It's also beautiful. Low, deep, like an old-fashioned country singer. Rich in tone. Twangy, but not too much. He sounds like a mix of Clint Black and Conway Twitty—and thinking that makes Hallelujah smile a little, because Jonah's the reason she knows who those guys are in the first place.

Hearing him sing takes her right back to ninth-grade choir. The two of them sang a duet in the holiday concert that year. "O Holy Night." It's one of her best memories.

Now he's singing "Rocky Top." But not the twangy bluegrass version. Not the pumped-up University of Tennessee fight song version, either. He's singing it slow, drawing out the vowels. It sounds just right for tonight. Lonesome. Wistful.

"Hal? Is something wrong?" Rachel's voice. Worried.

"No, sorry. I was just . . . listening. To Jonah."

"Oh. Can we . . . ?"

"Yeah."

Rachel and Hallelujah pick their way to a point where the fire is a red glow through the trees behind them. They can still get back. Rachel ducks behind a tree, and Hallelujah turns her back and focuses on the sound of Jonah's voice and the owls calling to each other and the wind rustling the leaves. But she still hears the zipper and Rachel's soft exhale of relief and it causes her own bladder to twinge in response.

A few more painful seconds and then footsteps behind her. Rachel taps her on the shoulder. "Stall's open," she says softly.

Hallelujah finds her own tree and wriggles her jeans down, leaning back for balance.

Jonah has reached the verse about strangers never making it back from Rocky Top. Given where they are right now, Hallelujah kind of wishes he'd skipped that part.

She finishes and pulls her pants back on. She finds Rachel and they walk carefully back to the clearing.

Jonah has added more wood to the fire. It's burning a little brighter now. He's also cleared a wider berth between the fire and the trees. Something Hallelujah hadn't even thought of: not setting the mountain on fire. She's grateful.

"My turn," Jonah says, and strides off into the woods.

"Want one of us to come along?" Rachel calls out to his back.

"Nah. Easier for me than for you." He picks up "Rocky Top" where he left off.

They listen to him walk away.

"How does he know all the words?" Rachel wonders.

"How do you know all the words to 'I've Got a Lovely Bunch of Coconuts'?"

"If I told you, I'd have to kill you." Rachel sits by the fire, wrapping her arms around her knees. After a few minutes, she speaks up again. "You're next. Sing."

Anxiety grips Hallelujah's chest, squeezing. "I don't sing," she says.

"C'mon, it doesn't matter if you're bad. It's not like this is a concert hall—"

"She's not bad." Jonah's back. "She has a great voice."

Rachel swings around to look from Jonah to Hallelujah. "Really? Now you *have* to—"

"No."

"But—"

"I don't sing," Hallelujah repeats, turning away.

Jonah joins them by the fire. The silence stretches out. Except it's not really silent, not with the birds and wind and fire and how loud Hallelujah's heart is beating. And then Jonah clears his throat. "You used to sing," he says. "You were great."

Hallelujah ignores the compliment. She looks into the

fire. She feels the last of the day's happiness fading away, already a memory.

"Why'd you quit?" Jonah asks. "Was it 'cause of Luke?"

Hallelujah inhales deeply. She feels the familiar spark of anger in her gut. "Yes," she says. "It was because of Luke. And you. And everyone else. So thanks for that." Jonah's face drops. She can see that she's hit a nerve. Well, he hurt her first. The way he took Luke's side, shutting her out. The loss of his friendship, when she needed a friend most. The loss of their voices harmonizing, when she needed music most. How she just hurt him can't begin to compare to all of that.

She stretches out on the hard ground. The grass tickles the back of her neck, under her ponytail. It's the least-comfortable bed ever. But it's all they've got. Rachel lies down next to her. Close, but not touching. It's almost weirder than if they were actually curled up together.

Jonah stays over by the fire. "I'll stay up and keep an eye on this for a while," he says. "You two get some sleep."

Hallelujah closes her eyes. The night sounds and the fire crackling seem even louder with her eyes shut. She's not sure how she'll ever fall asleep. Plus, her body hurts from so much hiking. She tries to will her tense, sore muscles to relax. She feels Rachel shifting beside her, probably doing the same thing. Their arms brush, coats making a swishing noise. They both pull away, back to not-touching. Then all is quiet.

*She remembers rehearsals. Wrong notes turning to right ones, dissonance becoming harmony. She remembers "O Holy Night" sounding so perfect, in the end, her voice wrapping itself around Jonah's like they were created just for this. She remembers his smile at her from across their shared mic.*

*She remembers getting asked to reprise her duet with Jonah a year later. Just after everything happened with Luke. But then Mr. Boyden took her aside. Told her that Jonah had backed out. He'd said he was too busy for extra rehearsals, but she knew: it was because of her. She saw it in Jonah's face, in the way he avoided her eyes. She saw it in everyone else's faces too. She was a bullet he'd just dodged.*

*She remembers standing up for the solo she was given instead—her last performance before she quit choir. She remembers opening her mouth, nothing coming out. She'd cleared her throat, tried again. Her voice emerged, but all wrong: small and shaky and sharp. With everyone looking at her, with the rumors still swirling, she felt exposed. She felt small and shaky and sharp. Vulnerable, but made of angles and thorns.*

the
**third**
day

# 1

A RUMBLE IN THE DISTANCE.

In spite of the birds calling to each other, in spite of the wind rustling leaves overhead, in spite of the cracking of branches and the buzzing of insects, it's the rumble that wakes her. It rolls, builds, and fades away. A few seconds later, it rolls again.

Hallelujah flips over, wondering why her bed is so hard, why her neck is so stiff. Then she remembers. No bed; only dirt and rock. No pillow; only leaves. And that rumbling, the sound that pulled her out of her dreams—thunder.

It sounds again.

She sits up, rubbing her eyes, returning to reality. The sky overhead is gray-blue, but to her right, beyond the peak of the mountain, it's nearly black. And she can see the dark clouds racing toward her, riding the wind.

It's going to rain.

It's going to rain soon.

"Jonah," she says. "Rachel."

They stir. Rachel groans. Jonah mumbles something.

She says their names again: "Rachel. Jonah."

Jonah sits up. Yawns. "What?"

Thunder rolls again. It's closer. Louder. More a clap than a rumble.

Jonah says, simply, "Oh." But he stands quickly, studying the sky.

Rachel sits up, looking groggy. Her ponytail is matted off to one side of her head. She has a leaf stuck to her face. "What's going on?" she asks, wiping it away with a grimace.

"Storm," Hallelujah says. She glances at Jonah.

"Looks bad," Jonah says. "We should get moving."

The wind picks up. Hallelujah has goosebumps, even under her jeans and jacket and long-sleeved shirt.

The three of them pull their backpacks down from the tree, sling them onto their backs, and start walking. They move quietly and quickly, scrambling over roots, ducking under branches, heading back to the trail they left last night.

The blackness is almost overhead. The sun has vanished. The birds are silent.

There's a bolt of lightning over a nearby mountaintop. Another clap of thunder.

And then Hallelujah can hear drops falling. Can't feel them yet, but can hear them pattering on leaves, on ground. It's a beautiful sound, a soft sound, a peaceful sound.

The air smells clean. Fresh. Like water.

They've reached the trail. They stand for a second, looking right and left. No one wants to make a mistake again. But then Jonah says, "Left," and there's absolutely no doubt in his voice, and so they move.

The drops are louder. Closer.

And then lightning splits the sky apart, directly overhead. The resulting thunder is deafening. It feels like the ground trembles in response. The trees tremble. Hallelujah trembles.

The first drop lands on Hallelujah's arm. More drops spatter her face, blown in on the wind. Soon she can no longer tell one drop from the next. It's just waves of water.

For a second, she can't see trees or leaves or ground or sky or Jonah or Rachel. Just rain, and the pink of Rachel's jacket and the blue of Jonah's jacket, bright against the gray-green landscape. The rain pounds her. Punishes her. It slams into her and pushes her forward and knocks her back. When she breathes, she's breathing water.

She ducks her head and moves, feet sliding on the wet ground. She trips and falls, knees first. She lands in mud. She stands, takes a few steps, falls again. Grabs a branch to pull herself up. Digs the toes of her boots into the mucky hillside.

She follows the curve of the trail. Where the path twists back on itself, there's an overlook. The ground seems to fall away. Hallelujah steps toward the edge, daring herself to look. The mountainside is quickly becoming a waterfall, a stream of rain and mud and leaves pouring into a ravine. It's a long way down, and seeing it makes Hallelujah dizzy.

Thunder roars overhead, sounding like the voice of an angry God. A vengeful, grudge-holding Old Testament God. The kind of God who would let her suffer while Luke got away with everything.

A scream cuts the air. Rachel. She's lost her footing. She tumbles past Hallelujah. Hallelujah reaches out to grab her, but misses, and the effort throws her off the trail and down the mountainside as well. They both roll down, down, clutching at everything in sight. It all slips out of their grasp. The world is green and brown and wet and spinning.

Grass and mud become slick rock. Rock becomes air. Hallelujah is floating, just for a second, and then she lands on her back, hard, gasping and tasting mud and water. Rachel is lying a foot away. Their eyes meet. Neither of them moves.

The ravine rises up around them. Where they fell: a tall cliff face, slick gray rock. On the other side: a gentler slope, moving away from the trail they were on. Rainwater is pouring in from both directions, from ground and sky.

What happens next comes in flashes.

Lightning, bright and blinding.

A crack, terrifyingly close.

A splitting sound. Groaning. Leaves on leaves. Air moving.

Above Hallelujah's head, the leaves are getting closer.

She realizes, and she screams, "Rachel!" Her voice is

swallowed by the storm, and so she rolls away, pulling Rachel with her.

The lightning-struck limb crashes to the ground, not far from where they'd been lying. Rachel's backpack is pinned down.

Hallelujah can't take her eyes off of the limb. There's a nest in one crook. Two broken eggs, their contents already washed away by the rain.

"Hallie!" Her name is barely there over the storm, carried downhill on the wind. Hallelujah rolls over to see Jonah skidding down the mountainside. "Hallie!" he calls again. "Rachel!" He's almost there. Hallelujah struggles to sit up. Helps Rachel to sit, too. Jonah jumps down from the high rocks and lands on his feet, staggers, falls to his knees. "I heard the lightning and I saw——"

Thunder drowns him out. Lightning takes out another tree, not far away. The crack is the same. And the groaning, like a dying breath.

"We're okay," Hallelujah says. And it's true. She's soaked, and bruised, and still a little out of breath, but she is not broken. "Right, Rachel?"

Rachel is staring, wide-eyed, at the limb next to her. It's easily as big around as she is. "That almost . . ." she says, her voice wavering and low. "We almost . . ."

"But it didn't. We weren't." Hallelujah says it more firmly than she feels it. Because if she stops to think about how similar she is to those eggshells, how easily she herself could be cracked in half and washed away, she's done for.

# 2

Jonah paces back and forth in front of the rock wall that rises up between where they landed and the trail above. He runs his fingers over the slick rocks like he's looking for handholds. He takes a few steps back, and then runs at the cliff, jumping high. His fingertips don't quite reach the top.

After a few more attempts, he shakes his head. He turns and yells, to be heard over the wind and the rain, "We'll have to find another way back up!" He starts walking, keeping the rocks on his left. Hallelujah and Rachel follow.

Where the rocks end, there's a wall of rhododendron—almost as intimidating. Jonah stops. He stares at the thick shrubs. Then he looks back at Hallelujah and Rachel. "Through?" he shouts. "The trail's up there." He points beyond the rhododendron, up the steep mountainside.

Hallelujah hesitates. The thicket is dark with leaves and twisting branches, but it's not so tangled that they can't force their way through. And it might be their only way back to the trail. She nods, and seeing her nod, Rachel nods. They move forward.

It's slow going. They have to drop to hands and knees just a few feet in. They push branches aside, climb over, slither under. The long, thick leaves protect them from the pounding of the rain, but they also block most of the light. As they crawl, Hallelujah feels the branches closing in like a loss of air.

Just when she's sure they're going in circles, the leaves part. She pushes aside the one branch still in her way and then she's out of the thicket. Jonah holds out a hand to help her to her feet.

They move, staying much closer together, treading much more carefully, up and up and up against the rain pounding down. Hallelujah climbs on all fours, hand grabbing this rock, toes wedging under that exposed root. She's determined not to fall again. And the hill is maybe a forty-five-degree incline. She slides on wet grass and leaves, on surface mud. But she climbs.

They have one plan. Find the trail, hike, hope.

Hope that the storm will pass. That the rain will stop.

Hope that miraculously, there will be an abandoned shack or a lean-to around the next bend. Somewhere to rest. Somewhere to wait.

Hope that even more miraculously, they're only steps from civilization. A warm, dry cabin. A parking lot filled with cars. People.

But Hallelujah doesn't believe in that kind of miracle. They got themselves into this mess, and they're going to have to find their own way out. That's what she tells herself as the thunder and lightning move on, away from them, but the rain continues pouring from the gray sky.

She is wet through. Jacket, long-sleeved shirt, tank top,

jeans, socks, shoes, underwear, and bra. Her hair sticks to her neck. She feels heavy. Her backpack is heavy. Her feet are heavy. Even her heart feels waterlogged.

They climb. They try, fail, to wipe the rain from their eyes. Scrape their hands on rocks and branches. Land knees-down in the mud. Face-plant. Again and again.

Hallelujah's vision narrows. She sees the ground in front of her feet. She sees her feet searching for firmness and safety on that ground. And when she falls, she sees it in slow motion: the sliding of her foot, the streak of the ground changing, the shift of her sightline from ground to trees to sky, a sideways panorama.

But she gets up again. Follows Jonah's blue and Rachel's pink and keeps going. Pushes forward.

Her legs burn. Her lungs burn.

And still the rain falls.


# 3


When Hallelujah was little, one of her Sunday school teachers said that a big storm like this was God watering his garden. And Hallelujah had asked, "What about the desert? What about plants that don't need any more water? What about when people get wet? Are we God's garden?" She'd really wanted to know. The teacher had laughed and moved on.

Now, Hallelujah thinks, the storm feels more like neglect. If God knows they're out here, knows what this rain is doing to them, then he's not the friendly caretaker she was told about in Sunday school. He's inattentive. Careless. Left the hose on, went inside for a glass of sweet tea, and ended up watching SEC football on TV.

They've been climbing for an hour. Maybe longer. Through sheets of rain. And it has occurred to Hallelujah, which means it has probably also occurred to Rachel and Jonah, that they should have found the trail by now. Did they cross right over it, a thin, washed-out dirt stripe in the sea of green? Did they fall farther than they thought?

Or did they climb the wrong hill entirely?

It's a chilling thought. A slice of icy rain, down to the bone.

Because that means that while before, they were just off-course, now, they are lost.

Lost.

Hallelujah has felt lost for the past six months. Since Luke. But now she almost wants to laugh, because clearly, she had no idea what lost was.

"We're lost," she says aloud. Trying out the words.

Jonah turns to look at her. He cocks his head, like he didn't hear what she said.

"We're lost," Hallelujah says again. Louder. She enunciates. "Lost."

And Jonah visibly deflates. Exhales. "I think so, yeah."

"What do you mean?" Rachel is on Hallelujah's other

side. She gets right up in Jonah's face. "I thought you knew where we were going! I thought you knew where the trail was! You said——" Her voice is rising. "You said left!"

"That was before you two fell down the mountain." Jonah's voice is calm, but his eyes are worried. "Before we cut through those bushes. I think we got turned around. Maybe the trail is over there." He points to another hillside. It looks incredibly far away.

"No!" Rachel starts climbing. "It's up here. It has to be!"

Jonah reaches out with one long arm to grab her leg. "We messed up," he says.

Hallelujah, frozen in position, still feeling the icy pellets of perspective raining down on her, repeats, "We're lost."

Rachel curses. And curses again. And again. Screams at the sky. Rips up a wad of grass with one hand and throws it. Curses a few more times. And then sags back against the ground, eyes closed.

That knocks Hallelujah out of her trance. She and Jonah stare. Hallelujah feels a smile in one corner of her mouth. It feels wrong there, like there's a crazy laugh inside that's trying to climb out. She bites her lip. This isn't funny. But the laugh keeps tickling. Maybe Rachel isn't the only one who's a little hysterical.

"Feel better?" Jonah asks.

Rachel nods.

Hallelujah scrambles up to sit next to her. She looks down at Jonah.

Jonah is smiling for real. Shaking his head. "Rachel, you

sure you came on the right hiking trip? I haven't heard words like that in church since——" He makes eye contact with Hallelujah, and they say it together: "George Hays."

A beat. Then Rachel says, equal parts begrudging and curious, "And what happened to him?"

"Dropped a giant box of hymnals on his foot."

Hallelujah picks up the story, the memory making the laugh she's been keeping in escape. "And then he was hopping around, holding his foot like a cartoon character, and he fell down the stairs in front of the pulpit." She pauses, adding, "He was fine."

"Cursed like a sailor," Jonah says. "But not as good as you." He eyes Rachel sidelong. "The church leaders made him apologize publicly to the congregation. What should we do to you?"

"Bite me," Rachel says. But she's smiling now too.

"Not till we run out of energy bars," Jonah answers, his voice softer. The gravity of the situation settles back in.

Hallelujah asks, "What do we do now?"

Jonah squints at the sky. It's nothing but rain clouds. "We find shelter," he says. "We stay put, make a decision when it stops raining."

"Shouldn't we keep moving?" Rachel argues. "Better chance of finding the trail?"

"Or of getting more lost. Or breaking our necks with another long fall."

Rachel looks down the mountain. Down to the crashed limb. "Oh."

"So we'll look for shelter," Hallelujah says. "And we'll wait out the storm. Or maybe we should just stay put altogether? Let the rescuers come to us?"

Rachel pulls her eyes away from the ravine. "We'll get home faster if we find them first," she says. She sounds sure, but Hallelujah doesn't trust Rachel's certainty as much as she did yesterday. She looks to Jonah.

He meets her eyes. "We'll decide once the rain stops."

# 4

AFTER ANOTHER TWENTY MINUTES OF CLIMBING, THEY find a muddy overhang. An ancient tree's thick roots spread wide, but something has dug away the ground underneath. The burrow is only about two feet deep, but it's just wide enough that they can sit side by side. There's a carpet of green that looks soft and inviting. They wedge themselves and their backpacks inside, pulling their feet close.

When Hallelujah looks up, she sees a rare view: a living tree from beneath. The trunk is bigger than the three of them together. The roots, their canopy, dwindle away to nothing where the soil isn't there anymore, but the tree still seems strong. And it covers them almost entirely.

Hallelujah feels like a hobbit.

She looks at Jonah and Rachel. They look back at her. Their faces show a mix of shock and relief, and she's sure her own looks the same.

And then Rachel bursts out laughing. "This," she manages between giggles, teeth chattering, "is ridiculous." She picks at her soaked shorts, at her failure of a rain jacket. "I don't think there's an inch of me that's not wet."

"Same." Jonah pulls his sodden shirt away from his body and wrings it out. "Okay over there, Hallie?"

"Yeah." She squeezes a stream of water from her ponytail and then unzips her backpack. Digs around. Pulls out the smashed, damp remains of what was once an energy bar. Now it's an energy lump. She holds it up. "Who's hungry?"

Rachel grabs it. "Me. I am." She peels open the wrapper and tears off a piece. She pops it in her mouth and chews, making exaggerated "Mmm" noises. "Now if I only had some coffee . . ."

Hallelujah hands Jonah an energy bar and starts eating her own, trying to take small bites to make it last longer. She tries to imagine that instead of oats and dried fruit, she's eating the warm zucchini bread she made last week. With butter. And the coffee Rachel mentioned. Hallelujah wants the taste of coffee in her mouth, the scent in her nostrils, the feel of the warm mug between her hands.

Her stomach growls, and she forces coffee and oven-fresh bread out of her mind. At least they have the carton of orange juice. She gets it out, inserts the tiny straw, takes a small sip. Passes it around.

The rain falls.

"Tomorrow, we are totally going to laugh about this,"

Rachel says. "After a good night's sleep and an awesome hot breakfast. Omelets. Biscuits. And bacon."

"Bacon," echoes Jonah reverently. Hallelujah is glad she wasn't the only one fantasizing about food.

"But do you think . . ." Rachel hesitates. "The search party—they'll be out in the rain, right?"

"Of course," Jonah says immediately. "They're probably on their way now."

Hallelujah watches the rain spatter on the ground. She watches, and she wonders. "Do you think this storm is washing away our trail?" she asks Jonah. "Not *the* trail, but ours—the evidence that we were there. Footprints. The fire."

"They're on their way," Jonah says. His voice is firm. "I've heard about things like this. There's a pattern to how they search. And they use dogs. Those guys can smell us through the rain."

Hallelujah nods, trying to silence her doubts. She leans back into their tiny shelter, pulling her knees toward her chin until the only rain landing on her is ricocheting from the ground or dripping from the ceiling overhead.

She isn't dry, but she isn't getting any wetter, either.

The rain on the leaves and the ground is white noise, a continuous soft shushing. It's a comforting sound, a soothing sound, and with a soft wall to lean on and a warm body beside her and a few bites of food in her stomach, Hallelujah watches the drops fall until she drops off to sleep.

# 5

SHE DREAMS OF RAIN, AND SHE WAKES, SHIVERING AND CHAT-
tering, sitting in two inches of muddy water. Rachel is asleep
with her head on Hallelujah's shoulder. Jonah has his chin on
his knees, watching them.

"How long . . . ?" Hallelujah asks. Her voice is hoarse.
Her mouth feels parched. She reaches for her water bottle.

"About an hour," Jonah says.

"Did it stop at all?" She motions toward the rain. It looks
the same out there as when she dozed off.

"Nope. I don't know where it's all coming from."

"The sky," Hallelujah says, smiling a little.

"Har, har." It wasn't that funny, but Jonah grins
anyway.

"You were keeping watch?"

"Yup. For wild animals. Or rescue. Or whatever."

"Thanks."

"No problem."

Hallelujah takes a swig of water, belatedly realizing that
the bottle, almost empty before, is now full. She looks at it,
and then at Jonah.

"Rain," he says. "I filled up our bottles while y'all were
sleeping."

"Oh." She never would've thought of that. "Thanks," she
says again.

"Drink up. We'll refill."

"Okay." She drinks, feeling the coolness slide down her throat.

They fall silent. Thunder crashes over the mountains. Hallelujah thinks about how the problem with not talking a lot, with being out of practice, is that when you're with another quiet person, you both tend to just sit there. Then again, this silence with Jonah is something new—not the flowing conversation they used to share, but not the pointed not-talking of the past six months, either.

She doesn't know how to feel about it. She wonders if she should shake Rachel awake. Rachel doesn't seem to have a problem filling silence.

As if she heard Hallelujah thinking, Rachel snorts and sits upright so fast she bumps the lip of ceiling that's sheltering them. A few chunks of earth fall on their heads.

"Whoa there," Jonah says, putting his hand on Rachel's shoulder.

Rachel looks around wildly, then her eyes seem to focus. "Oh," she says. "I dreamed I was back at home."

"Lucky," Hallelujah says. "I dreamed about rain. And then I woke up and it was still raining."

"So should we look for somewhere else to wait it out? Somewhere . . . drier?" Rachel asks.

"I think, in this rain, this might be as dry as we're gonna get," Jonah says. Then his stomach growls, loud enough for everyone to hear. He actually blushes. "Sorry."

"I know," Hallelujah says. "But we have to save the food. Right?"

"What do we have left?" Rachel asks.

And so they take inventory again. As if, by magic, something will have appeared that wasn't there last night.

No such luck. They're down to one banana, eight energy bars, and a Diet Coke.

This time it's Hallelujah who goes a little nuts. She's looking at the Diet Coke, and suddenly it's the funniest thing she's ever seen. A Diet Coke! They're lost in the mountains, in the middle of a storm that won't end, and Rachel has a Diet Coke.

The laughter bursts out of her, the kind of laughter that hurts, that takes her breath, that's part sob. She clutches her stomach. Tears roll down her face. Jonah and Rachel stare at her, open-mouthed, but she can't stop laughing because, *We might never get home, but at least we have a Diet Coke!*

Jonah moves around to face her. He grabs her shoulders. "Hallie. Calm down."

"Can't," she gasps. But the laughter is just a wheeze now. She feels like she pulled a stomach muscle.

"Breathe, Hallie." He holds her shoulders, looks into her eyes. "We're gonna be fine. We'll stay here till the rain stops. Then we'll go out and see if we can find the search party. Or the trail. We'll be home soon."

She nods. She gulps. Her eyes well up. He's looking at her with so much compassion. Like he knows what she's going through. Like he cares about her. This is what she wanted to see after everything happened with Luke. Instead, she saw Jonah's back, every time he turned and walked away from her.

She blurts, "Why are you being nice to me?"

She regrets it immediately. It's the vulnerability talking. The fear. The adrenaline. For a second, she forgot the aloof, thick-skinned Hallelujah she needs to be.

Jonah relaxes his grip. He looks away, out into the wet woods. He waits a long time before speaking. "Luke told me."

Hallelujah is instantly tense. "Luke told you what?"

Another long pause. "That he lied. About what happened that night."

"What happened?" Rachel cuts in. "What'd Luke lie about?"

Hallelujah ignores her. She stays focused on Jonah, even though he won't look at her. "What'd he tell you originally?"

Jonah flinches. "He made it . . . worse. Than what he told the adults. He said that that wasn't the first time. And he said that you—"

"Never mind," Hallelujah cuts in. "I can guess." She's heard the rumors. The persistent ones and the surprising, weird, creative ones. She bets there are a lot that she hasn't heard, too. "None of that happened," she says softly but firmly, certain without even knowing exactly what Luke said. What Jonah heard. "None of it."

"That's what he told me yesterday. I wanted to know why he was still—" He swallows, his Adam's apple moving up and down. "I'd heard him and Brad laughing about what they were gonna do to you this week, and I was like, enough is enough. Time to let it go. So I asked him what was up.

Why he was still messing with you."

"And?" Hallelujah asks.

"And he told me the truth: that he'd made most of it up. He said he had to keep you quiet. Plus, um. He said messing with you was fun."

Hallelujah lets that sink in. "You really didn't know it was a lie? You believed him this whole time?"

Jonah suddenly looks right at her. His eyes plead. "I *saw* you, Hallie. And Luke was the only one of the two of you with a story to explain it."

"So you stopped talking to me and started treating me like crap instead of asking me what happened?" She feels her voice getting higher. Hotter. "Because whatever he said just *seemed* like something I would do?"

"Hallie, it's more complicated than—"

"How? How is it more complicated? How is that any kind of excuse?"

"Hallie—"

"So now you're being nice to me because you feel bad."

"What do you want me to say?" Jonah's voice rises to meet hers. "Yeah, I feel bad. I feel really awful. Okay?"

Hallelujah forges on: "Or is it some kind of penance thing? Keep me from dying in the mountains and you'll be forgiven for everything else?"

"That's not fair—"

"You know what? I don't want to hear it. I just want to go home. And if it takes us working together, we'll work together. But we aren't friends. We stay alive, we get home, and then you never talk to me again. My choice this time."

Hallelujah slumps back against the dugout's dirt wall. The emotion of it, all of the fear and pain bursting to the surface—she's exhausted. Then she notices Rachel looking back and forth between the two of them. She was so focused on Jonah, she almost forgot Rachel was there.

"Hal?" Rachel says softly.

"Not now." Hallelujah pulls her knees to her chest, wraps her arms around her legs, and drops her head. The tears come slowly at first, like the first raindrops this morning. And then her shoulders are shaking—by themselves, she can't help it—and the tears fall.

She hears Jonah say, "I'm going for a walk." Then a rustling, his heavy steps moving away.

She hears Rachel cry out, scared, "Wait! Don't leave us—" and Jonah's answer, "I just have to—" and then it's just the rain.

The rain that won't stop, will probably never stop.

And the tears fall.

# 6

Time passes. Rain. Rain. Rachel puts her hand on Hallelujah's back.

The tears eventually dry up, and then it's just ragged breath for a few minutes, and then that stops too.

Hallelujah sits up. She feels wrung out.

She meets Rachel's eyes and Rachel says, "Better?"

A shrug.

"Looks like that was a long time coming."

A nod.

Rachel pats her own shoulder, and, surprising herself, Hallelujah leans in and drops her head.

"We're gonna get out of here," Rachel says. "Even though we're both apparently really bad in a crisis. Brought all our baggage along." She adds, a little hesitantly, "If you want to talk about it . . . while he's not here, I mean . . ."

Hallelujah can see Jonah sitting under a tree a short distance away. His back is a blue dot in the sea of green and brown. Despite everything, that blue dot is reassuring. He didn't leave. She didn't run him off.

"Okay," Rachel goes on, "I'll tell you about *my* baggage. Or some of it, anyway. We can talk about the God thing later."

"The God thing?" Hallelujah asks.

"Later," Rachel repeats. "So my parents separated a couple months ago. They should've done it sooner, honestly; they were miserable. They hate each other. But still."

"I'm sorry," Hallelujah says.

"Thanks. The thing is," Rachel goes on, her voice light but brittle, "I'm an only child. And they both wanted out so bad, they'd fight over me, too. Not who got to keep me, but who—" A gulp. "Who got to leave and start fresh. Like I didn't matter. Like I was the furniture. Let the court decide. I don't think they really meant it like that, they just couldn't see beyond—" Another gulp.

"Anyway, Mom lost and she won me—lucky her—and we moved to Bristol, where she grew up. Just after Christmas. I had to leave my school and my friends in Nashville and—and she didn't care how hard it was on me. And even once we moved, I could tell I was reminding her of Dad, all the time. I started looking for things to do over spring break. To get away. Give her some time alone. This girl I used to go to church with posted about this trip online, and I checked out the website and it looked cool. So I signed up. Of course, she ended up not coming, but I'd already paid my deposit when she bailed, so here I am. And I thought—I thought maybe after a week alone, Mom would miss me. Maybe things would get better."

Hallelujah keeps her head still on Rachel's shoulder. She listens.

"I know lots of people's parents get divorced. No big deal. But it sucks, and I just want it to stop sucking. I thought maybe this week wouldn't suck." A laugh, sharp and bitter. "So much for that. Your parents still together?"

Hallelujah nods. "Yeah. Almost thirty years."

"Do they fight?"

"Sometimes. But they always talk it out. 'Don't let the sun go down on your anger,' and all that stuff."

"My parents' motto was 'Don't let the sun go down

until you have the last word.'" Now Rachel's laugh is more genuine.

Hallelujah sits up. She wipes the tear crust from under her eyes.

"Okay," Rachel says. "Your turn."

"I'm just not used to—" *Talking about it. Wanting to talk. Having someone to talk to.* "—talking," Hallelujah finishes lamely. Understatement of the year.

"No kidding. I mean, when I first saw you, I thought you looked a little lonely. But the more I talked to you, I was like, this is either the saddest girl on the planet or the lamest. No offense."

Hallelujah feels embarrassment wash over her. "I wasn't always like this," she murmurs. "I used to be normal."

Rachel waves a hand, like, *Whatever.* "No such thing," she says. "Honestly, it made me want to figure you out, what was making you tick. And I think—I think we're gonna get along. Some people talk too much. I talk too much. But you know how to listen. I can tell." Hesitantly, she adds, "I think Jonah listens too."

Hallelujah doesn't answer.

"I think he's really torn up about . . . whatever happened with you and Luke," Rachel goes on. "You didn't see his face when you were crying. . . ."

"Because he made me cry," Hallelujah points out. It's a low blow, but she doesn't want to think of him as a nice guy who has feelings. Not yet.

"We agreed that that was a built-up cry," Rachel shoots

back. "About more than Jonah."

Hallelujah nods. She could argue, but Rachel is right. She would never have cried if it weren't for the storm, the lightning-struck limb, the night on hard ground, her empty stomach, Luke's dropping her in the creek yesterday. Never mind the past six months.

"We should go get him," Rachel says.

"Why?" Hallelujah still feels raw. Not ready.

"Because he's upset, and we have to be a team." Rachel is matter-of-fact. "And because he's the one who knows how to make a fire and keep our food away from bears."

"Okay." Hallelujah checks her backpack, eases her way out of the dugout, and gets to her feet. She takes a few steps away from their burrow, testing her pins-and-needles legs. She's surprised to find how sore her muscles are; the soreness didn't register this morning, during their frantic climb. Her upper back aches where she slammed into the ground after her tumble downhill. She itches, too. Mostly on her hands. Too much nature.

As Rachel crawls out from under the tree, her backpack hits the root-and-dirt ceiling. Clumps of dirt drop. Large clumps, head-size clumps. The roots sink where the earth has fallen away. Hallelujah sees the tree trunk tilting, its bulk no longer supported. Their dugout is getting smaller by the second.

Rachel sees it happening too, and jumps aside. The tree doesn't crash to the ground, but stops at a crazy diagonal, thick roots touching the ground where they were just sitting.

The roots still in the earth bend and twist, but don't snap.

"So much for that hiding place," Rachel says with a shaky smile.

Hallelujah nods, staring at the roots that are holding the tree in the ground. They're deep and thick, but flexible. Bent, but not broken. Because of them, the tree will survive.

# 7

JONAH IS WAITING FOR THEM. HE'S SITTING ON A ROCK, watching them walk toward him. When they're close enough to speak without shouting, he says, "How'd you pull that off?" He nods toward the diagonal tree.

Hallelujah stays quiet.

Rachel pipes up, "My fault. I shouldn't be allowed to touch anything."

The rain has dropped to a gentle drizzle. The sun is peeking out from behind a cloud. The world is misty and surreal, soft-focus. Once again, Hallelujah is overwhelmed by how beautiful it is. All of it. Away from the trail, away from any sign of other people, it's overgrown and wild and lovely.

But that wild beauty is a double-edged sword. Because they're still lost.

"What do we do now?" she asks. Her voice sounds harsh, wrong over the birds chirping and drizzle hitting leaves, like she doesn't belong. But maybe that feeling's because of Jonah. Because of what he did to her, after Luke. Because of what she said to him, just now.

She did see his face. Rachel was right. He's really upset. God only knows why.

"Well, we finally got a break." Jonah's voice is wry. "It's *almost* not raining."

The clouds are moving fast overhead, but they're white now, rather than the dull, dangerous gray of this morning.

This morning. Now, judging by the sun, it's midafternoon. Hallelujah's stomach is a gaping hole.

"So we move?" Rachel asks.

"Yep." Jonah doesn't elaborate.

And so Hallelujah asks him, "Where?" She doesn't bring up her earlier plan to stay in one place. She doesn't feel like arguing anymore. And she trusts Jonah's judgment. In this, if nothing else.

"Up," Jonah says. "I want to find somewhere we can see a long way. Make a fire. Try to send a smoke signal." He stands, slings his backpack on, turns, and walks, without waiting to see if Hallelujah and Rachel are following him.

They climb. Feet more sure on sun-drying ground. Legs wobbly and aching. With hunger and fear gnawing around the edges.

Hallelujah is third again. She doesn't mind. She climbs, watching Jonah's and Rachel's backs. She fixes her eyes on each of them in turn. Lets the scenery around her blur. Doesn't want to fall behind.

She focuses on small details. Jonah's muscular legs are scratched up, probably from his race down the hill after them earlier. His hiking socks don't match—different cuffs. The mud on Rachel's legs is smeared around, like she tried to wipe herself clean but only made it worse. There are a few streaks where she scratched, white skin peeking through. She looks like she had a self-tanning accident. And on her butt: two muddy circles, drying and crusting.

Hallelujah bets her own butt looks the same. And while the warmth of the sun is drying her top half, Hallelujah's jeans remain stubbornly damp. They're rubbing her inner thighs raw. Her feet are still damp, too. She can feel a blister forming on her heel.

She hikes. Up and over and around and under, a winding path between trees and bushes. A path to nowhere. Except that Jonah seems to have a plan.

It's easier to think about hiking *to* somewhere. Because *to* eventually leads home.

Hallelujah wants to ask Jonah for more information. But Jonah hasn't said a word to her since they started climbing, and Hallelujah doesn't want to make things worse by opening her mouth. Not again.

She and Jonah were sharing something. Something tentative, something new and familiar at the same time. And she had to go and—

But she *had* to. Jonah can't just decide to be her friend again. Not now. Not after everything. She can't just let him in. She can't.

Can she?

Hallelujah runs directly into Rachel's back.

"Hey," Rachel says softly, putting out a hand to steady herself on a tree. "Careful." It's not a warning, not an admonishment, just a statement of fact. They both know what careless means out here.

"What's he doing?" Hallelujah asks, just as softly. Jonah has gone ahead, but for some reason Rachel isn't following.

"He thought he saw something. An animal. Told me to wait here. To be still."

*Be still.* Hallelujah freezes midfidget, as if the command came from above. Was it a bear? A deer? She's seen both in Cades Cove, and that's the tourist part of the park.

"Side note," Rachel says, scratching the back of one leg with the front of the other foot. "I think I'm allergic to something out here. My legs totally itch."

Hallelujah wants to shush Rachel. This is her idea of still and quiet? Surely whatever Jonah saw can hear them. Is watching them. Is waiting for the right moment.

But then Jonah reappears. "All clear," he says. "It's gone."

"What was it?" Hallelujah asks.

"Bear. A cub."

"Are you sure they're gone?" Hallelujah says "they" intentionally. A cub isn't dangerous, but it means the mother's nearby. And she is dangerous.

"I'm sure. And anyway, we are on their turf." Jonah looks over his shoulder, up the hill. "C'mon. We're almost at the top." He glances back at Hallelujah, and their eyes meet for the first time since their confrontation in the dugout. He holds her gaze for a second, and then nods, turns, and starts walking.

# 8

THE VIEW IS INCREDIBLE. A 360 PANORAMA. IF THIS WERE A movie, the camera would sweep around and around, taking in their wide eyes along with the mountains rolling into the distance. There would be a swell of strings, a breathless final swoop before the dialogue, soft and awestruck.

It's not the tallest peak. Not by a long shot. They're at the top of what can't even really be called a mountain, not with everything else around. There are mountains visible behind other mountains, rising up behind valleys, peeking out, hills upon hills upon hills. The green mounds look so much softer and gentler from a distance. Almost like a blanket that someone left rumpled. Or that someone's still sleeping under.

And there are so many trees. So many shades of green. Sunlit green and shadowed green. Grass green and moss green and pine green and the greens of every variety of leaf.

Hallelujah turns in a circle. Mountain. Mountain. Valley. Mountain. Mountain. "What are we looking for?" she asks Jonah.

"Anything. A trail. Campfire smoke. People. The color

orange—the rescue squads and dogs wear orange jackets. Usually. I think."

"Right." She starts scanning.

Rachel joins her, eyes trailing Hallelujah's. "Should we shout or something?"

"Yeah, probably." Hallelujah feels a little silly that they didn't think of that before. "Hello!" she calls. "Up here!"

Rachel starts yelling too. "Anyone out there? Hello!"

As they call out, Hallelujah keeps turning in slow circles. Twice she thinks she sees something. A wisp of smoke. A flash of bright orange. Far away. But she blinks and they're gone, vanished into the sea of green. Twice she almost says something. But she can't find them again. She's not even sure they were ever there.

Eventually, Rachel sits down and begins using her backpack to try to wipe the dried mud off her legs. Hallelujah sits beside her, elbows on knees, scratching idly at her palms. Her eyes are tired. Her voice is tired. But she doesn't want to stop looking. Or stop shouting. They can't have gone so far from civilization that there's *nothing* out there.

"We'll try again later," Rachel says, patting Hallelujah on the shoulder.

Behind them, Jonah paces. Like an animal. Caged by all this openness.

Then he starts gathering wood. Scuffing away the grass from a clear area. Setting up the sticks in the dirt, careful to stay well away from the few bare trees that stick straight up from the hilltop. "It's okay that it's wet, actually," he says, kind of to himself.

After a second, Hallelujah asks, "Why?"

"It's harder to light, but wet wood smokes more when you burn it."

Hallelujah nods, understanding. A better smoke signal.

"Also, we'll be less likely to start a forest fire," Jonah adds, piling up more sticks.

"Um, guys? Y'all have to look at this. . . ." Rachel is staring in horror at her legs. She's wiped off the mud to reveal angry red welts. The surrounding skin looks extra pale in contrast. "Oh my God!" she wails. "It itches so bad!"

Jonah walks over and squats down. "Looks like poison ivy," he says. "You must've sat in it."

With dawning realization, Hallelujah stares at her itching hands. They're covered in a spotty red rash. She thinks of the soft green plant carpet beneath the tree roots, and she knows. "Under the tree," she says.

"Yeah, probably." Jonah starts examining his legs. He has a few red splotches on his calves, but nothing major. "You're lucky you're in jeans."

Hallelujah thinks of her raw, chafed inner thighs. Luck is relative. But she holds up her hands, the palms red and puffy, and says, "I still touched it."

"What am I going to do?" Rachel spits through clenched teeth. She's breathing heavily, like it's taking a lot of effort not to scratch.

"Did the mud help?" Jonah asks. "Did it itch less before you cleaned your legs?"

"Yes—no—I don't know!" Rachel throws her hands in the air.

Hallelujah scoops up a handful of damp earth and runs it through her hands like she's lathering soap. The itch lessens. Just a little. "Try it," she says to Rachel.

Rachel slaps mud onto her thighs, grumbling something about just getting clean and not being able to handle this. Once her legs are covered, she says, loud, "Can we at least eat something?"

Hallelujah's stomach growls in reaction. Breakfast—so small—seems so long ago. She digs out an energy bar for each of them. Rachel tears into hers, wolflike. Jonah takes two bites and folds the package closed, sticks the remainder in his pocket, goes back to the fire preparations. Hallelujah eats hers slowly, trying to savor it, to make it bigger than it is. Also trying not to touch anything but the wrapper with her muddy hands. And trying not to think about the fact that they're down to five now. Five energy bars and a banana.

And that stupid Diet Coke. It doesn't even have any sugar in it. It's useless.

*Like me*, Hallelujah thinks before she can help it. And just like that, she decides not to be useless anymore. It isn't only up to Jonah to get them out. Or up to the rescuers to find them. She can do more than just keep from falling behind.

She stands. Holds on to a tree until the light-headed feeling of standing too fast passes. Her stomach, having taken in three hundred calories, wants more, more, more, but she ignores it. She walks over to Jonah.

"What kind of wood do you need?" she asks.

He looks at her. Then says, "Try for damp, not soggy. And not rotting."

She nods, looking down at the pile. She tries to memorize the appearance of those branches. Then she walks downhill.

Jonah lets her go. But at the last minute, he adds, "Stay close."

# 9

SHE'S CARRYING A HEAVY LOAD OF STICKS AND BRANCHES, trying to ignore the burning where her palms touch the rough wood, where the mud has smeared, when she sees it. A patch of bright yellow dandelions. She stares. A scene pops into her head: her middle school graduation dinner, a fancy restaurant, the salad arriving with dandelions on top. Leaves and petals. Her dad refusing to eat them. "Weeds. I'm not eating weeds." But she'd tried them. They tasted like lettuce, but with a sharp bite. She's been meaning to use them in a recipe of her own.

She looks around for a landmark. That crooked tree. The dandelions are by that crooked tree.

She stumbles over her feet getting back to the top of the

mountain, to their small camp. She drops the wood in a pile next to Jonah's fire pit.

He glances up. "Thanks." Then he really looks at her. "Everything okay?"

"I think I found something." She's a little out of breath, not from the hiking but from the excitement. Her hands tingle. "Something we can *eat*."

"Seriously?"

Hallelujah nods.

"Show me."

Rachel looks up, interested. But she doesn't move from her mud-covered seat.

Jonah says, over his shoulder, "Watch the fire. We'll be right back."

Hallelujah leads him back to the crooked tree. Her stomach flips at the sight of the dandelions. She didn't realize she was this hungry, still, but of course she is because she's had two energy bars and a few sips of orange juice today and nothing else, and they've walked and walked and walked.

"Here," she says. "Do your Boy Scout thing."

"Dandelions?" he asks. He raises an eyebrow, picks a flower, and examines it. Smelling. Studying. His tongue darts out to touch the stem, the petals, the leaves.

Hallelujah can barely stand it. "I had them once with my parents. In a salad." She feels like an animal. She wants to tear the flowers from the ground and stuff them into her mouth until her stomach is full.

"I think it's okay," Jonah says.

"You think?"

"Well, seeing as I don't have a field guide to edible plants on me . . ." He flashes her an annoyed look. "It's kind of a risk."

"Yeah, but we—" Hallelujah lowers her voice. Not that Rachel is likely to hear her from this distance, but still. "Even if we cut meals in half, we run out of food tomorrow. What if they don't find us? What if—"

Jonah cuts her off. "Right. You're right. Anyway, I don't think these'll kill us. At most, we'll get the runs. Which isn't great, but we can get more water tomorrow."

Hallelujah grimaces. For everything good, there's a possible side effect.

"Get as many as you can carry." Jonah starts to pull the flowers out by the roots.

"Um. Maybe I shouldn't touch them." She shows Jonah her muddy, poison ivy–covered palms. "We probably don't want to eat . . . all this. Right?"

"Good call. Can we use your jacket?"

Hallelujah nods. She slips out of her jacket and lets Jonah drop handful after handful onto the fabric. Then she carefully wraps up the bundle of dandelions and carries the jacket back to their camp, Jonah right behind her.

When Rachel sees their bounty, her eyes go wide. Her mouth actually forms a round *O*.

"Rachel, I've got a job for you," Jonah says. He takes

Hallelujah's jacket and plops it down in front of Rachel. "Can you get the dirt off these? And Hallie, can you find some more wood?"

They work. By the time the sun is hanging low in the late-afternoon sky, Jonah has a good-size fire going. Smoke rises in a column, blowing lazily in the breeze. They all move upwind of it.

Jonah looks satisfied. "If anyone's looking for us—which they are, for sure—they'll see the smoke coming from up here where there's no campsite, shouldn't be any people, and then it's just a matter of getting to us. Plus," he adds, "from here we should see 'em coming."

Hallelujah's arms ache from carrying wood. Her legs ache from climbing all day. Her back still feels bruised from her fall into the ravine. Her hands itch so, so much. The skin on her thighs burns from being chafed by wet denim. Her heel blister has popped, and she thinks her sock has stuck to it. But she's pleased with their work. Proud. The emotions from earlier, the hysterical laughter and tears, they're gone. Replaced by a sense of peace. They did what they could do today. Beat Mother Nature.

She deliberately pushes tomorrow out of her head.

They sit next to the fire as the air grows chill, as the sun drops even lower toward the horizon. They each have one-third of Jonah's banana, one-third of an energy bar, and handful after handful of bitter dandelions.

It rains on them again, just once. A sudden, short storm. They don't even bother to look for shelter. Just hold their water bottles to the sky and let it happen.

Jonah stares at his fire as it goes out. He takes off his jacket and throws it over the remaining wood, tucking the edges like he's tucking a child into bed. And then he waits. When it's been a good five minutes without rain, he starts a new fire on top of the smoldering, wet remains of his earlier work.

Hallelujah doesn't ask what she can do to help this time. She can sense that he needs to do this alone. Plus, it's not like she can find good wood now, at twilight, after a storm like that. They'll have to use what they've got. What Jonah saved.

She huddles next to Rachel. It's getting colder and colder, and she can feel Rachel shivering. She wraps her coat around them both, trying to share body heat without touching Rachel's hive-covered legs. She doesn't want to get any more poison ivy rash than she already has.

Jonah rebuilds. Hallelujah watches him. Rachel stares into the place where the fire was. No one says a word.

# 10

THE SUN SETS. THE NIGHT SOUNDS START UP, ANIMALS CALLING back and forth. On their little mountaintop, Hallelujah feels like she, Jonah, and Rachel are the only people in the world. Prehistoric. Or survivors on a deserted island. In the dark, the wind on leaves is like the ocean, a rushing and a whisper.

The stars are very close.

It's cold. Even with the fire rebuilt, even wearing her tank top, swim T-shirt, and long-sleeved shirt under her jacket, Hallelujah has goosebumps. She sits as near to the flames as she dares—so near, a spark jumps over to her jeans and she has to hurriedly pat it out. The burn is sudden, over quickly, remains as only a small stinging on her thigh—a sign that she's still alive.

They're still alive. More than twenty-four hours in the mountains with no map, no camping supplies, definitely not enough food. It feels like longer. Like they've been out here for days. Weeks. Forever. In this darkness, with the tree-waves cresting and crashing on the mountains all around them, with *something* howling on one of the other peaks, home seems like a dream.

Hallelujah feels strange. She feels like she's watching a TV show with herself in it, wondering how it will all turn out. *Will they be rescued? Tune in next time.*

Rachel interrupts her thoughts. "I have to go to the bathroom." She stands up. Her red-and-white legs glow in the firelight and moonlight.

Hallelujah stands too. "I'll come with you."

"You don't have to."

"I have to go too." She does. Only a little.

They walk to the edge of the clearing. Look out into the shadows.

Rachel goes first. She picks her steps carefully. Hallelujah steps where Rachel stepped until the fire is just a flickering red through the trees behind them.

"I'm going . . . over there," Rachel says, gesturing vaguely. "I'll call out. Let you know I'm not dead. And who knows—maybe someone else'll hear us yelling too."

"Okay." Hallelujah watches Rachel's back as she moves away. Then she can't see her at all.

The trees surround her, and so she looks up. Turns in a circle. The stars blink down at her through the branches. If the trees are too close, are suffocating her, the sky looks too big, impossibly big.

"I'm still alive!" Rachel calls from somewhere to Hallelujah's right.

"Me too!" she calls back, unzipping her jeans with her swollen, itchy fingers. The wind is ice against her bare skin. She moves fast. She's dressed again in seconds.

"Hal?" Rachel is coming closer.

"Here." Hallelujah moves toward the voice, feeling with her feet to keep from having to put her raw palms against the bark of trunks and branches. She crosses her arms, tucking her hands into her armpits.

It's a mistake. Because when she trips over something she can't see, she's not ready. She stumbles forward, and her left foot catches on something, and her boot gets wedged, and her body lands but her foot stays put.

She feels the ankle pop.

She hits the ground hard.

For a second, she's just trying to breathe. Then she feels the sharp, hot stab of pain inside her ankle. It's like there's a knife in her hiking boot.

She whimpers.

Rachel appears. "Hal? You okay?"

Hallelujah doesn't move. She doesn't want to make it worse. The pain shoots up her leg. "My ankle," she says softly. Talking louder would make it hurt more.

Rachel rushes to kneel next to Hallelujah. "Which foot?"

"Left."

Rachel gently runs her hands down Hallelujah's leg, stopping when she reaches the wounded ankle. Hallelujah gasps at the pressure. "Okay," Rachel says. "Um. Do you think you can walk on it?"

"I don't know. But it's stuck." And throbbing. And throbbing.

"If I lift the root, can you pull your foot out?"

"I can try." Hallelujah sits up carefully and inches closer to the root, letting her knee bend. She grasps her left thigh with both hands, ready to pull. "Go," she says, gritting her teeth in anticipation.

"One, two . . . three!" Rachel groans as she pulls at the root. But it moves, loosens its grip on Hallelujah's boot, and she pulls her leg, and she feels her ankle pop again and her foot is free. Hallelujah falls back onto her elbows.

"I'll help you up." Rachel scrambles to her feet.

Hallelujah blinks back tears. "I can't," she says.

"Come on, Hal," Rachel says. "I've got you."

So Hallelujah extends her hand.

# 11

THE HIKE BACK UP THE HILL IS GRUELING. HALLELUJAH can barely breathe through the pain of each step. Rachel is panting from the effort of holding Hallelujah up. Still, when they get closer to the clearing, Rachel manages to call out: "Jonah! Help!"

There's a rustling noise up ahead. Twigs snapping. And then Jonah appears. His face is in shadow, but his voice is worried: "What happened?"

"I turned my ankle," Hallelujah says. "I'm okay."

"She's not okay," Rachel gasps. "She can't put weight on it. Can you carry her?"

Jonah doesn't hesitate. He wraps one arm around Hallelujah's waist, and then he scoops up her legs with the other. In a single, fluid motion, she's off the ground. She holds on to his shoulders. For a second, she thinks about how strange this is—to be held like this, to be held by Jonah. Then he starts moving, and she can't think of anything but the pain.

When they reach the clearing, Jonah lowers Hallelujah to the ground near the fire. He takes a step back. "Are you bleeding?"

"I don't think so."

"I'll take a look." Rachel squats down and rolls up Hallelujah's jeans leg. She loosens the laces of Hallelujah's hiking boot and slides it off. She folds down her sock.

Hallelujah leans back on her elbows and stares up. She knows they have to see what's going on, but her ankle *hurts*. The tears well up again, and she squeezes her eyes closed to hold them in.

Until: "This isn't good." Rachel's voice is low and serious. And so Hallelujah forces herself to open her eyes and sit up and look.

In the light of the fire, it's easy to see the swelling. The inside of her left ankle, where there should be just the tiny ankle-bone bump, is darkening and growing puffy.

"We have to elevate it," Rachel says. She looks at Jonah for confirmation. He's still standing about a foot away. Not helping. Hallelujah thinks, *Why isn't he helping?* Rachel must be thinking the same thing, because she pauses for a second and then says, "Jonah, we need to get her foot above her heart. Can you find, I don't know, a rock or a pile of branches or something?"

"Sure. Yes." Jonah vanishes into the woods.

Rachel turns back to Hallelujah. "Put your foot in my lap," she says. "Lie back."

Hallelujah does as she's told, a patient on an exam table.

The knife-pain is lessening, but the throbbing is still strong. She feels it reverberating up and down her body. She feels it behind her eyes, deep in her skull. She focuses on breathing in and out.

Footsteps. Jonah's back. "This all right?" he asks.

Hallelujah cranes her neck to see. He's holding a rock the size of a toddler.

"Looks good," Rachel says. "Maybe find something soft to put over it?"

"Thought of that." Jonah sets the rock down carefully. Hallelujah can see that his fingers are muddy, fingernails cracked and split, like he dug the rock up with his hands. "There's some pine needles over that way. Should make an okay pillow." He strides back off the way he came.

Rachel has pulled her backpack toward her and is rummaging through it. She gets out a pink one-piece swimsuit with tie straps. She stretches and pulls at it, appraising.

"What's that for?" Hallelujah croaks. Her nose is starting to run. She wipes it on one sleeve.

"Bandage. We've got to wrap your ankle to try to keep the swelling down."

"Oh." Hallelujah leans her head back again, letting it rest on the hard ground. "How do you know so much about sprained ankles?"

"I want to be a physical therapist," Rachel says. She carefully lifts Hallelujah's leg and sets the swimsuit underneath. "At my old school, they let me shadow the trainer for the girls' sports teams." She wraps the suit around and around Hallelujah's ankle, aligning the bra cups with the worst of the swelling. "I don't know much. But I've wrapped a few ankles." She pulls the spandex snug but not too snug and ties the straps securely. As an afterthought, she moves the knot so it's not directly on top of the swollen area. "How's that?" she asks.

Hallelujah looks down at her foot. It looks ridiculous, a puffy, pink polka-dot bandage. But it feels sturdy. "I think it's good," she says. "Thanks."

When Jonah returns, arms full of pine boughs, he doesn't even blink at Hallelujah's pink ankle wrap. He uses the boughs to create a pine-needle cushion on top of the rock, and then helps Hallelujah move closer so her leg is as comfortable as possible.

"There," Rachel says. She sits back. "Are you okay?"

Hallelujah nods. Her eyes well up again. Jonah and Rachel stare down at her. Having their eyes on her reminds her, abruptly, of that night with Luke, and she has to shake her head to clear that image out. "I'm fine," she says. She closes her eyes and tries to will the throbbing to stop.

It doesn't.

Which is why, God knows how long later, after Rachel has fallen asleep on the ground next to her, Hallelujah is still awake. Watching the fire flicker.

"Jonah?" she says softly. She can't see him. He could be asleep too.

But he's not. He stirs. "Yeah?"

"I can't sleep."

"Does it hurt bad?"

"It's . . ." She manages a small snort. "It's not good."

A shifting behind her. Jonah's shadow comes into her line of vision. Jonah himself follows. He sits next to her, careful not to block the fire's warmth from reaching her. Hallelujah pushes up to sitting. Jonah smells unwashed, like sweat and dirt and mildew. Hallelujah knows she probably smells the same.

"We'll get found tomorrow, right?" she asks.

"Yeah." Jonah's voice is soft but fierce. Like he's challenging the universe. Challenging God. "We will get found tomorrow." Because saying it makes it seem true.

It's late, and the wind is cold. It's hours until dawn. Until the sun. They stare into the fire. Their arms are touching, and Hallelujah can feel waves of emotion rolling off Jonah, hitting her.

Out of nowhere, he says, voice breaking, "I'm sorry."

"Me too." And she means it. Before doesn't matter in this moment. It certainly doesn't help.

Jonah pokes at the fire with a stick. His shoulders are hunched. He looks young. He looks vulnerable. He says it again: "I'm sorry."

"Me too," Hallelujah repeats. She hesitates for a second, then puts her arm around him, just across his back. It feels both totally wrong and completely right—to be sitting here, now, under an open sky, raw and injured and exposed, to be comforting Jonah, to be apologized to. She doesn't know if it feels wrong or right to him, because they don't talk after that. Jonah adds a few more branches to the fire. After a while they lie down, closer this time, careful not to disturb Rachel, whose sleep exhales puff white and frosty in the mountain air.

She remembers talking to God a lot right after everything happened with Luke. She remembers crying and asking why, over and over. Asking for help, for strength, for understanding. Apologizing for what she did wrong. Talking through everything she could have, should have done differently. Begging for the torment to stop.

She remembers belief and trust slowly turning sour. Still, she kept talking to God out of habit. And because she didn't have anyone else to talk to. At night, in the dark sanctuary of her bedroom, alone, she could say the things she'd been keeping quiet. But she stopped expecting an answer. Stopped hoping for one.

After a while, God felt as distant, as uncaring, as everyone else.

And her prayers faded away.

the
fourth
day

# 1

SHE WAKES WITH THE SUN. HALLELUJAH CAN FEEL IT through her eyelids, in that split second between asleep and awake. She wants to pull the covers over her head. She wishes she *had* covers.

She's stiff. So stiff. Everything hurts. Her left ankle especially, though last night's angry throb is now just a dull ache. Her hands, meanwhile, feel thick and scaly.

When she yawns, she feels the dried tears crack on her cheeks.

Rachel is asleep, mouth open.

Jonah is squatting by what's left of their fire. "Morning," he says softly.

"Morning," Hallelujah murmurs back.

"How are you feeling?" Jonah asks. He comes over and takes her by one arm to help her slide toward the fire.

"I'm okay," Hallelujah says. But the movement makes her ankle *ping* and she bites her lip, waiting for it to pass. "I'm okay," she says again.

Jonah watches her. "Liar," he says. "You don't have to fake it, you know. You're allowed to hurt."

"Maybe I can"—another *ping*—"trick myself. Into being okay."

Jonah nods. "Sure. But tell me if you need anything."

"Okay. I will."

Jonah pulls his flint and steel out of his back pocket and starts striking it over a small pile of wood. He frowns a little, pursing his lips in total concentration. With his hair sticking up and sleep lines on his face, he looks much younger. And adorable—as much as she hates to admit it. Watching him work like this, Hallelujah feels like she's witnessing something intimate, something she shouldn't be seeing. Peeking into his bedroom while he's sleeping. That thought makes her blush, and she looks away.

For a second, she wonders if morning-Hallelujah is as attractive in her rumpled, dirty, matted-hair state. She doubts it. Not that it matters.

The scenery is enough to distract her. Sunrise over the mountains, all pinks and purples and peaches with white cotton-ball clouds. The clouds are low, so low Hallelujah feels like she could reach up and grab one. Light streams down, split into actual shining rays. The sea of trees is a vivid, happy green in the early morning light, a stark contrast to last night's dark, threatening void.

The hills still stretch out in all directions, but now they look bright and new. And for just a moment, Hallelujah feels hope burble up in her chest, fresh and sharp and cold as a mountain spring. Anything could happen today. Great things could happen today. Rescue—improbable as it seemed last night—*could happen today.* And she is hit by such a strong sense of *everything's going to be okay* that she gasps.

Jonah rushes over. "What's up?"

"It's just . . . really beautiful," she answers. That's not it, not really, but it's where the feeling came from. Maybe Jonah can feel it too.

"Oh." Jonah sounds surprised. He looks out over the landscape, considering. "Yeah, it is." He sits down next to her. Shoulder to shoulder, arm to arm, thigh to thigh. He feels warm and solid and safe. And she feels warm and solid and safe, for the first time in a long time.

It's not just Jonah giving her that feeling. It's something else, too.

"I feel like—" She stops, not sure how to put it, not sure she wants to put it into words at all.

Jonah glances over at her, waiting.

"I feel like we're safe. Right now. I feel like—" She stops again. Then says, softly, "Do you think God is watching out for us?"

She wants to take it back immediately. She waits for him to laugh. To make fun of her.

But he doesn't. He just says, "I sure hope he is." And he doesn't say it like he's being sarcastic.

Which gives Hallelujah the courage to ask, "Do you ever, you know, feel God?" She cringes. It sounds so . . . earnest.

Like something her parents would say. Or Luke's dad, from the pulpit. She tries again. "I mean, in church they say we should be trying to feel God's presence. Look for signs that he's there. So—do you feel it?"

"Do I feel God?" Jonah repeats. He pulls his long legs up and leans forward to rest his chin on his knees. "Maybe?" He pauses, frowning a little. "I guess I don't know what God is supposed to feel like. And sometimes things go really great and sometimes they don't, and sometimes you get something you pray for and sometimes you don't, but it's not like I feel this *feeling* like 'God is here with me right now.'"

"Do you still believe he is? Even if you can't feel it?"

"Yeah, sure." He says it quickly, easily, with a shrug. "Why?"

Hallelujah looks down at her hands. "I used to feel something, I don't know, bigger than me. Especially when I was singing. I would get this sense of being in the right place, doing what I was supposed to be doing. This sense that everything was aligned just right. And when I'd feel that, I thought maybe I was feeling God."

Jonah nudges her with his shoulder. "Thought?" he says softly. "Not 'think'?"

"I haven't felt that way in a while."

The words *since Luke* hover between them.

Jonah pushes them aside. "But you feel it now? Or, you felt it a minute ago?"

"Maybe. Yeah."

They're both quiet for a second. Then Jonah says, "So do

you think there's some kind of plan? To us being out here? Not rescued yet?"

"I don't know. Do you?"

"No idea. But if there is a plan, I hope he gets to the point soon. How's that?"

Hallelujah looks at Jonah and sees him smiling. He looks hopeful. She can't help but smile back. "Me too."

Then Jonah does something Hallelujah would have never predicted. He stands up, looks up. "God," he says, speaking directly to the low-hanging clouds, "if you're listening right now, I just wanted to tell you we're ready to go home. We're hungry and it was pretty cold last night and Hallie needs a doctor for her ankle. So we'd like to be rescued." He looks down at Hallelujah. "Anything to add?"

She clears her throat. It takes her a second to find the right words. To push past the doubt, the frustration, the uncertainty that she feels. She tries to latch on to Jonah's belief. She tries to recapture the calm, safe, hopeful feeling she had a few minutes ago.

"Um. God, thanks for not waking us up with a thunderstorm. Thanks for this beautiful morning. I'm honestly really glad I got to see this sunrise, from this spot." She pauses, a little choked up. "But like Jonah said, we're pretty much ready to be rescued. I don't know—I don't know how much longer we can last. Without help." Now she's really choked up.

Another surprise: Jonah reaches down and squeezes her shoulder.

He finishes the prayer: "Amen."

They stay still for a second. Hallelujah is not sure what to do next. She feels like crying. She hopes, so desperately, that they were heard. She wishes she could be sure.

Jonah says, "Breakfast? I'm starving."

Hallelujah nods.

Jonah walks past Rachel, who's still sound asleep, around to the other side of the fire. He shows Hallelujah some dandelions he's piled on a piece of bark. "Thought we might see how they taste cooked," he says.

"Should be good." Hallelujah hasn't seen a recipe for cooked dandelions, but plenty of greens are good warm and wilted. Of course, they usually have butter and oil and garlic and other amazing stuff added in. With a sigh, she digs out the remaining energy bars from her bag and stares at them. Four.

She breaks one in half. Hands the other half to Jonah.

And they sit, nibbling, savoring, waiting for their dandelions to cook, as the sky finishes changing from pink and orange to blue, and the day arrives.

# 2

RACHEL WAKES UP. SHE YAWNS AND STRETCHES. THE RASH ON her legs is a dull red in the morning light. There are a few blisters behind her knees. Her first word of the day is *ugh*. Then she says, "Hey." Nods at Jonah and Hallelujah.

"Morning," Hallelujah says. "How are your legs?"

"They itch. A lot." Rachel crab-walks over to sit by Hallelujah. "How's your ankle? Did my bandage hold up overnight?"

Hallelujah lifts her left leg so Rachel can see the swimsuit still wrapped securely around her ankle. "It hurts. But I'll live."

"I'll check the swelling after breakfast. What's on the menu?" A beat. "That's a joke. I already know."

"Here." Hallelujah hands her an energy bar. "Save some of it for lunch, okay?"

"More dandelions, too?" Rachel asks.

"Yup," Jonah says. He serves her a pile on a bark platter.

"Fancy." Rachel munches her meal, staring out across the landscape. "Some view," she says a second later.

"Yeah. We saw the sun rise and everything."

"Cool."

"And Jonah's going to build another signal fire," Hallelujah continues.

"Great." Rachel closes her eyes and opens them again, looking pained. "I hate to ask you this while we're eating, but how big are the blisters on the back of my legs? I'm really . . . not comfortable." She props her legs up on Hallelujah's rock pillow.

Hallelujah leans down to look. "Um," she says.

"How bad?" Rachel's voice is flat.

"It's not pretty. Lots of little blisters, and four really big ones. Like the size of a quarter?"

"Ugh. Do I pop 'em?"

"No!" Jonah speaks up from gathering sticks. "Don't. You could get infected. Right, Hallie?"

"I guess." She sits up.

Rachel gulps. "So I just leave them?" She looks a little green now. Then she visibly shakes herself out of it. She eats her last few bites, then says, "Your turn, Hal." She pats her lap. "Leg here, please."

Hallelujah slides forward a few feet. She lifts her foot carefully into Rachel's lap. Rachel unties the straps and gently unwinds the fabric.

The air hits Hallelujah's ankle and the throb starts again. Far off, but coming closer. Hallelujah can't help but hiss a little, through her teeth.

"Sorry," Rachel says. She keeps her eyes on her work. Hallelujah tries to focus on what Jonah's doing. Dropping sticks into a pile, one by one. And she listens to the birds and the wind and all of the other forest sounds.

Her ankle emerges from its cocoon. It's swollen. Purple and green and deep blue, radiating out from the ankle bone on the inside. It feels warm. But the outside of the ankle is skin-colored, mostly, and the foot itself looks fine.

"I think you'll live," Rachel says. "Jonah, come take a look."

Hallelujah twists her head to see Jonah. He's gone pale.

"Jonah?" Rachel says again.

He mutters something.

"What?" Rachel asks.

"I'm, uh, not great with blood."

"There's no blood," Rachel says. "Just swelling. And bruising."

"Bruising *is* blood," Jonah mutters.

"Are you telling me you're afraid of blood? And bruises?" Rachel sounds genuinely incredulous. "Don't you play sports?"

"Yes." Jonah clamps his mouth shut, shaking his head. Then he adds, almost under his breath, "I can deal with bruises and stuff if I have to. I just don't like it, okay?"

"Don't worry about it," Hallelujah says, wondering how she didn't know this about Jonah already. How it never once came up. "Rachel will take care of me."

"Thanks, Hallie," Jonah says. He looks mortified.

But Rachel can't seem to let it go. "So you get light-headed, or what? Do you throw up? Pass out?"

"Rachel," Hallelujah says.

"I just need to know what I'm dealing with, you know?" Rachel shoots back. "What if one of us gets cut and starts bleeding? What if we need you?"

"I'll be fine," Jonah says, sounding like he wishes he'd never brought it up.

Rachel relaxes abruptly. "Sorry," she says. "I'm just . . . anxious."

"We all are," Hallelujah says. Jonah says nothing.

Hallelujah studies her ankle, making a mental note of how the swelling looks and where it starts and stops. She wishes she had a camera. But her memory will have to do.

She watches Rachel wrap the swimsuit-bandage around and around. Then she leans her head back and closes her eyes until the throbbing ebbs.

# 3

"So, what's on the agenda for the day?" Rachel asks, like she's starting a business meeting. "Does anyone move that we get rescued?"

"Sure," Jonah says. "Let's get rescued."

"You have to say 'I move' and then whatever," Rachel cuts in. "It's one of the rules of parliamentary procedure."

Hallelujah and Jonah just look at her. "Seriously?" Jonah asks.

"Yes. We have to maintain order, so we don't go all *Lord of the Flies*."

Hallelujah snorts. "Okay. I move that we get rescued. Today."

Rachel's hand shoots into the air. "Seconded."

Jonah adds tentatively, "Thirded?"

"That's not a word, Jonah." Rachel sticks her tongue out.

"If 'seconded' is a word," Jonah argues, "why isn't 'thirded'?"

"'To second' is a verb, in a meeting like this." Rachel spreads her arms wide to indicate their makeshift mountain-top boardroom. "'To third' is not a verb."

"Well, maybe it should be."

"Also, 'thirded' sounds weird and gross. Like, 'Who thirded?'" Rachel wrinkles her nose.

Jonah laughs out loud. "Wasn't me."

Hallelujah giggles too. Then she forces herself to focus. "So, Jonah, you're rebuilding the signal fire," she says, even though she knows that's the case. "We have two and a half energy bars left, plus one full bottle of water, a Diet Coke, and some dandelions."

"Right," Jonah says, resetting his features to Serious.

"So we need more water and more food."

"Yes. In case we don't get rescued."

"So that *when* we get rescued, today," Hallelujah corrects him, "we can yell and jump up and down and run to them."

"I like how you think, Hal," Rachel says.

"So," Hallelujah goes on, "Jonah: we stay here with the fire until . . . ?"

He thinks for a second. "Lunchtime," he says. "We let the smoke signal go for a few hours, hope that it doesn't rain again, split a meal, and then head down toward water. Unless it does rain—then we'll have water. But we'll still need food. Anyway, hopefully, we'll see people before then, or they'll see our fire." He pauses. "Maybe, if we find a creek, I can catch a fish or something."

"Way to go, Mr. Eagle Scout!" Rachel claps.

"I never said I was an Eagle Scout." Jonah clears his throat. "And I said maybe."

"You'll catch a fish," Rachel says. "You'll catch lots of

fish. We'll have a good old-fashioned fish fry." She shivers a little. "Are y'all cold?"

Hallelujah looks up at the sun. It's still shining down. "Not really," she says.

"Oh." Rachel pauses. "Can I borrow a jacket from one of you? If you aren't cold?"

Jonah hands over his jacket, and then stands up and walks to the edge of their small campsite. "I'm gonna get more wood," he says.

Rachel wraps Jonah's jacket around her legs. She shivers again, pulling her own jacket tight.

Hallelujah takes off her jacket and peels off her long-sleeved shirt, holding it out. "Want this?"

Rachel shakes her head. "No. But thanks."

Hallelujah feels the sun on her bare arms for the first time in two days. It feels good. She has goosebumps, but they're warmth goosebumps, like her skin is coming alive again after being cold and wet all day yesterday.

She stuffs the shirt into her backpack instead of putting it back on.

"Maybe you'll get a tan," Rachel cracks. She wriggles around to sit next to Hallelujah. She lies back on the ground. Looks at the sky. "Join me, Hal," she says, patting the ground beside her.

Hallelujah spreads her jacket out on the grass and lies back on it, looking up.

"I spy a rabbit," Rachel says, squinting.

"Where?"

Rachel points.

Hallelujah squints too. The cloud in question does look sort of like a deformed rabbit. With too many legs. "I spy a sailboat," she shoots back.

"That?" Rachel points again. Hallelujah nods. "That's not a sailboat, that's, like, an upside-down ice cream cone."

"What?" Hallelujah twists her head around. "No way. I stand by my sailboat."

"Fair enough." Rachel is quiet for a minute. "I used to play this game with my dad. When I was little. We had this big backyard and we'd lie in a different place every day. Dad convinced me that you could see different cloud formations from different spots."

Hallelujah waits a second, then scooches her body a few inches to the left. "You're right," she says. "That *is* an upside-down ice cream cone."

"Ha-ha." Rachel punches her arm. "I haven't seen my dad since Mom and I moved. He's had a lot of work stuff. Or at least that's what he says. And I can't stop thinking, if we don't get found soon——" She breaks off.

"You'll see him again." Jonah's voice, behind them, followed by the sound of wood hitting the ground.

"Sure. Of course." Rachel nods. But Hallelujah can see her eyes glistening in the sunlight.

Imagining Rachel as a kid, studying the clouds with her dad, makes Hallelujah think about her own parents. The good things. Her dad's corny jokes, and the way he used to laugh at them himself even if no one else laughed. The

Beatles songs her mom used to sing to her at bedtime. Her dad's patience with her when it took her weeks and weeks to learn to ride her bike. Her mom making up stories about the flowers in their garden, to get Hallelujah to help her pull weeds.

Her parents seem different now, and it's not just because she's older. What happened with Luke changed them, just like it changed her. Or maybe it changed them *because* it changed her.

"I just miss him a lot," Rachel goes on. "And what's weird is, I don't just miss the version of Dad before my parents started hating each other. I actually miss the yelling. Is that crazy?" She turns her head to look at Hallelujah.

"That's not crazy," Hallelujah says. She pauses, adds quietly, "Or if it is, we all have something that makes us crazy."

"Yeah? Your turn. I've been waiting for *days*. What makes you crazy, Hal?"

Hallelujah considers for a second. Should she? Then she throws caution to the wind, watches it sail out over the trees, over the hills. "Luke Willis," she says. "I hate him." She repeats it louder. "I hate him!" She shouts it at the sky, even though it's hard to shout lying down: "I! Hate! Luke! Willis!"

Rachel asks, "But what did he *do*?"

Hallelujah can hear Jonah waiting for her answer. She knows he's waiting because he's stopped making fire-building noises. He's silent. Completely.

She takes a deep breath. "He told a lie about me. Actually,

a lot of lies. And people believed him. The grown-ups, because he's the preacher's son and he'd *never* do something bad. And everyone our age—because he's popular and you don't question the popular guy, because if you do, you'll stop being popular yourself. Or you'll never get the chance. And because of what he said, my parents stopped trusting me. I lost friends. I was just this loser who—"

She breaks off. Now she's talking to Jonah. Even though he's behind her and she can't see him. "It doesn't matter what you saw that night, or what he told you happened. Luke treated me like I was nothing, and you let him do it."

Jonah doesn't answer.

"But that's not what makes me the maddest," Hallelujah continues, pushing up to sit. "What makes me the maddest is that I let it happen too. I didn't stand up for myself. And when someone did tell me to stand up for myself, I got so mad—"

*Sarah.* She feels the emotion of their argument wash over her, fresh.

"I pushed her away. I told her she didn't understand anything. But she was right. I became this girl who wouldn't stand up for herself. The quiet girl. The *nothing* girl. I just wanted it all to stop, but from the outside, without me having to make it stop. And I wanted to get away, but I figured, hey, college will get here eventually and then I'll be away, I just have to get there, and all the while I'm miserable, and I'm *letting* you guys make me miserable, letting you make me think I'm *supposed* to be miserable, that I'm *supposed* to be quiet, and I'm shutting people out, people who maybe actually care, and I hate myself for it." An abrupt stop. The train of thought hits a wall.

She's never said that before. Never thought it before. Not consciously.

But she knows, deeper than she's ever known anything, that it's true.

Hallelujah has spent six months hating herself for being weak and silent and for letting bad things happen and for not fighting.

But she didn't know what else to do.

Doesn't know what else to do.

Or does she?

She's not being silent now, far from it, and nothing's happening. Jonah and Rachel aren't laughing. The ground has not opened up to swallow her. She said how she was feeling, out loud, to people, and they listened. They listened.

She wonders, suddenly, if her parents would have listened. Would listen now.

Yes, they screwed up. They failed her. It's not just that she broke the rules and got punished for it—it's that in believing Luke's story, her parents believed the worst of her. She'd never given them a reason not to trust her before, and yet when something did go wrong, they weren't on her side. Not like they should have been.

But they were shocked. And embarrassed. And she never did tell them her version of what happened that night. Not really. When she couldn't get through to them right away, she stopped trying. Accepted her punishments—including a *no dating* rule that was almost funny, given the circumstances—in silence.

She's never once told them how bad things have gotten. In fact, she's gone out of her way to keep them from finding out. At home, she forces herself to smile. She gets her homework done and makes good grades. She cooks a few nights a week. She's the ideal daughter, just like she was before Luke screwed everything up. Her one big indiscretion is in the past. She's changed.

They just don't know how much.

They aren't bad people, her parents. They want the best for her. They always have.

Maybe they honestly can't see what's right in front of them—the current of misery just beneath the surface. Maybe they figured that since she hadn't said she *wasn't* okay, she was okay. And maybe it's time to stop blaming them and say something.

"Hal?" Rachel asks. She touches Hallelujah's arm lightly, hesitantly, like she's not sure how Hallelujah will react.

Hallelujah shakes herself out of her thoughts. She looks over at Rachel.

"Are you okay?" Rachel asks.

"Yeah. Thanks." Hallelujah turns to look at Jonah. He's standing, arms dropped by his sides, next to the smoldering fire. He's looking off into the distance.

She doesn't want to blame him anymore, either. She

wants to forgive him. To let that anger go.

She doesn't want to forgive Luke, probably won't ever forgive Luke, but she sees now that he's the one who's nothing. His opinion of her doesn't matter. She gave him power he shouldn't have.

Jonah is something. Jonah's opinion matters. And she doesn't want him to hurt because of her.

She and Jonah will never be what they were. Too much has happened. But maybe they could become something else.

She decides to take the first step. "Jonah," she says.

He looks over at her. "I'm sorry," he says, voice low.

"Don't be. I forgive you," she tells him. It sounds so formal. *I forgive you.* But it helps to say it out loud.

"Thanks. I don't know if I deserve that. But thanks."

"You do. Of course you do." Hallelujah says it firmly. "And—I want to." *I've missed you*, she adds silently. She's not ready to say that part. Not yet. She goes on, "And I don't want to be that girl anymore. I don't."

Rachel squeezes Hallelujah's arm. "So don't be," she says.

With those three words, Hallelujah feels something lifted, a heavy coat shrugged off. *So don't be.* Like that's all there is to it.

But is it that easy? Can she just decide not to be that person anymore—the one she hates? Can she really move on?

# 4

HALLELUJAH IS SCRATCHING AT HER PALMS, FEELING RAW AND relieved and itchy and alive, when she sees it.

A flash of orange in the distance.

Neon orange.

A color *definitely* not found in nature. Not in the Smoky Mountains.

She sees it again.

It looks . . . it looks person-size.

She's standing before she realizes what she's doing. "Hey!" she yells, waving her arms, wobbling on her good leg. "We're up here! We're up here! Hey!"

"Hallie, what—" Realization dawns on Jonah's face. He's by Hallelujah's side in an instant. "Hey!" he yells. "Up here! Up here!" He pulls his jacket from Rachel's legs and starts fanning the smoke from his signal fire.

Rachel's on her feet too, and then they're all calling, a jumble of words. "Help! Help! Up here! We're up here!"

Waving arms. Whistling. Screaming.

Hallelujah is scanning for another flash of orange.

Green. Green. Green.

"Help us! Please!"

No response comes back at them from the woods below. Just birdcalls and the roar of an animal, she can't tell what animal, but at least it sounds far away.

She stops, drops her arms. Her throat feels ripped apart. Her ankle throbs.

"What did you see?" Jonah asks. He looks where she's looking.

"Orange," she says. That's all she can get out. The tears are welling up. She has to put a hand on his shoulder to stay steady.

"Orange, like rescue orange?" he confirms. He takes her hand from his shoulder and helps her lower herself to the ground.

Hallelujah nods.

"Are you sure?" Rachel asks.

Hallelujah nods again. She is sure. Completely sure.

"Then we have to go that way." Jonah starts stamping out his fire.

"Jonah, the signal—" Rachel sounds scared.

"It'll smoke for a while. Hopefully it'll draw them toward us. And we'll be walking toward them." He pauses, one foot in midair, thinking. Then he brings the foot down hard on the ashes. "And if we go the wrong way, anyone who comes across this spot will see that someone was here, and they'll be able to see where we're headed next."

"How?"

"Three starving kids, one with a bum ankle?" Jonah's voice is biting. Then he snorts. "We're not exactly *Last of the Mohicans* here. We'll leave a trail."

"What can I do?" Hallelujah asks, tearing her eyes away from the sea of green below, the sea of green where she knows—she *knows*—she just saw the color orange.

"Just what you're doing. Look for landmarks down there that we can head toward. Where you saw . . . what you saw." He gets back to work, then adds, "See if you can get your boot back on."

Hallelujah slips into her jacket and then picks up her boot and looks at it. She bends her left knee, bringing her foot closer. She loosens the boot laces as much as she can. She slides her toes inside, wincing. She has to wiggle her foot a little to get another inch or so into the thick shoe. And then there's a stab of pain. It starts deep inside her ankle joint. Travels up. She freezes, biting her lip.

"I can't," she says.

Rachel looks up from stuffing dandelions into her backpack. "I'll help you." She scoots over, picks up Hallelujah's foot, and pulls the tongue of the boot way out. She inserts Hallelujah's foot fast, and the pain is like a Band-Aid ripping off: sharp and then over, with just a little after-stinging. But the boot won't close around her swollen ankle. Not even close. Rachel frowns. "Maybe we shouldn't have let you sleep without your boot on," she says slowly.

"I thought you had to wrap my ankle."

Rachel looks at Hallelujah's foot from all sides. The pink swimsuit puffs out the top of the boot, padding her ankle where the boot might touch it. "Well, that's what you do in sports . . . but maybe not in hiking?" She meets Hallelujah's eyes, then looks down. "I think I made it worse."

"No, I'm sure you didn't. . . ." Hallelujah tries lifting her foot. The heavy boot pulls at the injured muscles. "Maybe this'll protect it. Can you get it tied?"

Rachel nods and ties the loose laces into a double knot. Hallelujah sits back and tries to follow Jonah's first instruction. She tries to find landmarks between them and that flash of orange. She picks out a forked tree with a big knothole on one side. Then a lightning-struck tree beyond that, split in half and blackened. Then a big, beautiful pine, a gigantic Christmas tree without its lights. And in case she loses sight of those trees, Hallelujah tries to memorize the shape of the mountains ahead, so they can keep moving in the right direction.

Toward those trees. Toward the next hill. Toward rescue. Toward home.

## 5

AND THEN THEY'RE READY. JONAH HOISTS HALLELUJAH ONTO his back. He wears his backpack on his chest. Rachel carries her own backpack on one side and Hallelujah's on the other. They take one last look around their little camp at the top of the world.

And then they move forward. Down.

They thrash through the uncut woods. Zigzag looking for the easiest path. Jonah leads, so that Hallelujah can watch for her trees. Rachel follows. Every step jolts Hallelujah's ankle. She feels her foot flopping at the end of her leg, the boot weighing it down, and it hurts, hurts, hurts, but she keeps her mouth shut. Stifles the squeaks that want to escape. There's no time to stop and adjust, no time to rest.

As they hike, they call out to the invisible people in orange.

They reach the forked knothole tree. Hallelujah puts her hand on it as they pass, thanking it for being there, for staying put.

They reach the lightning-struck tree, and again, Hallelujah says a silent thank-you.

They reach the giant Christmas tree. Hallelujah can see the shapes of the mountains beyond, the shapes she memorized, though they look different from below than from above. Jonah pauses to catch his breath. He shifts Hallelujah's weight on his back. She can feel his sweat dampening the front of her shirt. His muscles flex and strain, holding her.

"Do you need to put me down?" she asks softly.

"I'm good," he says. He looks behind them. There's a thin column of smoke at the top of the hill where they came from. The smoke winds up into the air, a snake charmed by the wind. It looks so far away.

They walk again. Down and down until the ground levels out a little. Still calling for help. And what started as a hopeful noise turns desperate. Their voices break off and rise again. They crack. Rachel stops first. Then Jonah.

Hallelujah tries to keep yelling, but her mouth is cotton and her throat is raw and she's never wanted anything as badly as she wants a long, cool drink of water and then a cup of hot tea with honey.

The sounds of the woods finally drown them out.

"We must . . ." Rachel gasps, "be going . . . the same direction . . . as them."

"Maybe," Jonah grunts.

"I saw it," Hallelujah whispers into Jonah's back. "I saw it," she tells each tree they pass. "I saw it!" she tells the hawk that flies overhead. "I saw it. I know I did." With each declaration, she believes herself less. Believes *in* herself less.

They walk. Slower now. The exhilaration is gone. Reality is setting in.

If it was there, that flash of orange, it's gone now. Nobody heard them. Nobody saw them. Their lonely smoke signal rises up from the mountaintop where they spent the night, but from down here it's nothing more than a thread. Easy to miss.

Jonah stops abruptly. "I need a break." He lowers Hallelujah from his back, not letting go until he's sure she's steady on her good foot. Then he sinks, spaghetti-limbed, to the ground. His face is bright red. His shirt is soaked with sweat. His hair is dripping.

Hallelujah's legs feel like Jell-O from gripping Jonah's waist as they ran. She's also starving. *What time is it?* The sun is high overhead—lunchtime.

"If I sit down now," Rachel croaks, "I'm not getting up."

She's shaking all over, like a rabbit, or a tiny short-haired dog in winter.

Jonah nods. "Okay. Just give me a second."

Hallelujah stares at her mountain shapes. The orange was this way. Or it wasn't. They can't stop until they know.

# 6

THE SUN MOVES IN THE SKY. OTHERWISE, EVERYTHING looks and feels the same. Trees and trees and trees. Bushes and vines and grass and dirt and a few spring flowers. If Hallelujah never sees the color green again, it will be too soon.

They walk until they reach a creek with a small clearing on one side. In unspoken agreement, they set their things down. They each eat a third of an energy bar and some dandelions. Since it hasn't rained yet today and they're all sweating from their downhill hike, they fill their water bottles with creek water. Hallelujah tries not to think about germs and parasites. She's too thirsty.

No one says anything about rescue. About the color orange.

All the same, Hallelujah feels a familiar sense of shame settling over her. This is her fault. She led them on a wild goose chase. She made everyone more tired, took them from their hilltop vantage point, for nothing.

Jonah stands up, puts a hand on her shoulder, and says,

"We needed water and more food anyway."

It doesn't help.

"I'll be right back. Need to get wood for a fire. And, uh, use the bathroom." Jonah takes a few steps, then adds, "Put your foot up, Hallie."

"Okay," Hallelujah says. But she doesn't move.

She looks at the canopy of branches overhead. The trees go up and up and up. Through the crisscrossing limbs, she can see clouds blowing across the sky. She looks down at the creek. The trees are reflected in the water.

"I'm going to take a bath."

Hallelujah spins to stare at Rachel, startled. "Here?"

"Yup."

"Why?"

Rachel doesn't look at her. Her voice is glass, close to shattering. "Because I'm in a very bad mood, Hal. And I'm trying really hard not to take it out on anyone. I'm scared and I'm exhausted and I'm starving and my legs feel like they're on fire and I look like I have leprosy and—and—it will help to be clean. Clean-ish." She pauses. "Plus, maybe it'll stop the itching."

"Oh," Hallelujah says. She feels very small. Her internal voice repeats, *Your fault, your fault, your fault.* "But . . . the water's really cold."

"The sun is out. I'll live."

Hallelujah gestures at her ankle. The swimsuit. "Do you need this?"

"Nah." Rachel shakes off her jacket. She peels off her

tank top. Then, to Hallelujah's astonishment, she slips out of her shorts. Rachel's standing there in her bra and under-wear and hiking boots like it's the most natural thing in the world. She leans forward, fiddling with her bootlaces. "I guess I should leave these on?"

Hallelujah blinks. "Probably. Yeah. I would. Don't want to cut your feet."

"Okay." Rachel straightens up. She looks at Hallelujah properly for the first time since they realized there were no rescuers. She's quiet for a second. Then she says, "You should join me. You could use a bath too. I'm not being mean. I think it'll help." She nods decisively. "You're coming in. You brought a swimsuit, right?"

"Okay," Hallelujah murmurs, not sure why she's saying okay other than that it does sound really good to rinse the mud and grime off and run water through her frizzed-out hair.

"Do you need help changing?"

"Just help me up. And turn your back."

Hallelujah digs her black one-piece and swim shorts out of her bag. She lets Rachel pull her to standing. She hops over to the nearest tree and manages to wriggle, slowly, out of her clothes and into her swimsuit and shorts, leaning on the trunk for balance. When she's dressed, she feels like she ran a marathon.

With a sigh, she calls out, "Okay . . . I'm ready!"

Rachel comes over. She helps Hallelujah wade into the creek, toward a shallow pool near the bank. When the icy water hits their feet, fills their hiking boots, reaches their calves, it's a shock. Hallelujah gasps, and Rachel lets out a stream of curses. But they keep moving. Rachel lowers Hallelujah down to a flat rock that's poking up from the creek. Hallelujah balances herself and stretches her legs out, letting her injured ankle float on the surface of the water. She dips her raw hands in the creek. The poison-ivy itch is replaced by a pleasant numbness.

"Not bad, right?" Rachel says. She scoops up a handful of water and starts rinsing her arms. When the water hits her skin, she curses again, gleefully this time.

That's when Jonah comes running out of the woods. "Are you okay?" he yells. "I heard cursing and I thought—" He breaks off, eyes widening at Rachel in her underwear and Hallelujah in her swimsuit and shorts. His eyes skim Rachel's body, but linger on Hallelujah's. Their eyes meet. Hallelujah squirms, feeling exposed. She crosses her arms in front of her chest.

"We wanted to clean up a little," Rachel says. "Want to join us?"

"Oh." Jonah seems frozen in place. Rooted. His eyes are still on Hallelujah. "Uh," he says. "No. Not now. I'm, uh, I have to, um . . ."

Hallelujah desperately wants her clothes back on. But she would have to hobble past Jonah in her swimsuit in order to get to her clothes. Why is he looking at her like that? Why won't he look away?

"Okay there, J?" Rachel asks. There's a laugh in her voice.

And Jonah visibly shakes himself out of whatever spell was keeping him still and tongue-tied. His shoulders drop about two inches. He loosens his death grip on his backpack. "I, uh, found some dandelions. For dinner."

"Dandelions. Joy." Rachel pours a handful of water over her head. She runs her fingers through her wet hair. Then she turns her attention to her muddy, blistered legs.

"Don't eat 'em if you don't want to," Jonah says, defensive. "I'll finish getting the fire ready, so when you two lunatics are done with your ice baths, you can warm up." He walks back into the woods the way he came.

Hallelujah watches him go. Then she realizes that she's done absolutely no washing up. And she's only getting colder. So she leans back and dunks her head into the running water. Every hair on her body stands on end. She's awake. She's alive. And in a few minutes, she'll be as clean as she's likely to get out here.

Rachel splashes her. "See?" she asks. "Better, right?"

Hallelujah nods. "Your lips are a little blue, though."

"It's the new fashion." Rachel strikes a pouty model pose, but loses her balance. She wobbles and sits down in the creek with a shriek. Almost immediately, she starts shivering. Violently. "Cold. Out. Now," she says through chattering teeth.

"Yes." Hallelujah's feet and ankles have gone numb. Her hands have also moved beyond the nice non-itch into can't-feel-them-at-all territory. She quickly pours water over her legs, wiping them down. She dips in one arm at a time.

Splashes her face. When she can't take it any longer, she says, "Okay."

"Okay," Rachel says. She hooks her shoulder under Hallelujah's arm, helps her to stand. They wade carefully out of the creek. On the bank, Rachel is small and dripping and shivering. Her bra and underwear are soaked through, translucent and sagging. "Don't suppose you have a towel?" she gasps.

"No, sorry. Use your jacket?" Hallelujah sits on her own jacket, reaches for her dry T-shirt, and starts patting herself down.

For a few moments, they're quiet. Then Rachel curses, soft and vehement.

"What?" Hallelujah asks.

"I can't put my clothes back on. My underwear's all wet."

Hallelujah thinks for a second. "Take off your bra, put on my long-sleeved shirt," she says. "We can lay your stuff out to dry."

"Thanks, Hal." Rachel starts to unhook her bra and Hallelujah turns around quickly. Behind her, Rachel laughs. "Sorry. Not trying to flash you or anything. I'm turned around now. So you can change too."

Hallelujah slides her tank top on, slipping out of the swimsuit underneath, changing back into her bra. The dry shirt feels like heaven.

"I'm done," Rachel says.

"I'm not." Hallelujah pulls off her boots and unties the pink swimsuit bandage. She sets that and her wet socks out to dry. Then, checking to see that Jonah is nowhere in sight, she peels off her swim gear. She lies flat on her back to carefully pull her underwear and jeans up over her legs. Her injured ankle hasn't yet passed from numb back into hurting, but she doesn't want to speed up the process by putting weight on it. She finishes by sliding off of her jacket and wrapping herself up in it. She pulls on her extra socks.

When she's dressed, she turns around to find Rachel flat on her back, soaking up sunlight. She looks peaceful.

And so Hallelujah joins her.

# 7

JONAH RETURNS TO FIND THEM LIKE THAT.

"Feel better?" he asks.

"Yeah," Hallelujah answers, opening her eyes. "Kind of."

"I'd be awesome if I could just get warm," Rachel mutters. She sits up, wrapping her arms around her knees. She makes a loud *Brrr!* noise. "Okay, so I was thinking. We've been out here for three days and I don't know anything about you. Either of you. Other than where you're from and that you're both mad at Luke. And all you know about me is that my parents suck, and are divorced, and that I'm handling it badly. So now's a good time for Twenty Questions."

"I have to build a fire," Jonah says.

"You can build and talk at the same time," Rachel

answers. "I'll go first. Hal, what's your favorite color?"

"Purple," Hallelujah says.

"Mine's pink. Now you get to ask one of us a question."

"Wait—don't you want to know what my favorite color is?" Jonah sounds fake-hurt. "Who made up these rules?"

"Fine," Rachel says. "Jonah, what's your favorite color?"

"Blue," Jonah says, and Hallelujah has a vision of him from fifth grade: the month when he tried to wear a different blue shirt every day. No repeats.

"Predictable," Rachel scoffs. "But now we know. Your turn."

"Okay." Jonah frowns. "Favorite . . . subject in school. Mine's history."

"English," Hallelujah answers. Once, she would've said choir. Before.

"Biology," Rachel says. "But I already told you about wanting to do physical therapy, so you're not really learning anything new there."

"Is that why you were making fun of me earlier?" Jonah asks. "About the blood thing?"

"I was making fun of you because you're this big, strong guy who can build fires and carry Hal on your back, but you're afraid of a bruise." Rachel laughs. "Nothing to do with me wanting to join the medical profession. Okay. Favorite . . . sport."

"None," Hallelujah says immediately. "Sorry."

"Soccer." Jonah grins. "I want to play in college. I'm hoping for a scholarship."

"He's really good," Hallelujah tells Rachel. "And he runs track."

They talk like this, about everything and nothing, for a while. They go in circles: favorite ice cream flavor leads to favorite food overall leads to worst school cafeteria meals leads back to academics and extracurriculars and hobbies. It isn't until the conversation shifts to friends that Hallelujah falls silent. She doesn't have friends anymore. And she doesn't know what Jonah is going to say. If he'll mention everything they used to share.

"We would just, you know, go to the mall and movies and the football games every Friday and the parties after the games," Rachel is saying, arms wrapped around her middle. "Stupid stuff. Normal stuff. But then my mom decided to move and we were gone, like, two weeks later and now all I want is that stupid stuff back. I want to have people to do nothing with. You know?"

"Yeah." Jonah nods. "But you don't seem like you have a lot of trouble making friends."

"I mean, I talk to people, sure," Rachel says, "but it's hard. Everyone has their in-jokes and their cliques. I'm still new at school, and I knew my other friends forever. We text and call each other, but I can't exactly go to the mall and try on clothes with my phone. Or I can, but it's not the same."

"I guess not," Jonah says.

Hallelujah thinks about her version of "stupid stuff"— the things she used to do with Sarah and Dani and Lynn. They'd see movies and go to the mall too. And to that local bookstore that opened up the summer before ninth grade. The four of them spent hours hanging out there, drinking coffee until they were practically vibrating. It drove Hallelujah's mom crazy. But she always said, when she came to pick Hallelujah up, *If this is the worst thing you're doing, I guess I'm lucky.*

And then there were the parties Dani and Lynn had started throwing in the spring of ninth grade. Parties Hallelujah's parents would never have approved of, if they knew what was really going on. Never mind that Hallelujah didn't drink, wasn't dating anyone, felt like she was only at those parties because she'd known Dani and Lynn forever. Her parents would have seen them as step one toward—well, what eventually happened with Luke. Or what they think happened. What they were told happened.

She was already kind of disappointing her parents—on a small scale, behind their backs—for months before she became a Disappointment. But they still shouldn't have believed the worst of her.

She realizes Jonah is talking. "Most of my friends are from sports. Now I just do soccer and track, but in middle school I did baseball, too. And Brad and Luke and I helped start a church dodgeball league a couple years ago. Youth group kids and their parents. Remember, Hallie?"

She nods. Her dad had played. She'd watched from the sidelines, handed out Gatorades. The memory of herself jumping up and down and cheering when their team scored—it feels off, now. Like she's picturing someone else.

"We weren't great, but we kicked First Presbyterian's butt." Jonah laughs. "So anyway, other than being in choir at school, I guess I'm a jock all the way through."

"A sensitive, musical jock." Rachel smiles mischievously. "Those are hard to find, outside of the movies."

Jonah grins, shaking his head. "I'm not that musical. Hallie's a way better singer. Back when we were—" He stops short, looking over at her. Like he's deciding how to fill in the blank. "When we used to hang out," he finishes, "Hallie was into music like no one I'd ever met. And when I heard her sing . . ." He whistles.

"Hal—" Rachel starts.

"No."

"Please?" Now Rachel bats her eyelashes.

"Sorry. It's just that . . ." Hallelujah doesn't know how to explain how singing was the thing that mattered the most, how it was her dream for herself, how hearing her voice soar felt like she was flying for real. How she used to practice until she was almost hoarse and then go on practicing inside her head. How much she'd loved the way her voice harmonized with Jonah's during their duet in ninth grade. How much she'd looked forward to singing with him again.

And she doesn't know how to explain how much she misses singing, even though when she quit in January, it was her own choice. Or how, despite missing it, she's scared of the idea of starting again. Or how she's even more scared that her voice, her raw talent, her training, everything— that it will all vanish. That she's wasting it.

143

"You don't have to," Jonah says. "But you should know that there are people who'd love to hear you again." He pauses. "I mean, I would. But not only me."

Hallelujah feels a lump in her throat. "I wish," she says around it, "everything could go back to how it was before. I didn't know how good it all was."

"I guess we never do," Rachel says. She sounds tired now. "Jonah, can you build the fire up more? I'm still freezing."

"That ice bath earlier was worth it, huh," Jonah teases.

"Shut up," Rachel says. But she doesn't sound mad. The breeze picks up, and she shivers, looking at Hallelujah. "You're not cold?"

"Just a little," Hallelujah says.

"Lucky." Rachel huddles in on herself. "So, Hal, if you don't hang out with friends and you don't do choir anymore, what *do* you do? Don't say homework."

"Um. No comment." Hallelujah lets out a small laugh. "I'm kind of into cooking lately. Not, like, culinary school into it, but it's something I enjoy doing." No one else knows this. No one but her parents, her guinea pigs. Out loud, it sounds stupid.

"Really?" Jonah asks. "You never told me that."

"I didn't start until . . . until after."

"Oh." There's a moment of awkwardness, and then he says, "Maybe you can cook for us? When we get home?"

"Okay," Hallelujah answers. "When we get home." It sounds possible, put like that. The three of them together, in her kitchen.

"What'll you make us? What's your best dish?" Rachel asks. "Describe it. I want to hear every last ingredient." She leans forward, eager. "I want you to make me *taste* it."

And so Hallelujah tells Jonah and Rachel about the chicken Parmesan she made a few weeks ago. The bread crumbs and the egg wash and the olive oil and the from-scratch tomato sauce. Her mouth waters as she talks, and Rachel closes her eyes and smiles, and Jonah just looks at her like the recipe is the most interesting thing he's ever heard. When she's finished, it's quiet. They sit, and they imagine.

That's when they hear it. A whirring, chopping sound. It disturbs the air. Sends birds bursting from the trees.

Jonah's on his feet in an instant, face toward the sky.

"Is that what I think it is?" Rachel asks, eyes wide.

"I think so." Hallelujah's voice comes out as a whisper. She stares up, afraid to trust her ears.

It sounds like a helicopter. But she can't tell where the noise is coming from. The sound bounces off the mountainsides, coming at them from all directions. It's getting louder, getting closer. But how close is it? Will it actually fly over them?

She can't see anything. The trees are too thick.

Jonah is waving his jacket at the fire, fanning the smoke into the wind. Rachel is on her feet, jumping and waving her arms. Hallelujah waves hers, too.

They try to make themselves seen. Jonah's blue jacket. Rachel's pink one. The thick, black smoke from their fire.

Movement and color where there shouldn't be movement and color.

And they yell, even though they know they won't be heard. Not over the motor, over the propeller. Not from up there, when they're down here.

The chopping sound is softer now. Farther away.

They keep yelling, waving, fanning the smoke.

The echoes fade. The helicopter is gone.

It passed them by.

Jonah drops his jacket on the ground. He stands, looking up, looking defeated.

Rachel bursts into tears. She wraps her arms around herself and sobs. When Jonah reaches out a hand to touch her shoulder, she shrugs him away.

Hallelujah feels numb. She can still hear the violent, thrashing helicopter, inside her head. It was so close, and then it wasn't. It was here, and then it was gone.

They weren't seen.

Jonah sits back down next to the fire. Rachel squats by the creek, splashes water on her face. Runs her wet hands over the angry red welts on the backs of her legs.

No one says anything. There's nothing to say.

The afternoon sun is orange, hanging low in the sky. There's a second sun reflected in the creek, shimmering, moving with the current. The orange sun and the orange reflection and the orange flames remind Hallelujah of rescue that hasn't come.

They're still out here. Still alone.

# 8

THE SUN DROPS LOWER AND LOWER. THEIR EYES ADJUST.

The temperature drops too. Hallelujah rubs her hands together, pretending the itch in her palms is the prickle of her skin warming up.

Dinner is the last energy bar and a half, with a side of dandelions. It's painfully small, even by their new standards.

"Tomorrow, I'll try fishing," Jonah says.

Hallelujah nods. She thinks about her chicken Parmesan. And her empty stomach.

Rachel stares into the fire. She chews, slowly, on her few bites of energy bar. At first, Hallelujah thinks she's just savoring it, but there's something in the movement that's weird. Uncontrolled. Like her head is bobbing along with her jaw. Like she's not quite all there.

The hunger must be getting to her, too. And the disappointment.

The night settles in around them. The world gets bluer and bluer. The creek sounds louder now that its waters are dark. The night birds start to call.

"Hallie, can I ask you something?" Jonah's face is in shadow. His voice is soft.

"Sure."

"This morning, what you said, on top of that mountain—that you thought maybe you felt God there?"

"Yeah?" The morning seems so long ago. That brightness and hope seem like a dream.

"Do you feel it now?"

Hallelujah takes in a breath. She closes her eyes, thinking.

She doesn't feel the same as she did this morning. Not at all. Up on that mountaintop, looking out over miles of untouched forest, she felt comforted and safe. She felt the promise of great things on the horizon. Now, after a day that didn't live up to the promise of its dawn, she doesn't feel comforted. She doesn't feel safe. She doesn't know what the horizon holds.

But does that mean God has left them alone in the wilderness?

She thinks about the difference between feeling God's presence and trusting that he's there, regardless. Jonah's easy *Yeah, sure*, this morning, when she asked if he still believes God's there. But if God is watching, and there was a possibility of rescue earlier, then what was he doing? How can he just be up there, looking down, and not guide them? How can he not help?

Just like that, Hallelujah is back in her bedroom, talking to the ceiling. To something she hopes for but can't feel. To a God who isn't listening when she needs him most.

Tears prick at her eyes, and she blinks rapidly.

"Hallie?"

The words come out in a rush. "I don't feel God right

now," she says. "If he's there, he's"—she takes a shaky breath—"really far away."

"Oh," Jonah says. Then, softer, "Me too."

Those two words feel like a punch to Hallelujah's gut. She's used to feeling alone, like God—like everyone—is far away. But it's scary to hear that feeling in someone else's voice. Especially Jonah's. So she keeps talking, trying to find something to say that will make it better.

"But we're alive," she says. "We're alive, and there are a million reasons we shouldn't be. Not after two and a half days out here. So there's that."

"So you do feel like we're being looked out for?"

"Maybe? I mean—I don't feel safe. I don't feel like we're in this little bubble. But maybe God knows we're here, and he's just waiting for the right moment. . . ." She fades off, thinking about how many times she asked God to punish Luke, to make him stop spreading lies about her, to expose him for who he really was. And she thinks about this morning, when she realized that she didn't want Luke to have power over her anymore. That she was ready to make it stop.

"What if," she says slowly, "whether or not we feel God, we're where we're supposed to be? Every step of the way, we've ended up where we needed to be."

"Rained on. With poison ivy. And out of food. And with your ankle sprained."

"I know, it doesn't make sense. I'm just thinking out loud. But maybe—maybe it's okay that things are so bad because we're where we're supposed to be. Like you said this morning, maybe there's a plan. Maybe something's supposed to happen."

Something *has* happened. She's changing. She's opening up.

Hallelujah glances up toward the sky, toward the bright stars, thinking, *Really?*

"I'm not trying to argue with you," Jonah says, "but isn't that kind of a stretch? No matter how bad it gets, if we make it home alive, we say it was God's plan?"

"That's not what I meant. Not exactly." Hallelujah lets out a puff of breath. "You asked me if I felt God. You asked."

"I did."

"Well, I don't feel him. Not how I want to. But maybe he's out there, watching. Maybe there's a plan. Though if there is, he's sure taking his time getting us home!" She raises her voice on that last part. The word *home* echoes in the air.

Rachel speaks up suddenly. "I don't think I believe in God."

"Really?" Hallelujah asks, surprised. "Why'd you come on a youth group retreat?"

"I've gone to church since I was a kid. I'm used to youth group stuff. A lot of my friends in Nashville were from church." Rachel pauses. "My mom isn't really into church anymore. She hasn't gone since she and my dad split up. When we first stopped going, it was nice to sleep in on Sunday mornings. Then I kind of missed it. Especially being in a youth group." Another pause. "But if I'm being honest, I missed the social part way more than the God part."

Rachel is shivering. A lot. She hugs her knees into her chest, rocking a little.

"The more I think about it," she goes on, "the less I believe that there's a God. It's not that I don't *want* to believe. It can be comforting, right? To believe in something taking care of you. But I don't feel anything watching out for me. I don't feel like I'm praying to anything. And looking at the past year, at what I prayed for—for my parents to stop hating each other, to not have to move over winter break, for my mom to act like she cared, at least a little, about how I was doing—praying definitely didn't help. And now we're lost and starving and I'm scared, and if God is supposed to help, where is he?

"If there is a God, why are we even lost out here? Why would he let this happen? Why are my parents so messed up? Why did he let Luke do whatever he did to you? Why does the world suck so much, for so many people?" Rachel's voice cracks. Now she's really shaking. "It would be great if God was out there. But maybe the only thing that makes sense is that he doesn't exist."

It's like the night grows darker with that sentence. The air grows colder.

After a few moments, Jonah asks, "So it's all chance? Luck? Stuff just happens?"

"I don't know, okay?" Rachel is slurring a little. But she keeps talking. "I just know that I don't feel anything. And I'm not sure I ever did."

Hallelujah is struggling to find words. She understands, completely, how awful it feels not to have prayers answered. To feel like you're shouting into a void. But being mad at God and deciding there *is* no God are two different things.

"Just because you don't feel God," Jonah says, "doesn't mean he doesn't exist."

"So my two options are that there is no God," Rachel says, "or that he's there but wants nothing to do with me. Life keeps getting better and better." She tries to stand up, but her legs don't support her. She crumples to the ground, still shivering all over.

"Rachel!" Hallelujah scrambles to Rachel's side.

"I'm really . . . cold. . . ." Rachel says. She curls into the fetal position. Her eyes look distant, like she's seeing Hallelujah from a long way away.

Hallelujah wraps her arms around Rachel as she shakes and shakes. Rachel's skin is cool. It feels colder than the breeze that's blowing past. Just touching Rachel gives Hallelujah a chill. "Jonah, what do we do?"

Jonah has jumped into action. He's piling more wood on the fire. He strips off his jacket and throws it at Hallelujah. "Put this on her legs. Cover her."

Hallelujah wraps Jonah's jacket around Rachel's thighs. She pulls her extra T-shirt over Rachel's exposed calves and ankles. And then she wraps her body around Rachel's and tries to absorb the shivering.

When the fire is roaring strong, Jonah squats down next to them. "Rachel?"

No answer. Just the chatter of teeth.

"Okay, Hallie. I'm going to move her closer to the fire."

Hallelujah rolls away from Rachel. Jonah scoops Rachel up as if she weighs next to nothing and sets her down gently a few feet over. Then he beckons to Hallelujah.

"We have to get her warm. You lie on one side and I'll lie on the other."

Hallelujah crawls over, ankle throbs and stomach pangs forgotten. She curls around Rachel's front side, hugging her. Jonah hugs Rachel from behind. Their eyes meet over Rachel's tucked-in head.

"Now what?" Hallelujah whispers as Rachel twitches in her arms.

"We wait," Jonah says, voice hollow. "We wait for her to stop."

# 9

IT FEELS LIKE HOURS, BUT IT CAN'T BE. IT CAN'T BE MORE than a few minutes.

Rachel slowly stops shivering. Her breathing calms. Her skin warms.

They lie there, listening to the fire pop and crack just inches from their heads, and Hallelujah can't shake the feeling of disaster narrowly averted. She feels breathless, weak, exhausted, and she wasn't even the one who went cold.

She *is* cold, now that the sun has set. Especially the parts of her not facing the fire, not holding Rachel. But clearly what she's feeling is a fraction of what Rachel just experienced.

Rachel mutters something into Hallelujah's chest.

Hallelujah pulls away a little. "Are you okay? What can we get you? Jonah, should we—"

"I expected," Rachel says, voice hoarse, "to get hit by lightning. Not to freeze."

It takes Hallelujah's panicked brain a few seconds to catch on. Lightning. Because of the God stuff. Right. Rachel's making a joke. Good sign.

But Jonah's not laughing. "Dang it, Rachel," he hiss-yells, "you had to get in the creek earlier, in your frickin' underwear, never mind that it's not exactly August out here, never mind that people die of exposure all the time; you *had* to—"

"I'm sorry." Now Rachel sounds small. And miserable.

"And you!" Jonah turns to Hallelujah. "You're smarter than that! You could've got hypothermia too, and you said it yourself—there's a million reasons we should be dead right now, and you two being stupid is one of 'em!"

"I'm sorry," Rachel repeats. She's shaking again, but now it's because she's started crying. Tears sideways down her face, into the dirt. "I'm sorry, okay?"

"We both are." Hallelujah looks into Jonah's eyes. She sees his fear fully for the first time. He's as scared as she is. He's just better at hiding it.

"I'm sorry too," he says. He squeezes his eyes closed, like his head hurts.

"You can let go of me now," Rachel says, sniffling. "I think I'm okay."

"We shouldn't. Not yet," Jonah answers. "You need to keep warm. We all do."

"Oh." Rachel is quiet for a second. "Talk to me, Hal. Tell me what happened to you. What really happened. Distract me from my own problems. Please."

Hallelujah twists her head to look up. The moon is shining white overhead. It looks like if she could just climb to the highest tree branch, she could touch it.

She thinks about everything the three of them have shared over the past few days. She thinks about how the walls she built up around herself have been crumbling. She thinks about being honest. Truly honest. What that means. How it would feel. And she knows she's ready. It's time.

"Okay," she says. "Here goes."

She sees Jonah's arms tense. When she glances at him, he meets her gaze head-on. But he doesn't say anything to stop her.

"All through freshman year," she begins, feeling absurdly like an epic storyteller, wanting to invoke the muse to make sure she gets the words out right, "I had a serious crush on Luke Willis. My friend Dani and I could talk for hours about how great he was. Don't get me wrong, I knew he was kind of a jerk. But he was really cute, and he could be completely charming when he wanted to be—still is, when it helps him get what he wants—and I guess I thought that side of him was stronger than the jerk part. I hoped it was. And freshman year he was pretty much instantly popular, and I was . . . not. Plus, he's your friend"—she meets Jonah's eyes—"so he had that going for him.

"Spring of freshman year, he was dating this girl Jen, from school, but they broke up over the summer. He went out with a couple other girls from church after that, but he was single when we went on our youth group retreat to Gatlinburg in October. On Saturday night, everyone tenth grade and up got some free time without all the chaperones tagging along. A bunch of us rode the ski-lift thing up the mountain to see the view. On the way back down, Luke asked me to ride with him. I couldn't believe it, but of course I said yes."

Hallelujah remembers every detail of that ride: the crisp autumn breeze as they started down the mountain, how their chair rocked whenever they moved their dangling legs, the way being up so high made even a tourist trap like Gatlinburg look like a magical village from a fairy tale.

"It was the most romantic thing that had ever happened to me," she says. "I know that sounds dumb, but it's true. I'd been on a few dates, but nothing that even came *close* to being that romantic. I looked over at Luke and he was just looking at me, smiling. And when I shivered a little, he put his arm around me. It was perfect. And so when he kissed me, I kissed him back."

She's imagined telling this story so many times. Every detail. Every feeling. She tried, right after it happened. With her parents. With Sarah. But she never got it all the way out.

Her words went wrong.

Now, with Jonah, Rachel, the night creatures, the trees, and the moon and stars listening, she knows she'll finish it.

"We kissed for—I don't know, it felt like a while, but it must've been just a few minutes. The ride isn't that long. When we got to the bottom, everyone was waiting."

"Jonah, you were there?" Rachel cuts in.

"Yeah. I was there."

Hallelujah waits to see if he'll say anything more. When he doesn't, she goes on, "Luke got off the ski lift first and held out his hand to help me. And then he put his arm around my waist while we walked back to the hotel."

She remembers how his arm felt, keeping her by his side. And how she'd felt knowing that the cutest, most popular guy in the youth group had chosen her. She'd felt excited. Proud. Special. She remembers not being able to stop smiling.

"We had some time before curfew, so a bunch of us went up to Luke's room to hang out. Your room too, I guess," Hallelujah adds belatedly, talking to Jonah. "And Brad's." The three musketeers, together as always. "We stayed there until the chaperones told us it was time for bed." Hallelujah remembers not wanting to go. Not wanting the night to end. "As I was leaving, Luke whispered in my ear, 'Come back and kiss me good night.' I started to kiss him right then, but he stopped me and said, 'Later.' And when I opened my mouth to ask when, how, he cut me off: 'After the first bed check. Say you forgot something. Improvise.' And I nodded, and then he let me go."

Hallelujah remembers the excruciating stretch of time in her own room, waiting for the chaperones to make the rounds and count heads. Her heart racing as she changed into the yoga pants and tank top she slept in, so the adults wouldn't be suspicious. Checking her hair and applying lip gloss and hoping she looked calmer than she felt.

She'd never snuck out before. She couldn't believe she was about to try. She couldn't wait.

"When the chaperones left us, I told my roommates I'd forgotten my phone in Luke's room. And they totally teased me about sneaking off to see him, but I just kept saying I'd be right back." She'd said it blushing. Grinning. And not only because of Luke. She liked the other girls' questions. She liked that they'd seen her kissing Luke, that they guessed what she was up to.

She looks back at her bright-eyed excitement, at her eagerness to take risks, to be the center of attention for once, and she wants to smack herself.

"I had to promise to tell my roommates everything to get them to let me leave." She'd known she was wasting precious minutes before the final chaperone check, when they were all expected to be in bed with the lights out. "I ran down the hallway. I knocked on Luke's door. And when he opened it, he said, 'Nice outfit,' kind of laughing, and pulled me inside. He sat me down on the bed. He sat next to me. He told me," she says to Jonah, "he asked you and Brad to leave for a while. Because I was coming over."

"That's what he said," Jonah confirms, his voice so low she can barely hear it.

"And then we were kissing. A lot. It wasn't as—as perfect as the ski lift." The fluorescent lights were too bright. The air conditioner in the window was making a weird clunking noise. The comforter on the bed was scratchy. And after Luke's comment about her outfit, her decision to show up in her pajamas felt completely wrong. "Still, I got caught up in it. Then he put his hand up the back of my shirt." His fingers were cold. His touch gave her goosebumps. "I was trying to decide if I was okay with that when he—he stuck his other hand down the waistband of my pants. That's when I told him to slow down." She'd scooted away from him on the bed. Fast. She'd repeated it: *We have to slow down.*

"Luke was like, 'Come on. We don't have time for this.' He gave me this . . . look." A look that made her feel so immature. Like she was overreacting. Like she was about to miss her chance with him. "He said, 'You came here for a reason. Right?' And I said—I said—" Hallelujah cringes. "I said, 'To kiss you good night?' And he laughed. And he patted the bed next to him, and said, all suave, 'So kiss me.' I moved back toward him, and we kissed, and then he slid his hand right back up under my shirt and unhooked my bra. One-handed." She smiles now, even though the memory isn't funny. "I can't even do that half the time. I guess he'd had a lot of practice."

She'd wrapped her arms around her body, a quick reflex action. She'd stood. She'd caught sight of a person she didn't recognize in the smudged mirror on the back of the closet door: a flushed, disheveled girl, hair tangled, tank top twisted up to show her bare stomach, one bra strap falling off her shoulder. She'd stared at her reflection. And she'd felt like an idiot. And she'd felt ashamed.

"I wanted to go in the bathroom to get myself together before going back to my room, but Luke grabbed my wrist. He asked me if I was seriously going to leave him hanging. I told him to let me go, and I tried to pull away, but he was holding me so tight. He said, 'You're not leaving here until you give me a real good night.' He yanked me toward him, and I fell and landed against him on the bed, and—"

That's when the panic had kicked in. The sudden realization that Luke had the upper hand, that he was bigger and stronger and that this, to him, seemed like no big deal.

"And then what?" Rachel asks, voice hushed.

Hallelujah breathes in deep. "And then the door opened."

Rachel gasps.

"Brad came in first, saying something about getting caught in the hall. Jonah was next. Then Rich and his wife, Jill. And my first thought was, *I'm safe now. It's okay.* It took a few seconds of everyone staring for me to realize what it looked like. Me, a complete mess, in my pajamas, my tank top all stretched out, my bra falling off—on Luke's bed. I was pretty much lying on him. And then I couldn't move. It was like I was frozen.

"Luke pushed me away, hard. He said, 'Hallie, I told you. No way.' He said it so loud, and he was making this face like I was—like I was so pitiful. Like he was so far out of my league. Like he felt sorry for me. Before I could think of a single thing to say, Jill grabbed my arm, stood me up, and marched me out the door."

In Rich and Jill's room, the lectures had started. Hallelujah doesn't remember the exact words, aside from *Unacceptable*, over and over, and *We're going to have to call your parents*. She does remember the looks of disapproval and disappointment. And feeling so overwhelmed at what had just happened, so numb. And spending the night on the adults' fold-out sofa.

She'd lain there, unable to sleep. Watching a slideshow of broken images. The romantic ski-lift ride. The magical view. Their first kisses, so perfect. The security of Luke's arm around her. The rush of sneaking to his room. And then the *too much* that came after. The sound of the door opening. Eyes focused on her.

"At breakfast the next morning, I had to sit at the chaperones' table. I wasn't supposed to talk to anyone. And everyone was staring. Whispering. Luke had already started telling people that I'd snuck over to his room, in my pajamas, and thrown myself at him. He was even saying I'd tried to give him my bra as a souvenir."

"Gross," Rachel murmurs.

"By the time I found out about the rumors, the whole thing was just so . . . big. Out of control. I didn't know how to defend myself. What to say. Because so many people saw me and Luke kissing on the ski lift. And because I *did* sneak out. My roommates knew it. Jonah and Brad knew it. Never mind getting 'caught in the act.'" Hallelujah makes quote fingers around that part. "Anyway, after breakfast, my parents showed up."

Cue what was without question the most uncomfortable car ride of Hallelujah's entire life. Her parents so upset. Trying to get her to tell them the truth. Unable to get past the fact that she was caught in Luke's room. And then, silence. Their unhappiness radiating. It had filled their small sedan, until Hallelujah felt like she might suffocate.

"When the rest of the youth group got home, we had a big meeting." Her parents. Luke's parents: the preacher and his wife. Rich and Jill and a few other church leaders. Some eyewitnesses, including Jonah and Brad, to confirm she'd been with Luke. Behaving inappropriately. "Luke said that he was surprised when I showed up at his room. That he hadn't meant to give me the wrong idea. That he would never have taken it beyond just kissing. And he looked so genuine. So trustworthy. So sorry about what had happened. He almost convinced *me* that I'd misread his signals." Hallelujah pauses. "The whole time, I kept my mouth shut. I wish I hadn't. But I was still so humiliated. And I felt guilty. I made out with him. I liked it. And no one made me go to his room."

Her voice breaks. She has to swallow past a lump in her throat.

"I know Luke's not a good guy. I know what he did isn't

my fault. It's his. But still, none of it would've happened if I hadn't gone to his room."

She's almost there. Almost done. Almost heard. Something deep inside her hurts like it hasn't hurt in a long time. But she knows that this gash had to reopen in order to heal. That's how wounds work. They need air.

"I knew I'd get punished, and I did. My parents grounded me. I was put on youth group probation. But I honestly thought Luke's lies would just fade away if I kept a low profile. There's always gossip about someone. This time it was me."

It's not like she was the first person in the history of their youth group to break curfew on a retreat. She wasn't even the first one to get caught. To get lectured and punished. But to get caught with Luke, in his hotel room, looking like she did—and with her having been one of the "good girls" up until that point—it was like the perfect storm.

Luke didn't get off scot-free. Not that he got in trouble for inviting her over, for pushing her too far, for lying. But he did get a slap on the wrist for letting her into his room, unchaperoned, after curfew. She wonders sometimes if her life would be easier if he hadn't gotten punished at all. Maybe he'd feel less inclined to punish her in return.

"Luke is *still* telling people about what supposedly happened that night," Hallelujah says. "And he makes fun of me. All the time. What I look like, what I say, my name. And he does this thing at church: whenever we sing a hymn with my name in it, he sings it like he's hooking up with me. He sings the word 'hallelujah' *at* me. He *moans* it. And I hate it." That's one of the reasons she stopped singing: his voice, his fake grunts of satisfaction, ruining the music she loved so much.

"You said," she says to Jonah, "he wanted to keep me upset. To keep me from telling anyone what really happened. Well, it worked." She pauses. "Until now."

"Until now," Rachel repeats. Then she curses. "I can't believe him. I can't believe he got away with it."

"I let him get away with it," Hallelujah says softly.

"No. He's the one who crossed the line. And okay, maybe you could've spoken up sooner. But if no one pushed you for your side of the story, that's on them." Rachel yawns and stretches. "And when we get home, we're going to set the record straight."

A cloud passes over the moon, changing the light. The fire crackles and burns, sending shadows dancing on the ground. An owl calls out, *Who, who?* from a nearby tree. Another owl answers.

Rachel said *we*.

Hallelujah doesn't want to think too much about telling this story again—telling her parents, Rich, her former friends, or anyone, really. But she'll have to, for it to end.

And Rachel said *we*.

"Thanks," she says. "For listening."

"Thanks for trusting us," Rachel murmurs. Her eyelids are drooping now. "We're gonna fix this. I promise."

Hallelujah just nods.

After a few minutes, Rachel falls asleep. Hallelujah can hear her breathing, slow and even. She can *feel* her breathing, her chest rising and falling under Hallelujah's arm.

In the silence, Hallelujah realizes that Jonah hasn't said a word since confirming that Luke kicked him and Brad out of their hotel room. He has his eyes closed, but he's definitely not sleeping. His mouth is tight. He's breathing deeply too, but it's on purpose. And when he opens his eyes to see Hallelujah looking at him, he gets up abruptly. He adds more wood to their fire. He paces a circle around their camp.

Then he says, in that low, dangerous voice Hallelujah heard for the first time at the party three nights ago, "I'm gonna kill him." He circles the campfire again.

A part of Hallelujah feels a little thrill at Jonah's anger. That he's this worked up on her behalf. The other part of her—a bigger part—doesn't like seeing him like this. She says, not because she believes it but because she wants to calm him down, "It's okay."

"It's not okay," Jonah says, but he stops pacing. He looks at her, and then at his fists. "Right. I won't kill him. But it would feel really good to punch him in the face." And then it's like the anger drains out of him. He shakes his head. He pops his knuckles, slowly, one by one. He returns to Hallelujah and Rachel and wraps himself around Rachel's body, but his eyes are on Hallelujah. He looks at her. She looks back.

# 10

"I HAVE TO TELL YOU SOMETHING." JONAH SPREADS HIS jacket over the three of them. Hallelujah tucks the sleeve under her body. It's like they're being held together. Embraced.

"I—" He takes a deep breath. "I really liked you. The whole time you liked Luke, I . . . I liked you. I was even going to ask you to ride on the ski lift with me in the fall, but Luke told me you'd already asked him."

Hallelujah is genuinely surprised. "He asked me."

"I know that now. I didn't know it then. And you didn't exactly look like you minded riding with him. Kissing him. And then when we walked in on you two—uh—making out—"

"We were *not* making out," Hallelujah cuts in. "I mean, not any more . . ."

"Right. But like I said, I didn't know that. You were practically on top of him, and you looked like—and Luke said it was all your idea, and you didn't say anything, not then and not after—" He breaks off. Picks up again. "I didn't like thinking about you doing something like that. I was mad. I wanted it to be me. That's why I didn't stand up for you. I liked you," Jonah repeats, "and I didn't want to still like you, because—"

"Because I was a slut?" Hallelujah asks quietly. Even

166

quiet, the word is harsh. It cuts the night. "Or because I was a slut with someone else?"

"Both, honestly." Jonah keeps his eyes on hers. "Don't look at me like that. Do you want me to lie?"

"No," she says after a moment. "No more lies."

Jonah nods, slowly. "Then I have to tell you something else. Just in case we don't make it home."

Hallelujah's stomach lurches. "What?"

Jonah breaks eye contact. He studies the top of Rachel's head. "I never stopped liking you," he mumbles. "I tried. I really did. I thought by ignoring you, by staying mad at you, I could make it go away. But I couldn't. So when Luke told me the truth on Monday, the first thing I thought was, *I missed my chance, she's different now*, and——" Now he looks at her. Right at her. "I helped do that to you, to someone I liked, and I have to carry that around——"

Rachel stirs, murmurs something, shifts in her sleep. Hallelujah adjusts the jacket over her back, just to have something to do that isn't stare at Jonah.

"Say something?" he asks.

She flounders. "You like me?" She's sure it's the night that's making him say this. The honest and open night, with its never-ending black sky and wind-swirling treetops and sense of danger just out of sight and earshot, in every direction. It made Rachel admit she doesn't feel God, doesn't believe there's anything there. It made Hallelujah tell Jonah and Rachel what really happened with Luke.

And now, Jonah, who looks hopeful despite everything,

but not hopeful for the things they all need—not hopeful for rescue, or food, or warmth. Hopeful for her.

If they'd been found by those rescue hikers earlier, if there actually were rescue hikers out there, or if the helicopter had seen them, they might never have had this conversation. She might never have known how he felt. How he feels. That thought makes her sad.

She was liked. Is liked. In that way.

He's still watching her. Waiting for her to say more. Guilt and hope flicker across his features like the shadows from their fire, light and dark. And she can't help but notice that he's good-looking. *Cute* isn't right; the shadows and moonlight make his face look contoured, mature, a man's face rather than a boy's. His biceps bulge where he's hugging Rachel's small body to keep her warm and protect her.

A flicker of a second: Hallelujah imagines his arms hugging her instead.

Her heart is a traitor. But she kind of doesn't care. Not in this moment. Not under this moon.

Still, she's not sure how to respond. "I didn't know. And this . . . it's a lot to process. I have to think." It comes out harsher-sounding than she means it to, so she repeats, more softly, "I just have to think."

Jonah clears his throat. "Okay." He sounds disappointed. "We should, um, go to sleep." He's ending the conversation. He's closing that door.

Somewhere not so deep inside her, she hopes it's just closed, not locked.

But the suggestion of sleep is enough to make her yawn. She curls up into Rachel's body, under Jonah's jacket, sharing the warmth. She nods off, into a dream world that's dark and insect-buzzing.

*She remembers her first kiss. It was sixth grade. With Ryan Lane, youngest son of her parents' oldest friends. In her backyard, on a cool, almost-winter evening. Their parents inside. She didn't like Ryan, not really, but they both wanted to get their first kiss over with. They agreed, after the fact, not to try again.*

*She remembers other kisses. Just a few. Shared after an early-evening movie date, before her dad showed up to drive her home. Stolen during the eighth-grade graduation dance when the chaperones' backs were turned. It wasn't that those kisses were bad. Or that she didn't like the boys she kissed. She just didn't feel a spark.*

*She remembers, will always remember, kissing Luke Willis. Their first touch of lips, in the air over the mountains with only the glittering landscape as witness—it feels crystallized in amber. She wants to feel that caught-in-amber perfection again. Not with Luke. Never with Luke. But with someone.*

the
# fifth
day

# 1

HALLELUJAH WAKES TO THE SOUND OF WHOOPING AND cheering. It startles her. Where is she? Who's yelling? Why is she looking up at trees?

The whooping becomes her name, loud and jubilant: "Hallie! Hallie!"

She struggles to sit up. She's so tired. Her head hurts. Her ankle hurts. Her stomach gapes.

"What's he yelling about?" Rachel moans.

"I don't know."

"Is it a helicopter?"

"No." The only sounds are the creek and the birds and the wind.

"Then tell him to shut up." Rachel throws one arm over her eyes.

Hallelujah struggles to stand. She stretches. Squints. The sun is bright and cheerful. The air is crisp and clean.

"Hallie!" Jonah calls again. He's standing in the creek a

little ways down. He's waving one arm in the air. He's soaking wet. "Hallie!"

"What?" Hallelujah yells. She takes an experimental step, and her ankle gives beneath her. She gasps, but manages to stay upright. "What is it?" she calls. She can see that he's holding something. Something shiny. Something . . . that's moving.

All at once, she knows.

A fish.

Jonah is holding a fish.

It's not as good as rescue, but it's close.

"Backpack!" he yells.

Hallelujah grabs his bag. Unzips it and empties it. Holds it in the air.

"Rachel?" Jonah asks.

Hallelujah looks down at Rachel. She thinks about last night. Rachel's small, shivering body. She's not going *near* the creek today. "I'll come!" she yells back.

The fish wriggles out of Jonah's grasp, but he manages to catch it again, scrambling. "Are you sure?" he calls, clutching the fish to his chest.

Hallelujah takes another halting step. She hops on her good foot. She tests her injured ankle again. This time, it holds her up. But it hurts, it hurts, it hurts. She thinks: *Fish. Fish.* She hobbles closer.

When she reaches Jonah, she has to sit down and catch her breath.

"Are you okay?" he asks, eyes worried.

"I'm okay. What do you need?"

Now Jonah beams. He looks proud. And excited. "Open the bag."

She holds the backpack open and Jonah sloshes over to her. He deposits the squirming fish inside and she zips the bag up fast. It flops around in her arms.

She is holding a backpack with a live fish in it. She laughs out loud. Jonah grins like a maniac, and then turns his back to her and wades out to the middle of the creek. He stares intently at the surface of the water and then plunges in. He comes up empty-handed, and immediately dives in the opposite direction. This time, he surfaces with another wriggling fish.

"Open the bag, open the bag, open the bag!" he says, bounding through the thigh-deep water. She does. He dumps the second fish inside, and she zips it closed.

"I didn't know you could do that!" Hallelujah calls out as Jonah splashes away from her again.

"Neither did I!" He lunges sideways with a loud whoop, misses his footing, and sits down in the water. He's up again in a second, shaking himself off like a dog. "But I'm not going to stop until the fish get smart enough to figure out what I'm doing and—" Lunge. Splash. Up. Shake. "—run away!"

"Run?"

"Whatever!"

Hallelujah can't stop smiling. Jonah puts another fish in her bag, and another, and another. The bag's getting heavy. It jerks and lurches, trying to escape her grip. She loops her arms through the shoulder straps, keeps her hand by the zipper. At the ready.

Jonah's hair sprays water each time he flips around, in search of another fish. Droplets shimmer on his skin. He's really cute. And Hallelujah can't help but think about last night. About him liking her. He flashes her a smile, and something inside her swoons.

The thrashing fish bring her back to reality. When she opens the bag to let Jonah put one more in, a fish escapes. It flops around on the ground by her feet, and she squeals. Jonah drops the fish he's holding into the bag and grabs at the one on the ground. It slips from his grip once, twice, but the third time he gets it.

"Bag bag bag bag bag!" he says, and she's right there.

When that fish is secure, Jonah sits down beside her. Both of them are panting a little, excitement and effort mingling. Hallelujah's heart is beating fast. She tells herself it has nothing to do with Jonah sitting next to her. Nothing at all.

Jonah catches his breath and then stands up, using her shoulder to ease himself back down into the creek. He wades out to the middle, looking around. "I don't see any more," he says. "How many did I get?"

"Six. I think." She's not opening up the bag to count.

"That's plenty. For now." He wades back over to the bank. He shakes himself off again. Says, "Brrrr!" Squeezes some water from his hair. Hoists the writhing backpack onto his back, and then extends his hand to Hallelujah to pull her up. He wraps an arm around her waist to help her back to their campsite. She can feel the backpack jerking back and forth beside her.

The fish, fighting to live. The prospect of eating an actual meal. Jonah's arm around her. The ease between them.

All little miracles.

# 2

JONAH PEELS OFF HIS WET SHIRT AND SPREADS IT OUT ON the ground in the sun. For a second, all Hallelujah can see is his bare skin. She blushes and looks away, not turning back until she hears the zip of his jacket closing. Now he's looking at her. She doesn't know if he caught her staring.

"That's better." He shivers a little, rubbing his hands on his arms. "I can't believe you two were in that cold water so long yesterday! At least it's getting warmer out." He jumps up and down in place like he's prepping for a run. "So I'll get more wood for the fire," he says, "if you figure out how to cook the fish. Chef Calhoun." He grins and heads into the woods.

Hallelujah smiles too, riding the high of fish, food, Jonah. She looks at the backpack. It rolls over onto one side, all on its own. That's when she remembers that she's never actually butchered a fish, much less killed one.

"Do you think they'll just . . . die?" she asks Rachel. "Or do we have to do it?"

Rachel still has one arm slung across her face, blocking the sun's light. "No idea," she says.

"And then, do you think I should cook them whole, or try and make fillets?"

"Don't ask me. You're the cook."

"Well, do you want to help? You like biology. Want to do some dissecting?"

"No."

Hallelujah's high drops, just a little. "Are you okay?"

"No, I'm not," Rachel snaps. "I'm starving and exhausted and I know Jonah said it's warming up but I still feel cold. Also, my legs itch and the blisters are going to pop and it's *disgusting*. And last night was really, really scary and I had awful dreams and—" Her voice catches. "And I just want to go home."

Hallelujah is quiet for a moment. Then, she hands over her jacket. "Put this on," she says. "I bet a hot breakfast will help. It'll help all of us. You just rest. Okay?"

A grunt from Rachel as she pulls the extra layer over herself like a blanket.

Jonah comes out of the woods with a huge pile of sticks. "Well, chef?" he asks.

"Um," Hallelujah says. "I didn't get very far." But she eyes a few of the long, sturdy sticks and gets an idea. "What if we sharpen some of those on one end and spike the fish? We can roast them? Like marshmallows?"

Jonah nods. "That should work."

"And then we can peel off the skin once they're

cooked. Pick out the bones."

"Sounds good." Jonah looks at Rachel. "No comments from the peanut gallery?"

"She's not feeling great," Hallelujah says, before Rachel can snap at him, too.

"Well. Food will help."

"That's what I said."

"Great minds." Jonah flashes Hallelujah another quick smile, and then he hands her his pocketknife and three sticks. "Here. Whittle these into skewers. Make a point, and peel off the bark. We should put the fish on clean wood. Ever use a pocketknife?"

She shakes her head no.

"Okay. Always push the blade out, away from you. Like this." He makes a slicing motion. "And keep your other hand out of the way. Think you can handle it?"

Now she sticks her tongue out at him. It just happens, and it clearly surprises him, because he laughs.

They get to work. Jonah rebuilds last night's embers into a new fire. Hallelujah whittles. And a few minutes later, she realizes she's humming. "Amazing Grace," of all things. She's timing the strokes of her knife to the song's 6/8 beat.

She's humming *out loud*. Sending notes into the air. She can hear herself.

Her chest constricts. She stops. "Sorry."

"Don't apologize," Jonah says.

"What's with all the flirting?" Rachel grumbles from the ground.

Hallelujah and Jonah swing around to look at her. Embarrassment fills the air. Jonah clears his throat and keeps fanning the little flames he's created. Hallelujah finishes one skewer, sets it in her lap, and begins another. She notices that the backpack is still.

When the fire is crackling and the skewers are done, Hallelujah unzips it. The fish lie in a heap. Hallelujah is surprised that there's not a fishy smell. Not even a little. The backpack smells like the creek, like mud and grass and fresh air.

"You do it," she blurts, handing Jonah one of her sharpened sticks. "I can't."

"Okay." He picks up a fish. Holds the stick in the other hand. Frowns. Nods. And then he skewers the fish from the tail to just below the head, longways. The stick makes a squishing sound when it goes in, and both of them wince. But he shakes the stick a little, and the fish stays on. "Here," he says, handing it to Hallelujah. She holds it over the fire.

He skewers two more fish. Starts roasting them. And they wait.

The fish droop on their sticks. Their skins brown. Juice drips into the fire, and it sizzles and smokes.

The scent is amazing. Maybe it's that they haven't had anything other than energy bars and dandelions and a banana and a peanut butter and jelly sandwich since Monday, but it's possibly the best smell Hallelujah has ever smelled. Her mouth is watering. Her stomach growls, loudly.

"Me too," Jonah answers, without taking his eyes off the fish.

Rachel finally sits up. "That smells good," she says, a little begrudgingly.

When the skins are almost black, Hallelujah pulls her fish back out of the fire. Jonah does the same. They set them down on a large leaf. Pull the skewers out. Hallelujah sucks her smarting fingers. They taste like food, and she almost can't stand it. Almost rips into the fish right then and there. Despite the bones. Despite the sizzling.

Jonah skewers the other three fish and hands one to Rachel. "Keep it turning," he says. "Hallie, you ready?"

"Yeah. Just letting them cool a little."

She washes her hands in the creek, and then she breaks the fish apart. She pulls flaky, white meat out, removes slender white bones, and scrapes the oily skin with her fingers. It's not pretty. But it's food.

When she's pulled out all the meat she can, she separates it into three equal piles on plates made from energy bar wrappers. Three deconstructed fish fillets.

"I think these are done," Jonah says, examining his fish. "How's yours?" he asks Rachel.

"Done." She's staring at the fish with raw desire.

"Great. We'll put them down over here and Hallie can—"

"Let's eat," Hallelujah interrupts. "While those cool. Please." She doesn't wait for an answer. She hands out the little piles.

They dig in. Fingers scooping up fish, tongues licking lips. The fish has no seasoning except the smoke from the fire, but it's warm and it's solid and it's delicious. Hallelujah barely stops to breathe before her pile is gone. She gasps. She licks each finger, slowly, savoring. She closes her eyes. Inhales the smell of burnt fish. Relishes the feeling of food in her belly.

Rachel burps. Loudly. It startles Hallelujah's eyes open. "Nice," she says.

"Sign of a satisfied diner," Rachel says. "Can we eat the other ones now?"

Hallelujah stares longingly at the three cooling fish. But she says, "We should probably save them for later. Right, Jonah?"

Rachel wrinkles her nose. "Fine." Then she grins. "Jonah, your name is Jonah, and you just fed us a bunch of fish."

Jonah pauses before saying, "And?"

"And it's funny. Jonah was eaten by a big fish. We just ate fish caught by Jonah."

"Because I've never heard that before. When eating fish."

"You know what I thought when I smelled it cooking?" Now Rachel grins at Hallelujah.

Hallelujah knows what's coming. "No," she says anyway.

"I thought, 'Hallelujah!'" Rachel crows. "Ladies and gentlemen, I'll be here all week. Wait—I've already been here all week."

Jonah is shaking his head. "You're nuts," he says to Rachel.

"You know you like it," Rachel says, voice breezy. She curls up on the ground, pulling Hallelujah's jacket tight around her. "I'm going back to sleep. So you two can get back to whatever you do while I'm not around."

Jonah almost chokes on his last bite of fish.

Hallelujah feels her face getting hot. Again. What's changed since yesterday? And is it so obvious that Rachel can sense it without being told? Or was she listening last night? No, she was asleep. Definitely asleep.

Hallelujah, meanwhile, feels more awake than she's ever felt in her life. She's filthy and scratched up and injured and scared, but the sun is warming the ground she's sitting on, warming her face, and her stomach is full of food they caught and prepared themselves, without anyone's help. She's alive, against the odds, and they're doing okay. It's a new day. A day when anything can happen.

*Anything*, she thinks, looking at Jonah. *Anything at all.*

# 3

RACHEL NAPS AS JONAH TURNS THEIR COOKING FIRE INTO A signal fire. She naps as Hallelujah dismantles the other three fish and puts the meat into a plastic sandwich bag that held a PB&J all those days ago. She naps as the sun rises higher in the sky.

Jonah and Hallelujah don't talk for a long time. They complete their tasks. They work with a quiet efficiency, both because they don't want to disturb the peace of this beautiful morning and because they still need to conserve energy. Even with fish for breakfast, even feeling pleasantly full for the first time in days, they're both very conscious of their bodies' weakness and exhaustion.

But eventually, there's nothing left to do. Jonah sits down next to Hallelujah. "It's weird," he says, "but this feels normal."

"We've been out here too long," Hallelujah answers. "Bet our beds will feel weird when we get home."

"Nope. No way." Jonah shakes his head emphatically. "My bed will feel *amazing*. You never got to lie in it, but if you did, you'd——" He stops abruptly. Clamps his mouth shut. Blinks a few times.

Hallelujah looks at him, curious. And then her mind catches up to his: *He imagined me in his bedroom.*

He sees her face change and it's like it flips a switch in him. "I didn't mean it like that. I meant my bed is so soft, you have to lie on it, like a science experiment, not like—not like——"

"Not like you want me in your bed," Hallelujah says softly. And then she feels giddy. She can't believe she just said that out loud.

"Well—I mean—I just——"

She can tell his mind's going all kinds of places. She kind of likes it. Feeling like she has this power over him. But after relishing it for a moment, she puts him out of his misery.

"I knew what you meant," she says, "and it's fine. Really."

He visibly exhales, all of him sagging back into his arms.

And he sits there, locked elbows, shoulders pushed up. "You feel it too," he says to the fire. "Right?"

She thinks about her answer. They might never go home. This might be it. She has to face that possibility. Every day out here is borrowed time.

"I feel it too," she says. The thing that's changed between them. The sparks that weren't there before. At least, not for Hallelujah.

"What do you think we should do?" His voice is not much more than a whisper.

Hallelujah glances at Rachel, sound asleep. "I don't know," she says. She can feel Jonah tense and warm beside her, the air between their arms crackling. "I don't know," she says again.

Silence. In Hallelujah's head, the creek becomes a roaring river. The birds in the trees overhead seem to multiply; their calls drown out her thoughts.

She doesn't know what she wants to happen. But she needs it to happen now. Right now.

Jonah moves first. He closes the few inches between them. His fingers brush her cheek, curve gently around the side of her neck. He makes eye contact, and then he pulls her to him. Their lips touch.

Hallelujah flinches. And Jonah jumps away from her like she burned him.

"I—"

"Sorry. Don't know what got into me." He mutters it at the ground.

"I—"

"Won't happen again. I promise, Hallie."

"I can't get hurt again!" It bursts out of her, sounding like a bad line from the sappy movies she used to make Jonah watch as retaliation for all of his ridiculous action films. But it's the first thing in her head to explain the flinch, to apologize for it.

Jonah's face hardens. "You think I'm going to hurt you?"

"No, I just—"

Rachel stirs in her sleep, and they both stop breathing, caught by her movement, her yawn. But she doesn't wake.

Hallelujah turns back to Jonah. "I don't think you're going to hurt me. Not anymore. I promise. But the last guy I kissed was Luke. So now, I'm—" She inhales. It's shaky. "I'm just a little overwhelmed."

To her surprise, Jonah cracks a small, hesitant smile. "I thought maybe it was my breath. You know, haven't brushed my teeth in four days, fish for breakfast . . ."

She mimics his light tone, grateful for it. "If the smell of your not having showered in four days didn't drive me away, your breath wasn't going to do it."

Jonah lifts an arm. Sniffs his armpit. Grimaces. "Ouch."

Hallelujah pats the ground beside her. Extends a hand to Jonah.

He takes it. Slides over.

They stare at the fire, follow the column of smoke up and up and up, to where it passes through the tree branches, becomes one with the clouds. A bird flies through the smoke, scattering it with its wings.

"Are we just feeling like this because we're out here, and it's scary and crazy?" Hallelujah asks. "Is it going to go away when we get home?"

"No," Jonah says simply.

"How do you know?"

"Hallie. I told you. I've liked you for more than a year. I didn't stop when Luke—did what he did. So I'm not going to stop liking you now that we're actually talking again, and now that you like me back." He smiles. Then, like he's realizing something, he gets very still. "Why? Is it gonna go away for you?"

"I don't know!" Hallelujah exhales in frustration. How can she be sure that feeling this—*this*—isn't just her being amazed that someone actually likes her, after everything, and that it's Jonah, and that he has for so long? And it's not like she's emotionally stable. "I mean, I'm happier right now than I've been in six months, which doesn't make any sense because I'm still hungry and my ankle hurts and we're still lost and we have no idea what to do next and the worst could happen at any minute!" She gulps. "I don't know what I'm feeling. Other than that I don't want to hurt you any more than I want you to hurt me."

Jonah is quiet for several seconds. "I think," he says slowly, "that you're overthinking this."

That's not what Hallelujah expected him to say.

"First of all, thanks for not wanting to string me along. I appreciate it." A crooked smile, with only one corner of his mouth. "Second, this is extreme for me, too. Being out here. With you. Talking like this. But isn't it good that everything's out in the open now? You said it yourself: you don't want to be that other girl anymore."

"I don't," Hallelujah echoes. It's the one thing she knows for sure.

"So who says the new you can't, you know . . . ?"

He doesn't finish the question, and Hallelujah mentally fills in the blanks. *Be with me. Kiss me.* Or maybe he was going to say something else entirely. Maybe that was the point. The open-endedness. If she's a new person, she can start from scratch. Rebuild atop the rubble of her old self. Remake herself in whatever image she chooses.

Is that even possible? If they go back, and Luke's the same, and her parents are the same, can she be different?

"All you can control is you," Jonah murmurs, and it's like he's read her mind, except when she looks over at him, he's not looking at her at all. He's looking up at the sky, where dark clouds are gathering.

# 4

"Rain," Jonah says. "Dang it." He scrambles to his feet.

"How come you don't curse?" Hallelujah asks.

Jonah glances at her, clearly confused. "You want me to curse?"

"Well, no. But lots of people do." She nods her head

toward Rachel. "Luke and Brad curse all the time, when there aren't adults around. And I know you don't have a problem watching movies or listening to music with cursing. So how come you don't?"

"You're asking me this now?" Jonah's zipping up their bags. He tosses her hers, and she's hit with the scent of the cooked fish inside. "With *that* coming at us?" He gestures up. Hallelujah follows his point. It looks like the apocalypse. She half expects four horsemen to come riding out. "Why?" Jonah asks.

"I don't know, I just want to . . . know more about you." She mutters the last part, suddenly embarrassed. "It was dumb. Sorry."

"Not dumb. Nice. Just—timing. Get Rachel up."

Hallelujah crawls over to Rachel. Gently shakes her shoulder.

"My dad's like Luke and Brad," Jonah says, walking a circle around their camp, squinting, looking out. "Curses up a storm when we're not in church. And I don't like it. Not that I think he's gonna be smote or anything. I mean, I get that God probably doesn't like it when people use his name as a curse word. I wouldn't like it if people yelled 'Jonah!' every time they stubbed their toe. But it's more that—" He turns to look at Hallelujah and Rachel. Walks over. "I know too many people who are one thing when they think it matters and another thing the rest of the time. And I don't want to be like that. So I don't curse at all. It's like—what you see is what you get."

Hallelujah looks up at him. She's amazed, all over again, at this Jonah she never knew existed.

He goes on, "I'm not perfect. Obviously. You know that as well as anyone. But at least I'm not pretending to be someone I'm not." He pokes Rachel's arm. "Rachel. Up."

The first roll of thunder sounds overhead. It's not far off.

"No." Rachel's voice is sleepy, thick. "I don't wanna get up."

"There's a storm. We have to find shelter."

Rachel opens her eyes. "A storm?" She jumps up. "We have to get moving."

Lightning brightens the dark sky. Thunder follows. It's hard to believe that not fifteen minutes ago, the day was clear. The sky was blue.

Hallelujah realizes she can't hear any birds. She's gotten so used to their chatter in the background out here that the silence is loud and harrowing.

"Hallie, can you walk?" Jonah asks.

"Not very fast."

"Okay. I've got you." Jonah helps her stand. He wraps an arm around her waist, taking the weight off her bad ankle. "Let's go. When I was getting wood yesterday, I saw some rocks we can hide under. Up the hill."

"Lead the way," Rachel says, eyes on the sky. She looks afraid.

The rain starts: sharp, hard drops that sting Hallelujah's arms. It feels like an attack. Like they let their guard down, and now nature is back with a vengeance.

But Hallelujah breathes in deep. Limps along. Tries to think of her skin as armor. The rain can't pierce her. It can't break her. She's not the same person she was two days ago. That girl ran from rain, fell down mountainsides, scrambled in the mud, blind and gasping and scared.

This girl, this new Hallelujah, is still scared, but she watches her footing, and she holds on to Jonah and Rachel instead of pushing them away. She watches the rocks grow closer. For once, she knows where she's going.

5

They're tucked into a crook between three large rocks, on the edge of a rhododendron thicket. One rock is on top of the other two, creating a roof that keeps the worst of the rain out. The rhododendron branches and leaves above them create a second barrier. Water drips down between the rocks, but the thin trails are nothing like the downpour outside, so they're able to stay pretty dry.

The rocks are old. The formation is old. It's not going anywhere. At least, not for a long, long time. The rainwater runs down grooves that are deep, like they've channeled many drips before. There's a thick coating of moss over the rocks, a heavy, insulating blanket of green and brown.

Rachel leans back against the cool stone and closes her eyes. "I'm going to rest a little," she says.

"Are you feeling okay?" Hallelujah asks. "Are you warm enough?"

"I'm okay," Rachel says without opening her eyes. "Just . . . tired."

Hallelujah and Jonah look at each other. "Should we be worried?" Hallelujah whispers. "She's sleeping a lot. And she's still cold, and it's not that cold out right now."

"Probably fallout from last night," Jonah says, though he doesn't sound sure. "Her body temp was so low . . . and without extra gear and more warm food . . ."

"I can hear you," Rachel murmurs.

"Right. Sorry."

"It's fine. I'm glad you care." Rachel yawns again and then is quiet. Her breathing evens out. She looks peaceful, but she also looks small and vulnerable. Her eyes are dark-circled. Her wrists, sticking out from Hallelujah's jacket sleeves, are bird bones.

Jonah turns his eyes on Hallelujah. "You could sleep too. If you want. We'll probably be here a while."

"I'm okay." In truth, she's exhausted. Today more than yesterday; yesterday more than the day before. But she doesn't feel like sleeping. Sitting is enough. Being quiet is enough.

Jonah shifts around in their tiny shelter to face her. He's going to say something. He'll pick up their conversation where it broke off before the storm.

"Lunchtime?"

Hallelujah feels a surge of disappointment, but she hides

it behind the mask of a smile. "The restaurant's serving fish today. With a side of dandelions."

"My favorite."

Hallelujah portions out two tiny meals and they eat quickly, without talking. The rain drips onto their stone roof, patters on the leaves of the trees all around them, spatters on the ground. Down the hill, Hallelujah can just barely see the clearing where they spent the night. The creek is rising with the storm. Water laps at the bank, overflows in places.

The weather gets worse into the afternoon. The wind roars past their little shelter, whistling through the cracks between the stones. The rain blows in sideways, from above, from below. The sky is black.

Hallelujah huddles ever closer to Jonah. Rachel sleeps through it. Her mouth is slightly open, and she breathes in short gasps. Her eyelids twitch and flicker, like she's dreaming.

When Hallelujah touches Rachel's forehead, just to see if she feels feverish, she starts to shiver. In her sleep.

Jonah's eyes widen. "Hold her," he says.

And so they squeeze on either side and wrap their arms around her. Hallelujah holds tight. She feels Rachel twitching, and then the shivering slows, and then Rachel is still except for her breath. Her eyes flutter open.

"Aw, I love you too," she says. Her voice is weak, but the laugh is still there.

Jonah and Hallelujah let go at the same time. "You were

shivering," Hallelujah says. "We were trying to keep you warm."

"Oh." Rachel looks more serious now. "Thanks." Her eyes well up, and she wipes at them with the backs of her hands. Angrily. "I hate this." She almost growls it. "I hate it so much." A deep breath. Then, in a very small voice: "Can I have my fish now?"

A crash of thunder.

Jonah hands over the last small pile of food. Rachel devours it, and doesn't speak again until she's licking her fingers. "Thanks," she says. "For catching that and cooking it and taking care of me . . ." She pauses. "I'm such a disaster."

"What? No!" Hallelujah is firm. "No way."

"What have I done but get us lost and more lost? And after that, I fell down a mountain and got poison ivy and hypothermia! I'm useless. I'm worse than useless."

"You wrapped my ankle. You knew what to do and you did it."

"Without me getting us lost, your ankle wouldn't have gotten hurt in the first place. And I messed up taking your boot off, too."

"Okay, this is not helping," Jonah cuts in. "We're here now, so we have to focus on getting home. If we can just——"

The wind roars, drowning out Jonah's words. The world churns and swirls. Leaves fly.

And then a bird is blown in. It hits the stone above Hallelujah's head with a crunch and drops to the ground. It's tiny. Brown. Trembling.

It's breathing. Being pelted with rain, dazed, and scared, but breathing. Seeing it, all three of them are struck silent.

Hallelujah leans over. Gently slides one hand under the bird. It weighs next to nothing. It lets out a chirp, ruffles its feathers and moves its feet like it's trying to get away. But it doesn't try to fly. And so she carefully moves it in out of the rain.

Jonah watches. Rachel watches.

Hallelujah finds one last dandelion under her backpack. She sets it gently on the ground in front of the bird, in its line of sight.

And then she lets it be.

# 6

JUST LIKE THAT, THE STORM IS OVER. ONE MINUTE, THE world is screaming around them, dark and angry, and the next, the sun comes out. Jonah unfolds himself from his seat. "I'm going to scope out the area. See if I can find anything useful. I'll be back soon."

"Okay," Hallelujah says.

"Okay," Rachel echoes.

Jonah climbs past Hallelujah. Even with her pulling her legs as close to her body as they'll go, he brushes them as he passes. He puts a hand on her knee for balance.

Then he's outside and walking away, humming to himself.

She can still feel his hand on her knee.

Rachel's the first one to speak. "So—he told you."

"Told me what?"

"Come on, Hal. What's changed since yesterday?" Rachel sneaks one arm out of her jacket cocoon to give Hallelujah a soft punch in the shoulder. "I may not be at my best right now, but I'm not blind." She pauses. "Or deaf."

Hallelujah feels her face get hot. "Oh. What did you hear?"

"Bits and pieces. I was really out of it last night, after . . . whatever that was. After almost freezing to death." Rachel shudders. "I have to say, it was totally obvious from the get-go that Jonah liked you."

"It was?" Hallelujah is still surprised. She still doesn't quite believe it.

"Um, yeah. Or did you think he's out here for me?" Rachel says slowly, as if to a child, "You followed me. He followed you."

"I didn't know. I don't know anything, apparently." Hallelujah leans back against the cold rock wall, listening to the birds calling again outside, heralding the end of the storm. But in the distance, thunder rumbles. She can't tell whether it's on its way out or on its way in. And she's so tired. Some little part of her is really starting to believe they aren't going to make it home. "I guess I just never thought about us like that."

"So how *did* you think about him?" Rachel asks.

Hallelujah shrugs. "We were friends. Good friends. He

knew—knows—a lot about me. I guess I know a lot about him. Stuff he likes and doesn't like."

Rachel looks skeptical. "And yet you never knew he liked *you*."

"No! I mean—when Jonah and I were friends, I liked Luke. So maybe I missed some signs."

"So you just . . . hung out? Platonically?"

"Yeah. I guess." Hallelujah thinks about how to explain it. How to distill a friendship down to its most basic components. "We had choir together last year. We talked. For kind of the first time, even though we'd been in church and school together since fourth grade."

"And, what, you found out you had *so much* in common?"

"Actually, no. But we started comparing music we liked, and a month into ninth grade, Jonah made me this mix of songs. Based on what we'd talked about. So then I made him a mix. And it grew from there. We'd go to each other's houses, watch movies, listen to music, that kind of thing. Hanging out."

"So tell me about Jonah. Something only you know."

"Um. He'd probably deny it, but he got really into the Harry Potter books. Like, *really* into them. I loaned him my box set last spring. He got so mad at me for not warning him how Book Six ends."

Rachel laughs. "He didn't see the movies?"

"No. But I told him we couldn't watch them until he'd finished the books."

"So what was Jonah like before high school? As a kid?"

"As a kid?" Hallelujah brings up the picture in her mind. "He was . . . sweet, I guess. Dorky. He'd wear these outfits his mom picked out—pleated khaki pants and polo shirts, with his hair slicked down with gel. And he would get really enthusiastic about things. Too enthusiastic. He went through this cowboy phase where he wore a cowboy hat and boots to school every day. Didn't care what anyone thought." The mental image makes her smile.

"And he and Luke were best friends?"

"Starting in middle school, yeah. They played soccer together."

"Huh." Rachel pauses. "So when did Jonah get cute?"

"He was still pretty short in middle school. And skinny. But he did start dressing better."

"No more pleated khakis?"

"No more pleated khakis. And then the summer before ninth grade, he had this growth spurt. And he started to, uh, fill out. So I guess ninth grade is when I noticed . . ." Hallelujah fades off. "This is embarrassing."

"No, it's not. This is what girls talk about." Rachel grins. "Besides. I wanted to see if you were paying as close attention to him as he was to you."

"I didn't realize I was. We were just friends."

"You can be friends and still objectively notice someone's cuteness. Anyway—you were in choir together. . . ."

"Yeah. I was so surprised to see him on the first day of school last year. He'd never told me he was interested in singing. And then his voice turned out to be really good."

She closes her eyes, hears him singing in her head. "We had so much fun in that class. Not just singing together. We did a lot of stuff as a group—pizza nights, movies, ice cream socials. Not to mention all the rehearsals. Mr. Boyden wanted us all to bond. He said it would help us perform better." Her smile drops. "I was really looking forward to this year. It started off so great."

And then Jonah's best friend made Hallelujah his personal punching bag and Jonah went along with it. And sure, now she knows why he pulled away, she knows that he was hurt too, but she's still not sure whether that excuses the betrayal.

*Betrayed.* That's the only word for how she felt when she tried to talk to Jonah the Monday after it happened, in the choir room, and he'd pretended she wasn't even there. And the times after that when she saw him at school, said his name, and he turned away. Actually looked the other way, like he was looking for someone else, someone better.

Thunder again. Definitely getting closer.

"Hal?"

Hallelujah realizes her eyes are wet. "Sorry," she says automatically. She blinks a few times, trying to will the tears to evaporate.

"It's okay." Rachel inches over until they're huddling together. "Do you like him back? Now?"

The answer's just as automatic as the apology. Still, it comes out as a whisper: "Yeah." She takes a deep breath, gives voice to some of the noise in her head. "But what if

I'm just feeling this because we're out here and it's scary and he feels safe? Or what if I'm just relieved to have my friend back, but I don't *like him* like him? I don't even know why he'd choose me. Then or now."

Rachel drops her head down onto Hallelujah's shoulder. She nuzzles into Hallelujah's neck, like a cat. "Hal, despite the giant prickly wall you've put up around yourself with the neon Off Limits sign flashing at the gate——"

Hallelujah lets out a small laugh at this picture of herself.

"——you're nice. Like I said when I told you about my parents, you listen. And you care. Which is more than I can say for about three-quarters of the high school population. And you're pretty. And while I've never heard you sing, obviously Jonah likes that about you. Speaking of which," Rachel says, "why'd you stop? For real?"

The question makes Hallelujah's mouth go dry. Why did she stop singing? Why did she stop doing something that she loved so much?

She remembers the first time she sang a solo in church after everything happened. The first time Luke pulled his "Hallelujah" stunt. She saw him, a few pews from the back, fake-moaning her name, rubbing his hands over his chest, the other youth group members either looking on in horror or stifling laughter. Hallelujah barely made it through the rest of the hymn. Tears in her eyes. Throat so tight she could barely squeeze out the notes.

She remembers her voice failing her more and more often after that. At first, only when she sang alone. Then every time she sang, even in a group. And finally the holiday concert, the duet she was supposed to sing with Jonah, turned into a solo after he refused. Her voice a shadow of its former self.

"Singing made people look at me," she tells Rachel. "It put me in the spotlight. And I didn't want to be in the spotlight anymore. I don't. I can't stand to have everyone looking at me. Laughing at me. That's why I quit."

"Okay, so you don't want to perform. But you stopped singing *entirely*."

"Yeah. Because it—it hurt. Too much."

"Do you miss it?" Rachel sounds sad.

"Every day." Even now, Hallelujah hears music in the air, in the whoosh of the wind through the leaves, in the calling of the birds, in the timpani sound of the thunder, in the soft patter of the drops that are starting, again, to fall. And sometimes in church on Sundays, she imagines her voice joining in, rising and falling and soaring with the voices around her. It would be like coming home.

Now, of course, coming home means something completely different. It means not starving and shivering, not being wet or scared. Not being terrified that the next choice they make will be the last one they ever make. At the same time, it means not going back the same person she was on Monday.

"Sing something for me?" Rachel murmurs.

Anxiety wraps its fingers around her heart, her lungs. "I . . . I can't."

"Yes, you can," Rachel says. But she doesn't push it. "I'm just going to . . ." She doesn't finish her sentence, dropping instead into a quiet, even breathing.

The storm settles in on top of them. Hallelujah's stomach growls. She reaches for her backpack. Opens it. Confirms that they are officially out of food.

She needs something to distract her from her hunger. And from all of the feelings that are threatening to drown her faster than the rain. She finds her water bottle. Unscrews its top. Holds it out into the rain. Even in the hard down-pour, it takes so long to feel the bottle grow heavy and full. Hallelujah's arm trembles. But she waits until she feels the splash of overflow on her hand before she pulls her arm back in. Jonah's water bottle sits on the ground across from her. He didn't take it with him. *Why didn't he take it? When is he coming back?*

She hopes he's okay. She hopes he didn't get turned around when the second storm rolled in. She hopes he'll come walking up the hill any second now. She hopes, even as her mind starts spinning worst-case scenarios.

To calm herself, she fills Jonah's water bottle and puts it into her backpack. She opens Rachel's bag. Finds her water bottle. Fills it. The effort of holding her arm out horizontal a third time is almost too much, and she's glad not to have to move much after that. As she puts Rachel's water bottle back, she feels something else in the bag. A can. Dented, but intact.

Hallelujah pulls out the Diet Coke and stares at it. She'd

almost forgotten about it. She holds it reverently, cradling it in her palms. It's caffeine—maybe a vital jolt of energy—but it's more than that. It's home. It's grocery stores and refrigerators. It's other people.

She wants to open it up right then, drink the entire thing in one gulp. Feel the carbonation tickle her teeth and bounce around inside her. Have the world's most satisfying belch. But something tells her not to drink. It's not time yet. They might need this. *You'll know when*, she tells herself. *Wait for the right time.*

And so she tucks the can gently back into Rachel's backpack, trying to ignore the part of her that's laughing at the ridiculousness of thinking their salvation might depend on a Diet Coke. Because you never know. You never know. *At the very least, it'll be a good last drink*, she thinks, and then hates that she thought it.

She stares out into the rain for a few minutes. She looks for the color blue. She knows she should be looking for orange—for rescue—but right now, all she wants to see is Jonah's blue jacket.

It's time for him to come back. She needs him to come back.

Not in a romantic way. Not even because he's the only one of them left who's not superweak or injured. She needs him to come back because with Rachel asleep, the silence is too loud. Surrounded by trees and trees and trees being battered by sheets of rain, she feels so small. She feels alone. She doesn't want to be alone. Not anymore.

"Where are you?" she asks aloud. It's reassuring to hear her voice over the storm. "Come back," she says. "Come back."

She tells herself that she's talking to Jonah, that her voice will be carried to him on this crazy wind and that he'll beeline back to these rocks. But she's also talking to God. Because she's alone and lost and tired, and now would be a great time to feel like there's someone watching over her, like everything's going to be okay. But she doesn't. It's like there's nothing there.

# 7

HALLELUJAH WAKES WITH A START. SHE DOESN'T REMEMBER dozing off. She's hugging Rachel like a human teddy bear. Her left arm, caught between Rachel and the rock, is asleep. But she doesn't want to let go. The space between Hallelujah's body and Rachel's body is warm, and everything else feels cold.

Jonah is not back.

She wonders how long she's been asleep. The rain has almost stopped; it's just a drizzle. The sun has moved. As Hallelujah scans the woods, craning her neck to avoid letting go of Rachel, a single ray of light pierces through the clouds, traveling down through the trees, between the branches, between the leaves, to land on the forest floor not too far away. It creates a little square that looks like summer.

Another ray cuts through the clouds and the trees. And then another. A leaf drifts toward her on the breeze, passing from sunlight to shadow, sunlight to shadow.

At Hallelujah's feet, the bird she pulled in out of the rain is stirring. Testing its wings. It lets out a few chirps.

She shakes Rachel gently, needing another human being to see what she's seeing. The beauty after the storm.

Rachel's awake in an instant. "What? What is it?"

But the light changes again. The beams vanish, all at once. And the moment Rachel speaks, the bird flies away into the trees. "Never mind," Hallelujah says.

Rachel yawns and stretches. "What time is it? How long did I sleep?"

"A while. I don't know . . ."

Jonah should be back by now. Something has happened. Hallelujah feels the certainty of it, deep in her gut. "Can you walk?" she asks Rachel.

"I think so. I feel okay." Rachel yawns again. She glances at Hallelujah's ankle, wrapped in its dirty pink bandage. "Can *you* walk?"

"I don't think I have a choice. We have to find Jonah."

"Well, let me look at your ankle first." Rachel shifts around to sit opposite Hallelujah and pats her lap. Hallelujah puts her foot on Rachel's legs. Rachel pulls off the boot and starts unwrapping the swimsuit. And Hallelujah's ankle emerges: red and blue and purple and green and, on the edges of the bruise, yellow. Hallelujah gasps at the sight of it, and Rachel looks up.

"Considering that we don't have ice or ibuprofen or a proper bandage, and that you've been walking on it," she says, "this is actually not so bad."

If this isn't so bad, Hallelujah thinks, she wouldn't want to see worse. But she just says, "Okay."

Rachel wraps Hallelujah's ankle back up, very carefully. Even the gentle touch hurts, though, and Hallelujah has to bite the inside of her cheek to keep from whimpering.

"Almost done," Rachel says. She ties the ties, slides Hallelujah's boot back on, and looks up. "There." A pause. "Now what?"

"We have to find Jonah."

"We don't . . . have any food left, do we?" Rachel says the last part quick and casual, like she just has the munchies. Nothing serious.

Hallelujah holds up the empty sandwich bag. There are a few morsels of fish clinging to the bottom. She and Rachel lock eyes. Hallelujah opens the bag and runs her finger through it. She hands the bag to Rachel, who does the same. They stick their fingers in their mouths and suck.

Hallelujah feels a sob bubbling up. She tries to talk it away. "When we find Jonah, we're not separating again. Whatever happens from here on out, we're together."

Rachel nods. She licks her lips like she's searching for the phantom taste of fish.

"Jonah's fine," Hallelujah goes on. "He's fine." Him not being fine is not an option. He didn't go far; he found something interesting; he lost track of time. She tries telling herself that he found people searching for them, that he found help. But she doesn't really believe it. If he had, they'd have been here by now. "He's fine," she repeats. It's the best she can do.

"He's totally fine," Rachel echoes. But Hallelujah can see the shadow of every possible catastrophe flickering in her eyes.

A cool breeze blows into their shelter. Hallelujah looks at their two backpacks. "Okay," she says. "You're going to put on all of my extra clothes. You'll be warmer and our bags will be lighter."

Rachel nods. She stands, slowly, bracing herself on the rock walls. She sways. She blinks. "Whoa," she whispers. At Hallelujah's worried look, she adds, "Just dizzy. I'm okay." She takes off her jacket and pulls on Hallelujah's swim shorts and long-sleeved shirt. They hang loosely on her tiny frame. She has to roll the waistband of the shorts down a couple times before they stay up. Then she puts on Hallelujah's extra T-shirt, with her jacket back over top of it all. "I look ridiculous," she says.

"You look warm."

"I know," Rachel says quickly. "Thanks. You ready?"

"As I'll ever be." Hallelujah extends her hands and braces her good foot on the ground. Rachel grabs hold and leans back, and through some miracle of physics, Hallelujah is upright. She slumps against the rock for a second. Catches her breath. Then, with the taste of fish in her mouth and a sense of doom in her stomach, she takes a hobbling step outside.

"Not so fast, Hal," Rachel says. She hooks her shoulder under Hallelujah's arm. She's smaller and shorter than Hallelujah, so she fits perfectly. Unfortunately, when Hallelujah puts her weight on Rachel for real, Rachel's knees buckle a little. The two of them stagger-hop over to a nearby tree. "Okay," Rachel says. "We can do this."

Hallelujah is already feeling discouraged. But she tries to tamp it down. "Jonah went that way." She points. "And I didn't see him cross back. So we'll start over there."

Rachel takes a step. Hallelujah hops, landing heavily and off-balance on the uneven ground. Rachel wavers. Barely keeps her balance. But she stays on her feet, so they try the same thing again. Step, step, hop, stumble, catch. Ten feet feels like a major accomplishment. Twenty feet feels like a miracle. And eventually they fall into a rhythm, and Hallelujah stops thinking of anything but moving forward and looking and listening for Jonah.

"Jonah!" she calls. She's already out of breath from the effort of hopping and holding Rachel up and staying up herself. Shouting hurts, deep in her chest. But she shouts again: "Jonah!"

The sky is turning the color of sunset. But it's a cloudless sky. No rain on the horizon.

"Jonah!" Step, step, hop, stumble, catch. The damp leaves are slick. It feels like the ground is shifting under their feet. A few times, Hallelujah is forced to put weight on her sprained ankle, and each time it's a new hit of pain. She knows that a wrong move from either of them could pull them both down. And they might not get up. But she keeps moving forward. Toward the clearing where they spent last night; it's as good a starting place as any. "Jonah!" she calls. Her voice cracks. She clears her throat and calls his name again. Rachel joins in. They call again. And again. And again.

# 8

SHE'S NOT SURE HOW LONG THEY'VE BEEN WALKING. THE SUN has almost vanished over the tall mountain behind her. Her voice is a husk, dry and rasping.

"Jonah!" she calls, and coughs. It hurts. She needs water, but she can't get a water bottle out of her bag without stopping, and stopping is not an option. Not yet. "Jonah! Answer me! Come on! Please!" The last word comes out as a squeak, mostly air with no sound behind it.

They've been following the creek downstream. It's Hallelujah's best guess at what Jonah might have done. This creek could lead to another body of water, and then another, and eventually, to civilization. A house. A fishing shack. A tubing business. Those are all over the Smokies. Kids floating down the river on rented inner tubes. Hallelujah fantasizes for a second about floating. Rachel in a tube on one side and Jonah on the other. Feeling weightless, letting the current cradle her and rock her. Her ankle twinges at the thought.

Of course, Jonah might not have followed the creek. It seems like what he would do, but can she really predict which of a hundred options he'd choose, alone in the mountains, caught in a sudden and violent storm?

But she will not give up. Will not stop calling until her voice gives out. Will not stop walking until her legs will no longer hold her up.

She inhales deeply. "Jonah!" Forces it out from her chest, rather than from her raw throat. Projects, like she learned how to do in choir. "Jonah, we're coming! Just tell us where you are!"

"Jonah!" Rachel's call is more of a stage whisper. But she's trying.

The area where they're walking is almost entirely in shadow now. The sky is a gorgeous blue-gray, purple around the edges. It's getting hard to see the ground clearly, and Hallelujah stumbles. Rachel keeps her upright, but she stands hard on her injured ankle. She has to stop. Let the pain wash over her. Nerve endings are firing from her forehead to her toes. The knife in her boot stabs her over and over. She squeezes her eyes closed and takes five deep breaths.

"Hal?" Rachel croaks.

Hallelujah bites her lip. The pain recedes a little. She opens her eyes.

And she sees it.

Jonah's blue jacket. Floating in the creek. Riding the lazy rapids, both sleeves extended. It looks almost black in the dusk, but she knows it's Jonah's. And he's not in it.

"Jonah!" she screams. She looks back and forth, up and down the creek, squinting. It's getting too dark. If he's passed out somewhere, if he's hurt, how is she supposed to—

"Hallie! Over here!"

She whips around. "Jonah?" The call came from ahead of them. Not too far.

"Hallie! I—I need help."

"Where are you?"

"By the water." His voice is softer now. Strained. Like the two shouts were all he had in him.

"Wave your arm or something!"

He does. Hallelujah sees it as a moving shadow across the creek. The larger shadow that's the rest of him is half in and half out of the water.

"I see you!" she calls. "I'm coming!"

The arm drops.

The creek isn't too wide here. It's not deep. The water's slow. But Hallelujah and Rachel aren't steady on their feet on land.

Rachel's eyes are wide. "I don't want to go in," she says, staring at the water. "I don't want to."

"We have to."

Rachel is already shivering, like just the thought of the cold water is chilling her. "I know," she says. "I just . . . don't want to."

"I know," Hallelujah says. She hugs Rachel close.

They slip and slide down the bank to the creek. At the water's edge, Hallelujah feels Rachel tense all over. She's still shivering, but she steps in. She helps Hallelujah limp in after her. The water rushes up around Hallelujah's boots, bitterly cold. So cold, like ice cutting through her skin.

There's no longer enough daylight for them to see the creek bed, so they feel their way carefully. Don't move until they're sure the ground's solid. Ankle-deep, calf-deep, knee-deep: halfway there. A few steps and they're calf-deep. Then ankle-deep again. Then at the bank.

Rachel collapses to the ground, shaking all over. She starts rubbing at her legs, trying to warm them. "Go," she says through chattering teeth.

Hallelujah hops over to Jonah. She lowers herself to sit beside him.

He's on his back, one hand gripping a thick root to stay on the bank. His legs are in the water up to his thighs. His face is shadowed, but even so, Hallelujah can see the grimace of pain. She's afraid to ask right away.

Instead, she leans over him and says, "Jonah. I'm here."

# 9

His eyes flutter open. "Hi."

"Sorry it took me so long."

"Don't apologize. I think I passed out. For a while." He's pale. His breathing is really shallow, almost panting. And his eyes—his eyes are scared.

"What happened?" Hallelujah asks.

Jonah shakes his head like he's trying to clear out the fog. "Hallie, I found—I followed the creek a little ways, and then went uphill—back there—" He waves one arm in the direction of upstream. "And you're not gonna believe it—I found a campsite!"

Hallelujah draws in a sharp breath. She spins and makes eye contact with Rachel, who's still curled up on the ground.

"There weren't any people there, but a campsite has to mean there's a trail nearby." Jonah takes a shuddering breath. "I ran back down the hill to get you two. And when I was crossing the creek, I thought, might as well catch some more fish. For dinner. So we can be ready to get up tomorrow and find our way out of here. Then that storm came up, out of nowhere. One second I was standing in a foot of water, two fish in my backpack, and the next there was this downpour, and all this water came at me, and it knocked me over. I got washed down here. Lost my backpack. And—" He nods in the direction of his legs.

"And?" Hallelujah echoes.

"Cut my leg on a rock." He doesn't elaborate. The sentence hangs in the air.

"What can I do?"

"Campsite's not far. I think we should spend the night there. If we can get back to it in the dark. And maybe you and Rachel can patch me up?"

"Of course." Hallelujah doesn't bring up how awful she's

feeling, how much her ankle is throbbing, how the mention of fish almost makes her delirious.

The last light is leaving. They don't have much time.

"Rachel?" Hallelujah looks over her shoulder again. Rachel is now lying on her stomach, dipping her water bottle into the creek and drinking the contents, over and over. "Be right there," Rachel says.

Jonah grabs Hallelujah's arm. "I tore strips off my T-shirt to mark the way back to the campsite."

"Good."

"We can use my watch for light." He holds up his wrist and shows Hallelujah the faint blue glow.

She repeats, "Good."

Rachel comes over to sit next to Hallelujah. She squints toward Jonah's legs. "Where'd you get cut?"

He pushes up onto his elbows. The movement makes him full-body cringe. He scoots back out of the water a few inches, gasping with each shift of weight. "Thigh," he grunts, jaw clenched. "Thought the water might . . . numb it."

"What do we use for a bandage?" Rachel asks.

"Use this." In one smooth motion, Jonah pulls his T-shirt off inside out. "I guess just wrap it around as tight as you can," he says. "Since it's not like we can get it clean."

Hallelujah takes the shirt. "Can I rip it up?" she asks. There's already a bit torn away near the bottom. She runs the fabric between two fingers.

"Go for it." Jonah pulls himself another few inches up the bank and then slumps back to the ground, closing his eyes. "Can you see it?" he asks Rachel.

"I think so." Rachel's got her face close to Jonah's leg.

"Okay. The blood . . . I mean, I can't . . ." He sounds queasy, on top of the pain. "I didn't really look at it yet."

"Hal, you need to see this." Rachel pulls Hallelujah closer. "Can I?" Without waiting for a response, she slides Jonah's watch from his wrist and points its tiny blue screen at Jonah's thigh.

And Hallelujah sees it. A jagged cut starting on his outer thigh, under the hem of his cargo shorts, and—she follows its path as Rachel moves the light—passing the knee to stop at the calf. Six inches, maybe seven. The skin is puckered, pulling away from the open wound. Watery blood is already trickling down Jonah's leg to join the dirt. It looks bad. It looks like it *hurts*.

Jonah's whole body is tense. "Oh man," he says. "Oh geez."

"You know," Hallelujah says, trying to sound light, like she's not on the verge of tears, "there are probably times when it's okay to curse. Like now."

"Just wrap it." Jonah's voice is tight. "Please."

"We have to lift your knee up. . . ." Rachel fades off. "Hal, are you ready?"

"One second." Hallelujah rips Jonah's T-shirt into long, wide strips. She holds them out. "Okay."

Rachel takes them. "Okay. You lift, I'll wrap."

Hallelujah nods. She slides her hands under Jonah's leg, one above the cut and one below. His skin is wet, and she doesn't know if it's creek water or blood, but it makes her heart beat faster and her stomach turn. She gulps and lifts Jonah's leg a few inches off the ground. Rachel presses a strip of T-shirt against the top of the cut.

Jonah inhales sharply. His hand grabs at Hallelujah's tank top, pulls at the fabric, squeezes tight.

Rachel begins wrapping his leg. Jonah's breath is coming in short bursts, in and out through his nose like his mouth is clamped shut. Then, all at once, he relaxes. His whole body goes limp.

"Jonah?" Hallelujah feels a wave of panic, but when she sets his foot down and holds her hand over his face, she feels breath. He's just passed out.

Rachel looks at her, hands frozen midwrap.

"He's breathing," Hallelujah whispers.

Rachel starts wrapping again. In the last bit of light, Hallelujah can see that she's crying, her tears landing on the dark spots that already stain Jonah's white bandage. "There," she says a second later. She's tucked the ends in tight.

A chilly breeze brushes Hallelujah's shoulders, giving her goosebumps. "He found a campsite," she says.

"I heard."

"We have to get him up. We have to get there."

"I don't know if I can—" Rachel stops. She breathes in, long and slow, and out again. "Let's go," she says.

"Jonah." Hallelujah shakes his shoulder. He moans. "Jonah. It's time to move." He doesn't open his eyes, so she climbs carefully over his legs to his other side. "Let's sit him up. On three." She slides her hands under his shoulder and back. Rachel does the same. "One, two, three." They lift, straining a little because he's dead weight—Hallelujah suddenly hates that phrase, "dead weight"—but they get him to a seated position.

His chin hits his chest, lolling. But then his head snaps back up. He looks around wildly, like he doesn't know where he is. Then his eyes focus. He sees Rachel and Hallelujah. He sees his leg. He looks away from it quickly.

"We need to find the campsite," Hallelujah tells him. "Before it's totally dark."

"Right."

Hallelujah rolls onto her hands and knees, and slowly, painfully stands upright. She balances on her good leg, holding her left foot just off the ground. She extends a hand to Jonah.

He looks at her hand. He looks down at her ankle, wrapped in its filthy pink bandage. His face crumples, just for a second, but then he pulls it together. He takes her hand. Puts his other hand on Rachel's shoulder. Brings in his left leg so the foot is flat on the ground. And then he pulls and he pushes and with a deep grunt, he stands. He wobbles. Hallelujah wobbles too. But they're both upright.

Rachel scrambles to her feet. She looks from Hallelujah to Jonah, eyes wide. They're both bigger than her, Jonah by a lot. They're both down to one good leg. "I—I don't know if I—" She sounds scared and exhausted and ashamed and like she's about to give up. "How are we gonna do this?"

"We hold each other up," Jonah says grimly. "Rachel, you're in the middle. Hallie's on your left." They line up. Rachel's small enough that she can wrap her arms around their waists. Jonah's left arm stretches across Rachel's shoulders; his hand rests on Hallelujah's back. He gives her shoulder a squeeze that is either meant to reassure her or is a reflex, a reaction to the pain that must be rolling through him.

They move even more slowly than Hallelujah and Rachel did earlier. Because of the dark. Because of the pain. Because they're so weak and tired.

But the moon comes out to help. It reflects in the creek and peers through the tree branches above. It helps them see the obstacles in their path. And it illuminates the strip of white T-shirt Jonah tied to a forked tree to show them where to turn.

They don't stop to catch their breath. They veer right.

Uphill is even harder. In addition to a throbbing ankle, Hallelujah now has burning thighs, burning shoulders, burning lungs. Her vision narrows until all she can see is what's right in front of her. Where she's stepping next.

There's an owl overhead, not far away. Its calling is rhythmic. Calm. And she hears the flapping of wings and a staccato birdcall and the chirping of crickets and some kind of buzzing. She lets the night music fill her head, blocking out Rachel's panting and sobbing and Jonah's groans and gasps of pain.

They climb. Hallelujah's heart feels like it's about to explode.

She can see a little plateau, lit by moonlight, not too far

ahead. Just a few more feet up. *Please let that be the campsite*, she thinks. Prays. *Please let that be it. Please.*

And then they're over the ledge. They're there.

Rachel drops to the ground immediately, crying and shaking. Jonah grabs for Hallelujah like he might drop too. She leans in, her good leg against his good leg, pain and fear forgotten, just for an instant.

It's an honest-to-God campsite. With a proper fire pit. A few logs cut in half longways for seating. A flat dirt area with holes around the perimeter that must've been made by tent stakes.

The trail—a trail, who knows what trail, who cares—can't be far away.

"You did it," she whispers to Jonah.

"Not yet," he whispers back. But she can hear the hope in his voice.

Hope bubbles up inside her, too. It feels strange and foolish and fragile, given everything that's happened and that could still happen. But it's there.

She hopes.

# 10

JONAH LOWERS HIMSELF TO THE GROUND, BACK AGAINST one of the log benches. Hallelujah sinks to the ground beside him. She's pretty sure she's never been this tired. She's so tired she's shaking almost as much as Rachel was last night.

"You don't have another shirt, do you?" Jonah asks.

Hallelujah is startled. She'd actually forgotten that Jonah is shirtless. But now that she remembers, she's not sure how she could have paid attention to anything else. She can see his skin and his muscles and—no, it's too dark to see his muscles. She's imagining them. But she's arm to bare arm with him and she's—she's staring. Oh no.

Rachel rescues her. "I think I'm wearing them all."

"Oh." Jonah is quiet for a second. "I lost my jacket in the water."

"We saw it," Rachel says.

Another few moments of silence. Jonah wraps his arms across his chest, rubbing his palms up and down on the opposite biceps.

"Here." Rachel crawls over, takes off her jacket, and peels off Hallelujah's extra T-shirt. She hands it over to Jonah, then zips her jacket back up again, tight.

"Thanks," he says. His teeth are starting to chatter, and the chattering is mixed with pained gasps, like each tremor pulls at the gash in his leg. He quickly puts the shirt on. "So can you two build a fire?"

Hallelujah's house doesn't have a working fireplace. It's the spot where her mom arranges plants in decorative flowerpots. "I don't know how," she says, staring into the empty fire pit.

"I don't either," Rachel says.

"Neither did I, before this week."

Rachel gapes at him. "But you said you were a Boy Scout."

"Yeah, but it's been a couple years since I tried to build a fire without a match or a lighter. I figured I could do it now, because I had to. And I was pretty relieved when that first fire caught and I didn't burn down the forest."

"What about that flint you have?" Rachel's leaning into Hallelujah like Hallelujah herself is giving off warmth. "You carry around a fire-starting tool? Just in case?"

Now Jonah sighs. "My dad gave that to me. Before this trip." He puts on a deeper, dad voice. "'I'm proud of you, son. You have a good time out there. God loves you, and your mother and I do too.'" He goes back to his normal voice. "Guess he thought it was outdoorsy. Manly. Maybe he meant for it to, I don't know, spark the flame of God inside me."

Rachel lets out a tiny noise that is almost a laugh.

Hallelujah is just sad. Before she left for this trip, her dad gave her a lecture on listening to the chaperones and staying on the girls' side of the lodge and staying out of trouble. Her mom said, "Bill, she knows." And then, "Have fun, Hallelujah." Which was nice, and surprising, even if it proved how out of touch her mom was with her life. She'd thought that was going to be it, but right before she got in the van with Luke, Brad, Jonah, and the others from their church, both parents had hugged her and said they would be praying for her to be safe.

She hopes they're still praying.

Jonah shifts to lean back a little farther, moaning as

he does. "Holy heck, my leg hurts," he says, still with that strained, forced lightness.

Again, Hallelujah mimics his tone. "'Holy heck'? That's cutting it close."

"I have a gash in my leg the size of the Mississippi. I can say whatever I want."

Hallelujah closes her eyes for a second, but sees a picture of her parents crying inside her eyelids. She opens her eyes again. It's just as dark. "I'm going to see about that fire," she says. "Rachel?" But Rachel's dozing off, and Hallelujah can't bear to wake her back up, so she slides her shoulder carefully out from under Rachel's head and moves away. Rachel collapses into Jonah's side, and he winces but shakes it off.

"Just look for dry wood," he says. "Twigs. Even dry leaves." Jonah keeps instructing her as she slowly circles the campsite on hands and knees, gathering materials. It takes a while to find wood that's dry enough to light, but she eventually has a small pile in the fire pit. Then, with great ceremony, Jonah hands her his flint and steel. "Strike it like this," he says, demonstrating.

She takes it with shaking hands, shifting to sit on the ground with her left leg out to one side. She strikes. And strikes. Just about the time she's ready to give up, to let them all freeze to death, she gets a spark.

"Jonah!" She's so excited she almost drops the flint.

"Okay, blow on it. Gently! Get some of those leaves to light."

She purses her lips and blows, just a little. The sparks

jump and multiply. And then: flames. Flames!

Once the fire's going, it spreads to the rest of the fire pit pretty quickly. Hallelujah watches the flames dance. She almost feels like dancing herself.

"Nice work," Jonah says. She tosses the flint to him and he catches it in one hand. "Maybe get a little more wood? If you can?"

"I can." She made fire out of nothing. She can take a little more pain. She gets up and limps around, scanning the area. She gathers more wood. Sets it by the fire pit. The work distracts her from the coldness of the air, from the knife in her ankle, from the fact that her stomach has just realized, again, that they have no food for dinner. Nothing. Not even a single dandelion.

Jonah must be thinking about that too. "You got any water?" he asks. He's been watching her work. She could feel his eyes on her as she piled up sticks and leaves.

Hallelujah turns, seeing him through the flames. "In my backpack," she says. "Two bottles of rain."

"Great," Jonah says, already rummaging through her bag. He pulls out his water bottle, unscrews it, takes a single, long swig.

Hallelujah has run out of jobs to do. Her fire-starting adrenaline is fading. She stands still for a second, and her eyes meet Jonah's. He pats the ground next to him. And so she hobbles over. Sits. The exhaustion descends immediately.

"Want to get some sleep?" Jonah asks.

"I think I'll stay up a little longer," Hallelujah says. As tired as she is, she wants to keep watch for a while. Jonah watched out for them the first few nights; it's her turn. Plus, they're in even worse shape than they were before. The less time they're all asleep—vulnerable to anything that might happen—the better. Or at least that's how it feels right now, with the night so dark and the trail home so tantalizingly close. "You can sleep," she tells Jonah.

"Not sure how much I'll get. With this." Jonah gestures at his leg. In the firelight, they both can see blood soaking through the thin T-shirt bandage. There's also a dark red stain on his shorts leg. Jonah flinches and looks up at the sky, taking a few wavering breaths. "Wish I had my coat," he says. "It'd be awesome to cover that up. So I didn't have to look at it."

"Just close your eyes," Hallelujah says gently. "Try to rest."

Jonah nods a few times, still looking up at the moon. When he looks down, it's at Hallelujah. He's holding it together. Barely. "Can I ask you something?"

"Yes," she answers. "Anything."

"Can you—I mean, will you—please—" He gulps. She actually sees his Adam's apple go up and down. "It really hurts, Hallie."

"I know. I'm sorry. I wish I could do something."

"Can you, maybe, just hold on to me for a little while? Till I fall asleep?" He looks away, like he's ashamed to ask.

Hallelujah hesitates. She held Rachel earlier. It's not any

different. It really isn't. She tries not to think about Jonah's arms around her. How that would feel. If she does this, it has nothing to do with how he feels about her. Or how she feels about him.

"Hallie?" Jonah's voice is just a breath. "You don't have to. Don't feel like—I mean, I'm fine. Don't worry about it."

"Jonah," she says, wrapping her arms around him, "it's okay. Go to sleep."

"But—"

"We'll talk in the morning," she says, leaning her head into his shoulder. He drops his head to rest on hers.

As she holds him, she feels him tremble. After a while, that stops. Then he twitches a few times, so hard she's amazed he doesn't wake himself back up. And then, all at once, his whole body relaxes. She can feel his rib cage expand and contract as he breathes, opening and closing her hug around him. His breathing is calm and regular, and it soothes her. Her head fits perfectly in the crook between his neck and shoulder.

She watches the fire. It crackles, sending sparks floating away on the breeze. She can see the smoke in the moonlight. The smell of charred wood drifts toward her, and she breathes it in, imagining it can warm her from the inside out. Her mouth waters at the scent, and she fantasizes about this morning's fish. That fish turns into a feast in her head: a full cookout, grilled vegetables and burgers and hot dogs and chicken and her mom's homemade French fries, all tasting of delicious grill char. With butter and salt and pepper and ketchup and cheese. On top of everything.

The wind changes and the fire smell drifts in the opposite direction. Just like that, the feast is gone. Hallelujah is left with a salivating mouth and an empty stomach.

Time passes. She checks Jonah's light-up watch once and it's 10:23 p.m. The next time she looks, it's almost 11:00. Then it's 11:07.

She blinks and forces her eyes to stay open.

*She remembers the last perfect evening before everything happened, perfect even though she didn't know everything was about to change. Karaoke night. A bunch of kids from choir cheering each other on. When it was her turn, Hallelujah belted out "Total Eclipse of the Heart." She went for every melodramatic note, closing her eyes and beating her chest. She got the whole group to sing along.*

*She remembers Jonah taking the stage next. When he sang the opening lines to Garth Brooks's "Friends in Low Places," the room went nuts. He put on a cowboy drawl and sent the low notes reverberating through the wooden floorboards. She remembers him tipping an imaginary Stetson at her when he was done.*

*In a week, Hallelujah would get caught making out with Luke Willis. He would humiliate her and start spreading lies about her. She would become someone quiet and sad and resentful. But right then, performance-flushed and surrounded by friends, she couldn't stop smiling.*

the
## sixth
day

# 1

THE NEXT TIME HALLELUJAH CHECKS JONAH'S WATCH, after holding out for what feels like an agonizingly long time, it's 12:06. A new day. She counts in her head: They arrived on Sunday night, which makes today Friday. Time to pack up and head for home.

She wonders what the rest of the week would've been like, if they hadn't ended up out here. It probably would've been miserable. Luke could've turned the whole group against her, chaperones included. He could've come up with new ways to torture her. Or she could've been ignored completely, a shadow on the trail and in the lodge, unseen and unheard. She could've gone home feeling even more alone than she felt in the van on the way there. Even angrier at God.

Instead, she's starving, exhausted, injured, and scared. But not alone. And much less angry.

Hallelujah swats at a bug that's flying around her face. It vanishes and then comes back, drawn by the light of the fire's last gasps, drawn by some scent on her goosebumped, sweat-dried skin. She swats again.

Jonah shifts in her arms. He mutters something. She looks down at him. He's frowning in his sleep. She hopes his leg isn't hurting too much. Hopes he'll be able to keep sleeping. He needs the rest.

She probably does too, but she still feels compelled to stay awake. They're so close to getting out of here. It feels like—like pushing her luck to let her guard down. And keeping her eyes open isn't so hard. It would be easier with a book or a movie, though. It would be easier with snacks.

Chocolate. Like M&Ms. And Oreos. And those chocolate-covered macadamia nuts her mom used to buy from the market for special occasions, to put in the crystal bowl on the coffee table in the living room. For guests. Those, too.

And popcorn! Oh, popcorn. Hallelujah's stomach gurgles, so loud she's sure it will wake Jonah up, but he doesn't move.

Her brain feels like popcorn, jumping around.

The bug is back, buzzing near her head. She blows at it. Bats it away with one arm, the arm that's not pinned behind Jonah. Finally, sheer luck, she manages to hit it. A tiny impact against the palm of her hand.

Hallelujah checks Jonah's watch again. 12:15. Nine minutes since last time.

As if on cue, her eyelids get heavy. She forces them open, and her eyes burn. She blinks. Squeezes her eyes shut and opens them wide: eye exercises.

There's a flutter overhead. The whoosh of wings. Hallelujah ducks as a bird swoops in low, scoops something from the ground on the other side of the fire, and flies off, a dark shadow near the moon. She wonders what it's holding. Whatever it is, she's glad she didn't have to fight it in the dark. Or even see it.

Another bird swoops in. Looking for leftovers.

*All we have is Diet Coke*, Hallelujah thinks. *No human food, no bird food, no nothing.*

Diet Coke. She could drink the Diet Coke and stay awake.

A yawn, wide-mouthed and croaking, convinces her. She leans as far away from Jonah as she can without actually wriggling her arm free. She stretches toward Rachel's backpack. She gets her fingertips and then her whole hand under one strap and pulls the bag toward her. It slides easily on the packed dirt. Then it's in her lap.

She unzips the bag. Pulls out the Diet Coke can. She's never been so happy to see a soft drink. She imagines the sensation of the bubbles against her teeth, and how the drink will fizz on her tongue. The can's a little banged up; she hopes it hasn't gone flat. She takes hold of the metal tab. Braces herself to pull. Prepares for the sweet, sweet whoosh of pressure leaving the can.

She hesitates. It's not even one a.m. yet. Maybe she should wait. If she wants to watch for a while longer, just to make sure they're safe, maybe she should put off the caffeine until she can't function without it. For best results.

"What do you think, Jonah?" she asks softly. He doesn't

wake up, so she answers for him. "I think it's smart to conserve your resources, Hallie," she says in a slightly deeper voice than her own. It sounds nothing like him, but that's not the point. "You might be able to stay awake without that." She pauses, says as herself, "Right, and we might need it tomorrow. For energy to get out. To get help." She looks at the can in her hand. It's not ice-cold, but its slick aluminum skin is still cool to the touch. She turns the cylinder around, running her fingers through the dents and dings. She feels the liquid slosh inside. "So I shouldn't drink it?" she asks sleeping Jonah. "No, wait for the right moment," she replies as him. "Okay. Thanks."

He exhales. He twitches and moans a little.

Hallelujah settles back against the log bench, shifting her seat against the ground. Her butt is falling asleep. She's going to have to get up and walk soon, before she loses feeling in her lower half entirely. But for now, she cradles the Diet Coke can close to her chest, leans her head onto Jonah's shoulder, and waits.

# 2

SHE WAKES WITH A JOLT SOMETIME LATER. THE GUILT SETS IN immediately, before she's even got her eyes fully open. She fell asleep. She was going to stay awake, and she couldn't. She failed Jonah and Rachel. She is a failure.

Her mouth tastes like dirt and her eyes are crusted over. Her hand is still clutching the Diet Coke, but she has a kink in her wrist. Her arm behind Jonah is pins and needles.

"Good. You're awake." The voice in her ear startles her, and she swings her head around to look at Jonah. He's sitting perfectly still, staring at her intently.

"Jonah, I'm so sorry I fell asleep, I don't know what happened, I just—"

"Not now," Jonah says through gritted teeth. "And keep it down."

Jonah is mad at her. At this point, when they've come this far, it feels like—

"I'm not mad at you," he hisses. "So stop making that face."

She blinks at him. "Is your leg hurting a lot?"

"Yes, but—" He gestures with his head and eyes, off to one side. Toward the campfire. "I'm more worried about that."

Hallelujah turns her head to look, rubbing her eyes. "About what . . . ?" The words die in her mouth.

Past the fire pit, a massive dark spot is moving. It takes a second for her to understand what she's seeing.

A bear.

A giant bear.

It has its face buried inside Hallelujah's backpack. It's making rooting noises. Snuffles and grunts and little growls. Each of its paws is the size of Hallelujah's head.

She lets out a whimper. She fell asleep, and the worst happened. "Has it seen us?"

"It looked at me, but it went straight for the bag," Jonah says, just above a whisper. "I think it must smell the fish."

Hallelujah sits as still as she can. Her heart is beating so heavy and loud, though, that she feels like the bear must be able to feel the vibration through the earth.

Rachel is waking up. She shifts and stretches and yawns. "What's going—"

Jonah and Hallelujah shush her. Jonah points and Rachel looks and sees and her eyes go wide and her mouth drops open. She curses softly.

The bear lifts its head up. Shakes the backpack free. The bag hits the ground, limp and empty. The bear walks back and forth over top of it a few times, like it's still searching for the source of the fish smell. It raises its snout into the air, sniffing.

Then it looks over at Hallelujah, Jonah, and Rachel. It cocks its head. It rises up onto its hind feet, as if to get a better view.

In the predawn darkness, with the moonlight fading and the sun not yet up, it looks as tall as the trees. A mythical creature.

It keeps sniffing.

It keeps looking at them.

Hallelujah feels like the air is sparking around her. Rachel is breathing in short, panicked gasps. Jonah is gripping Hallelujah's arm so tightly it hurts. His lips are pressed together.

234

White. She can't seem to close her own mouth. She feels her breath in and out, in and out. Her heart is banging in her ears.

This is what terror feels like.

The bear drops down onto four legs and takes a few steps toward them. Like it's curious.

Like it wonders what they're doing there.

And what they'll taste like.

Hallelujah can't help it—she reaches over, lightning-fast, and grabs Rachel's hand. It's clammy and cold, but now they're all linked.

The bear appears startled by the sudden movement. It sits on its rear end, like a cat, and looks right at Hallelujah. It's still too dark to see the bear's eyes. She can only see the shadows above its snout. That's almost worse.

*Oh God, oh God, oh God.* Hallelujah thinks she's thinking it, but a second later, she realizes Jonah is chanting it under his breath. *"Oh God, oh God, oh God."*

Hallelujah can't stare at those dark eye sockets any longer. She looks away. The bear growls a little, a low rumble that sounds deep and dark and primal. And it moves. She hears the padding of feet on dirt. One. Two. Three footfalls.

She looks up. The bear stops. It sits again.

Just a few feet away.

And looks at her.

That's when something inside Hallelujah snaps. This is the last straw. The rain and the cold and the energy bars and the dandelions and the poison ivy and her ankle and Rachel getting weaker and Jonah sliced apart—and now a bear. When they could not be any more vulnerable.

It makes her so angry.

Angry and reckless.

She will *not* get eaten by a bear. Not today. Not ever.

"Go away!" she shouts. The bear leans back. It bares its teeth. "Go away! Leave us alone!"

Jonah's muttering gets louder: *"Oh God, oh God, oh God."* Rachel sounds like she's hyperventilating.

"We don't have any food! And we're already starving, so, you know, we'd taste awful." Hallelujah barks out a laugh. "So just leave!"

The bear stands up. It walks in a half circle around the fire pit. Then it turns around and paces back the other direction. It makes a low, steady grumbling noise.

The sun is coming up. The light catches the bear's eyes and makes them glint like some kind of monster.

And Hallelujah wonders if she's made a terrible mistake. "What do I do now?" she asks, panic growing.

She's not expecting an answer. She isn't even sure who she's talking to. Herself. God. But Jonah speaks up, like the question knocked him back into reality.

"You've got its attention," he says. "Now you have to convince it you're the alpha. I think."

*He thinks.* "How?" It's a gasp more than a word.

"Pretend you're bigger and scarier than it is?"

"Can't." Hallelujah shakes her head back and forth, back and forth.

"Just"—Jonah's grip on her arm tightens as the bear paces another semicircle, this time coming a few feet closer to them—"try."

The bear stops to sniff at Hallelujah's backpack again. Then it looks over toward them, rises up on its hind legs, and lets out something that's not quite a roar, but the loudest noise it has made yet.

Hallelujah feels like she is going to throw up.

"I heard you say it: You're not going to get eaten by a bear. So don't!"

That was out loud? She doesn't remember that being out loud.

"And if you need to, you can grab Rachel and run."

"No. No, no, no, no, no."

The bear is still on its hind legs.

Hallelujah gets to her feet. Her legs wobble beneath her and her ankle twinges sharply, and she isn't sure she's going to stay upright, but she does. She climbs up onto the log bench, almost losing her balance but righting herself before she falls. She realizes she's still gripping the Diet Coke can.

The bear watches her.

And she gets an idea. How to make a big impact in a short amount of time.

She starts shaking the can. "Jonah. The flint. Now."

He hands it up to her, understanding dawning on his face like the sun over the mountain behind them.

She shakes the can. She starts waving her arms in the air. And yelling. No words. Just sounds. The loudest possible yells she can make. Yells that hurt her dry throat so much she's sure she'll never speak again. Much less sing. She jumps up and down on her good foot. The energy comes from somewhere, she doesn't know where, but she feels like she's jumping so high, reaching so far, shaking so hard. She is the beast, not the bear.

The bear drops to all fours. It backs up a few feet. It's still facing her, but it's definitely confused.

Hallelujah yells and yells. And, right when she can't yell for another second, she plunges the sharp edge of the flint into the aluminum can and rips. The can explodes in her hand, sending foam and liquid everywhere. With one final yell, Hallelujah heaves the spewing can toward the bear.

It grunts, turns, and runs into the woods.

The can hits the ground by her backpack. It fizzes for a few more seconds, and then drains out.

Hallelujah is covered in Diet Coke. Her hand is bleeding; she stabbed so hard with the flint that she went straight through the can to her palm on the other side.

She stands there for a second, watching the bear go. The morning light has truly arrived, and she can see the bear clearly, smaller and smaller and then hidden by trees.

She starts to tremble. She staggers. Falls off the log, hitting the ground hard. The panic-breath is back. Her eyes well up, and for a second she can't see anything, just her own tears. And she can't breathe. And she's shaking all over, jerky and painful, like Rachel was when she got too cold.

"Hallie!" She hears her own name as if from a distance,

through the roar of blood in her head. "Hallie, come here. Hallie!"

It's Jonah's voice.

There's something else: a low, keening, gasping sound.

"Hallie! I can't get over to you. You have to come to me."

It takes her a second to realize what he's saying. And to realize that the keening, the gasping, is her. She blinks enough to see Jonah reaching out for her.

She pulls herself in that direction. Her arms feel like newborn faun legs, spindly and weak. She has no strength left. The bear took it.

Jonah's arms go around her. He pulls her to his chest.

"Hey," he says. "Hey, it's okay. You did it. It's gone. It's okay."

He rocks her like a baby, holds her like she held him last night. There's no self-consciousness left. Just arms holding and voice soothing and hearts beating, and the hysteria passes and she drops off to sleep.

## 3

WHEN HALLELUJAH WAKES AGAIN, IT'S FULLY LIGHT. AND IT'S beautiful. The light makes the green leaves sparkle. The air is hazy. The ground of the campsite looks soft, like a tan carpet instead of dirt.

She blinks a few times, letting herself come to consciousness slowly. Like she's waking up in her bed at home on a Saturday with nowhere to go and nothing to do. Like she smells bacon cooking downstairs, and that's what brought her out of her dreams.

"Better?" Jonah asks.

"A little," Hallelujah answers. Her voice is hoarse. Her throat hurts.

"Good," he says. "Because Rachel's sick." He leans back so Hallelujah can peer around him to see Rachel. She's curled in the fetal position on the ground.

"I puked," Rachel mutters. She's gripping her stomach. And now that she's said it, Hallelujah can see the wet spot in the dirt not too far away. Rachel retches. It's a thick, wet, nasty sound. She turns her head and spits on the ground.

"Did you eat something?" Hallelujah asks, untangling herself from Jonah's arms.

"If I had, don't you think I would've shared it?" Rachel snaps. Then she moans, curling up even tighter. "Sorry. I just . . ." She grunts, pushes up onto hands and knees, tries to stand but isn't strong enough and collapses, body heaving as she spits up liquid and bile.

Hallelujah's stomach turns watching her. "Maybe it was the water? From the creek?"

"Maybe." Rachel wipes a hand across her face, removing snot and spit but adding a smear of dirt.

Hallelujah turns to Jonah. She sees his leg in daylight for the first time. The T-shirt, already dirty, is now crusted over with brown blood. Not only over the cut itself, but almost entirely around the leg. Jonah must have been bleeding most of the night. She reaches a hand toward his leg and Jonah flinches before she's anywhere close, so she pulls her hand back quickly.

"How bad?" she asks.

"It hurts," he says, not looking down at it. He's pale, with dark circles under his eyes. "It hurts so bad, for a few minutes, and then it . . . goes numb. Like I don't have a leg at all." He pauses. "I don't know which one's worse."

"We need help," Hallelujah says.

"Yup," Jonah answers. Rachel retches again.

Birds chirp, welcoming the day. A gentle breeze rustles the leaves. She can hear the creek water moving, just down the hill. It's like nature is mocking them.

Hallelujah looks back at Jonah's leg. It's not bleeding now, not much, but she can tell that if he tries to move—at all—the gash will open up again. And judging by how pale he is, he doesn't have much blood left to lose.

Rachel can barely sit up.

Jonah can't move.

They have no food. They have only half a canteen of rain water.

But there's a trail nearby. A trail that has to lead somewhere. Somewhere with people. On this beautiful spring day, there *have* to be people out there.

Hallelujah knows what she has to do. And she knows she's the only one of them who can do it.

"So where's the trail?" she asks Jonah.

He points. "I think it must be up the hill, maybe another thirty feet," he says. "See that break in the trees? But I don't think I can——"

"You don't have to. I'm going."

"Hallie——"

"No arguments. One way or the other, I have to run into someone. And if you two stay here, I can get help back to you."

Jonah's nodding. But he looks scared. And sad.

"It's the only way, Jonah," Hallelujah says, squeezing his shoulder. He leans his head over onto her hand.

"I know. You're right." He takes a breath. "I wanted to get us out of here. And I couldn't do it."

The guilt in his voice almost stops Hallelujah's breath. "Jonah," she says softly. "You kept us alive. You built the fires and caught the fish. You made me feel safe. You kept us alive," she repeats, "and now it's my turn."

"I know. And I know you can do it."

"Besides. You still have work to do. You and Rachel have to watch out for each other. But don't move. If your leg stays scabbed, you should make it until I come back."

"I'll keep him alive, Hal," Rachel croaks. "I promise."

All at once, Hallelujah is hit with a million thoughts and emotions.

"Hallie . . . ?" Jonah asks.

And the words rush out of her. "I feel like I'm ready to fight off another bear and then another one, and I feel like I'm going to pass out before I even get to the trail. And I know I have to go, but I don't want to leave." Her eyes fill with tears. She wipes them away, frustrated. "I don't know if I should be thanking God that we're alive and near a trail or cursing at him for letting it get to this point. I feel him watching, and then I don't, and then I feel him again, and then he's gone."

Jonah's quiet for a long time. "I still believe he's there."

"Even with your leg sliced open?"

He winces, but says, "Even with my leg sliced open." He pauses. "We can say a prayer before you go. If you want."

"Okay. Yeah. Can't hurt." She closes her eyes. Feels him take her hand.

"Wait!" Rachel blurts.

Hallelujah opens her eyes to see Rachel crawling over, cradling her stomach with one arm and using the other to pull herself across the dirt. Hallelujah reaches out the hand that Jonah's not holding and grabs Rachel's free hand.

"Not without me," Rachel says.

"I didn't think you'd want to," Hallelujah says.

"I want to." Rachel's voice is thick in her throat.

"Okay," Hallelujah says. She closes her eyes again. "God, this week has pretty much sucked."

Jonah makes a surprised noise, but he doesn't interrupt.

"But whether you got us into this or you didn't, whether you have a plan that includes us starving and getting sick and hurt and being scared or whether you're just seeing how everything plays out—please watch over me on the trail. And watch over Jonah and Rachel. Let me find help. Give me the strength to walk however far it takes. Because I'm really, really tired, and I want to go home." She pauses, feeling like maybe that was a terrible prayer. "Jonah?"

"Yeah. Um. God, please keep us safe today. Hallie on the trail, and me and Rachel here. And, uh, as crazy as the past few days have been, thanks for—" He clears his throat. "Thanks for giving me a chance to make up with Hallie, and to get to know Rachel. Thanks for helping Hallie forgive me. Amen."

Hallelujah opens her eyes to see Jonah looking at her.

"Was that okay?" he asks, sounding nervous.

She nods, swallowing past the sudden lump in her throat, not trusting herself to talk. She gets to her feet, pushing on Jonah's shoulder for balance. She hobbles over to the edge of the campsite and picks up a limb that's almost as tall as Rachel. She puts it on its end and leans on it like a crutch. It helps. She wonders why she didn't think of this before. But then, it's not like they've always been thinking clearly out here. They kept moving, instead of staying in one spot, easy to find. She and Rachel took that ice-cold creek bath. Jonah went off alone and got hurt. Rachel drank bad water. So many mistakes.

Hallelujah walks a slow circle around the fire pit, using her crutch. Everything aches. But she's still in one piece. Still standing. And she's stronger than she ever gave herself credit for.

"Do you want the water?" Jonah asks.

"No. You keep it. I'll be okay." *You can do this. You can do this. You can do this.* She feels her exhausted, sore muscles loosening up, firing, ready to move.

She pauses in front of Jonah. She looks down at him.

Then, without stopping to think about it, she drops to one knee, leans in and kisses him. Soft and slow. She feels his breath on her face, his fingers sliding up the back of her neck into her hair. His lips are a promise.

Her heart is beating really fast, but the moment feels like it's happening at half-speed. It's so hard to pull away.

She sits back, feeling her face flush. His eyes are still closed. He's smiling a little.

Rachel is staring. She manages a weak grin. "Hal—" she says, and then stops. "I was going to make a joke, but—" Her eyes well up.

Hallelujah pulls her into a hug. "I will be back with help. Today. I promise."

"Good luck," Rachel chokes out.

Hallelujah lets go of Rachel. She pushes herself to standing. She looks down at her friends.

Jonah reaches up and takes her hand. "Be safe." He meets her eyes, squeezes her hand, and lets his arm drop.

"You too," Hallelujah says.

She starts up the hill.

# 4

HALLELUJAH TURNS AROUND ONLY ONCE, JUST BEFORE SHE gets to the trail. Jonah and Rachel are huddling together below her. They're saying something she can't hear. The brownish red on his leg is an angry swipe of color against the sea of leaf green and dirt brown, of moss and bark and fire-pit ash.

They look so small from up here.

She stands, holding on to a low branch for balance, catching her breath, looking down. She wants Jonah to look up. To see her one more time before she goes. But he doesn't. And she doesn't want to yell down. Doesn't want to seem desperate. For attention, for approval, for love, for hope.

She also wants to leave their good-bye the way it was. Whatever happens next, she'll have that kiss.

She's getting a little dizzy, staring down the steep hill. So she turns, climbs another few feet, and is at the trail.

It's maybe two feet wide, and stretches off in both directions for several yards before disappearing around curves and behind trees. It's not perfectly flat, but it's seen many feet. It's cared for.

It's been waiting for this moment. For her.

She steps over a rotting tree stump and just like that, she's standing on the trail. She closes her eyes and thinks, *I'm going home. We're going home.* There's a thickness in her throat, a pounding in her chest that's more than just the uphill climb. It's also that she didn't quite believe there was a trail until she reached it. Like maybe it was a mirage, or wishful thinking on Jonah's part. Like maybe it would have vanished overnight.

But which way to go? Which way leads to civilization? To help?

Hallelujah looks right and left, assessing. Even though she's fairly high up, she can't see anything but trees and mountains, on and on and on. This bit of trail doesn't look like the one they took on Monday, but who's to say she remembers every foot and feature of their path? It could be the same trail. Or they could have fumbled through the woods, driven by rain and hunger and thirst and those imagined orange jackets, in completely the opposite direction.

For all she knows, they could be in North Carolina.

But she has to make a decision, has to get started, and so she turns right. The trail will curve and wind, she knows, but she will begin by going right.

She walks, using her crutch to swing herself along. She gets up good momentum. Despite the wobbly feeling in her legs. Despite her ankle, which is throbbing again. Despite her growling stomach, which knows that it's past breakfast time.

She's on the move. And the path does twist and turn a little, though for now it stays fairly flat. Small hills that feel easy after the hiking she's done. Weak as she is, she's stronger than before.

And yet the farther she walks away from Jonah and Rachel, the worse she feels. She's left them defenseless. What if the bear comes back? Or something else? What if Rachel gets sicker? What if Jonah's leg gets infected? What if it's already infected? She should be there. They should be together.

But she's also their only hope at this point. Clearly, the

rescue squad isn't going to just stumble upon them. It's their fifth day lost.

Even as she tells herself, *Forward, forward, forward,* something deep in her gut wants to go back. Or at least to look, to see if she can still see their campsite.

She doesn't look back. She moves.

# 5

HOURS PASS. THE SUN SHIFTS IN THE SKY. SHE HIKES UP and down and around. Her stomach aches and burns and then shrinks, empty and resentful. She trips over exposed roots, over rocks, over her own feet. The swimsuit bandage catches on brambles and twigs, pulling painfully. She tears the skin on her palms grabbing at branches to stay on her feet. The cut from the flint starts bleeding again.

She sees no one. Just woods and woods and woods.

Once, she hears a helicopter. But it's far away. A sound echoing from mountainside to mountainside. She hears it, and then it's gone.

By the time the sun is directly overhead, she's sweating. She wishes she wasn't, because she doesn't have any water, doesn't see any water anywhere nearby, but her body is following its own rules now. It's all she can do to keep picking her feet up and putting them down, inch by inch.

She stops on an overlook to catch her breath. Not to sit

down; she might not get up again. To breathe. And to look at the view. Look for signs. She scans the landscape below her, remembering that flash of orange two days ago. Now: nothing.

All at once, she's hit by how alone she is. Before, *they* were alone. Together. Now, *she* is one small speck in this giant mountain range, completely and totally by herself.

The air pulls away, leaving her gasping. The silence roars at her.

She staggers back from the overlook edge, eyes filling with tears. She turns onto the trail. She pushes forward.

She's alone. More alone than she's ever been. It's just her and the trees closing in and the sun beating down. The branches block her path, holding her back. The birds are laughing at her. The ground drops out from under her with no warning, and she stumbles. There's no one to catch her. She falls hard. She lies still for a moment, gasping, feeling pain and fear and hunger and panic roll across her in waves. Then she uses the nearest tree to pull herself back to her feet. She has to keep moving. No one else can help her do this. It's all up to her.

Her mind drifts to everything that led her here. She remembers the whispers. Friends turning away. Friends she pushed away. She remembers choir with Jonah. Singing with him, and then without him, and then not at all. She remembers talking to God. Pleading with him. And then feeling him at such a distance. She remembers her first kiss and the kisses that came after. And she remembers the perfect moments. Laughter and music. Once, she had the ability to be effortlessly happy. One day, maybe, she'll be effortlessly happy again.

Because now, everything is different. The five days she's been out here are a lifetime. Before is a memory. Before that—barely a dream. Now, there's only ahead. One foot in front of the other. This trail will lead somewhere. It has to.

She wipes her forearm across her face, feels tears and snot smear across the sleeve of her jacket. She blinks a few times, and her vision goes from cloudy to clear.

She used to think alone was the answer. Alone would stop the whispers and the taunts. Alone couldn't get her into any more trouble. Alone meant not getting hurt. Now, she'd give anything to see another human being. To hear someone call her name.

She settles for listening to her own voice. "Hello," she says aloud. Or tries to say. It's more of a hiss. Her throat is scratched raw. Her mouth is so dry. She licks her lips, trying to produce some spit. She thinks of food. Of hamburgers and grits and gravy and French fries and the world's biggest, freshest garden salad with balsamic vinaigrette dressing. And chocolate cake for dessert. Her mouth moistens, and she quickly swishes it around, washes it down her raw throat. "Hello!" she says again, louder.

She starts talking. She doesn't think about what she's saying. She only needs the sounds. Needs distraction. Needs to feel less alone.

"It's just past lunchtime, and—I guess you can't really

call it lunchtime without lunch, so I'll say it's just past noon. It's a beautiful day to be lost in the woods. The sun is shining and the birds are chirping. . . ."

She goes on and on. She tells the woods everything that happened between Monday morning and this moment. And it actually helps. Time seems to pass faster. She feels like she's moving faster.

"So, what's going to happen between me and Jonah? Are we going to be together, or what?" She pauses, creating suspense. Then lets the air out of the balloon with a slow whoosh. "I don't know. But I hope so. I do." The more she thinks about the two of them together—dating—the more right it seems. They already know so much about each other. And there's so much more to know. She wants to know it.

"But I have all of that other stuff to deal with when we get home." Handling Luke. Talking to her parents. And Sarah—she has to get in touch with Sarah. She has to apologize. She wants her friend back. "And I keep feeling like it's just like this with me and Jonah because we're in this mess, and we're all we've got out here. And that it might die as soon as we're home."

That word—*die*—hits her like a brick. She wishes so much that she hadn't said it. Jonah is fine. Jonah was alive when she left him, and he'll be alive when the rescuers get to him. Rachel, too.

They will all be okay. Hallelujah will not accept anything less than everyone being okay.

She takes a few steps in silence. Trips over a branch in

the trail and stumbles to stay upright, ankle singing its pain. Inhale, exhale.

She continues her conversation. "Jonah said he's liked me for more than a year. Which is crazy." It really is. Even when he didn't want to like her, he liked her. "How could I not know? Why didn't he ever say anything? Before it all went wrong?"

Around another curve. The path is sloping gently downward. "So what happens if we get home and he starts hanging out with Luke again? What if he doesn't like me as much as he used to? As much as I . . . as I think I like him?" Another pause. "I guess . . . I guess that would mean it wasn't meant to be."

That thought makes her sad. And angry.

And then she hears something that makes her forget everything else. A motor. Not like a helicopter—like a car. The sound is far away, and it's gone as soon as she realizes what it is.

Still, she starts running. Toward the sound. Toward the residue of the sound. Toward the memory of something already gone.

She can't move fast enough. She's too weak. Her feet drag. She loses her crutching rhythm. She's out of breath almost immediately. Not just a little out of breath—gasping, wheezing, choking out of breath. She gets a stabbing pain in her right side, so sharp she drops to her knees. She gulps in air. Sweat pours down her face into her mouth. She lets it. The salt tastes good.

She's seeing spots. She drops her head below her heart. Closes her eyes. Lets everything settle. Her head throbs. She hears the birds and the wind and everything else louder and softer, louder and softer.

*Okay. No more running. No more running.*

But she's close. She can feel it.

She gets to her feet. The stitch in her side twinges as she straightens up. She puts a hand there, presses in, willing the cramp to go away. It doesn't. She feels it in every inhale and exhale.

She walks. Downhill. Carefully. As fast as she dares.

The ground in front of her blurs. She blinks a few times, but the world doesn't come back into focus. It's like she's underwater.

She starts to feel like she's being propelled by invisible hands. Like she's no longer doing the walking herself. Her limbs just move.

She's lost her train of thought. All she can think is, *Help help help help.*

She hikes toward it.

# 6

THE FIRST THING SHE REGISTERS IS THE SPACE OPENING UP around her. The trees pulling away. Next, it's how the ground feels different beneath her feet.

Gravel. Packed gravel. With small grooves worn into it on either side.

The gravel area is maybe ten feet across. Maybe more.

It stretches off into the distance, right and left.

A road.

She takes a deep, shuddering breath, afraid to believe. Then she turns and sees a brown wooden sign marking the Hannah Mountain Trail. The trail she just walked. It crosses a road. This is real.

A road means cars. Cars mean people. People mean help.

Hallelujah lets out a whoop that quickly turns into a hacking cough. For a second, she can't breathe at all. When the fit subsides, she takes in a few deep gulps of air to compensate.

A road. All she has to do is pick which way to go.

To her right, the road stretches invitingly downhill. It goes uphill to the left. Downhill would be easier. But her gut is saying, *Go up*.

She turns left. It's a guess. She knows it's a guess. And she knows she'll wear out faster this way. But it feels right. Those invisible hands have turned her shoulders and she's walking, before she has time to change her mind.

Walking on gravel is different from walking on a dirt trail. It's also different from climbing through brush and over downed trees and pulling herself along on hands and knees. The gravel shifts around beneath her feet as she drags them. It makes a scraping noise that grates on her ears. She feels it in her teeth.

It only takes a few steps for her to need to hear something else. Anything else.

And then she knows: she needs to sing. The feeling hits her so hard she can't breathe for a second. The need knocks the wind out of her.

She's going to sing. She *has* to sing.

She doesn't let herself think beyond that. She takes a deep breath. Opens her mouth. Launches into the first song that enters her head: "O Holy Night."

She gets the first few lines out, laughing a little. At this choice: a Christmas carol, in April, a song about a holy night, with the sun shining down. But she doesn't stop. She finishes the whole thing, even though the high notes are nothing more than scratching breath in her throat.

The song reminds her of Jonah. Of what she's walking for.

And thinking of Jonah reminds her of the last song he sang to her, before everything happened with Luke: "Friends in Low Places." So she switches gears abruptly and starts wailing that song's chorus.

Then she moves into a few of the songs from the mix he made her at the start of ninth grade. A little country, a little classic rock. When she doesn't remember all the words, she hums, keeping time with her feet, until she can pick up again.

She sings, though her tongue feels like a log in her mouth and her raw throat aches. She sounds terrible, and feels terrible, and yet sounds and feels amazing. Because she is alive and she is singing and she *will* find help and she *will* get rescuers to Jonah and Rachel and it *will* be today.

The last song on Jonah's first mix was a country version of Leonard Cohen's "Hallelujah." She starts that one before realizing it's too slow, too sad, for this moment. She needs something up-tempo. Powerful music. A battle cry.

"The Battle Hymn of the Republic" pops into her head, which makes her laugh again. But she decides to go for it. She starts the first verse, imagining a full orchestra backing her up. When she comes to the chorus's "Glory, glory, hallelujah!" she hesitates. For a second, all she can see is Luke's face as he moans her name. His hands rubbing up and down his body, mocking her.

And then she pushes those thoughts aside and sings out the line. She feels a thrill. It feels good. The next time her name comes up, she doesn't hesitate at all. She sings it at the top of her nonexistent voice. When the verses are done, she repeats the chorus, over and over. Her feet and her crutch, gravel-scraping, are all the percussion she needs.

She is marching home.

# 7

MOTORS. COMING CLOSER.

Hallelujah almost falls down on the spot. But she doesn't want to be run over. Then she snorts, because that's what's in her head in possibly the most important moment of her entire life so far: *Don't get run over.*

She walks a little farther, just to the top of a small hill. In the distance, she can see two motorcycles approaching, side by side. Their engines rev to start up the incline.

Hallelujah lifts the arm that's not holding her crutch in the air and starts waving. She wants to jump up and down, but her feet won't leave the ground, and if she bends her knees too much, she's going to sit down. She yells, "Hey! Hello! Help!" a few times.

She sees one of the helmeted riders lift a hand from the handlebars and point at her. He glances over at his companion. They're close enough now that Hallelujah can see them nod.

She's been seen.

Now, finally, she allows herself to sink to the gravel road. She feels like she descends in slow motion, like she's riding a fluffy cloud. And yet, when she lands, it hurts a little. Her legs are jelly. She can't even move them out of the awkward position she sat down in. But she keeps waving.

The motorcycles pull up on either side of her in a cloud of gravel dust. The helmets come off to reveal a middle-aged man and woman. Neither of them looks like a Hell's Angel. He's got a dad-mustache and she has a chic short haircut that's flattened from the helmet.

They stare down at her with concern. And with something else—disbelief. Awe. The man's eyebrows go up and the woman's jaw drops. They look at each other, then back down at her, and that's when she realizes what's going on: *They know who she is.*

"You're one of those missing kids," the man says. "Your photo's all over the news."

"You're Hallelujah," the woman adds. "I wouldn't forget a name like that."

That's all it takes. Hallelujah covers her mouth with one hand, trying to keep the sobs in, but it just makes her body shake. Her eyes are still dry, but she feels like she's crying everywhere else. She looks up. "Water?" she croaks.

"Oh God, Charlie," the woman says in a flat northern accent. She starts fishing around in her bag. Pulls out a water bottle. Hands it down to Hallelujah.

Hallelujah drinks noisily. She lets it slosh on her face, wet her lips, run down her chest. She swishes it around in her mouth, relishing the clean flavor. She feels it fill her hollow stomach.

"Better?" the man—Charlie—asks.

Hallelujah nods. She stares at the water bottle. She can't believe she emptied it so fast. She wants more.

"Are you hurt?" the woman asks.

"Just my—" Even after the water, her voice comes out as a dry hiss. She clears her throat and tries again. "Just my ankle."

"Can you tell us where the others are? Are they . . . ?" Charlie fades off, but she knows how the question ends.

"They're still out there. Still alive." Hallelujah will *not* think about the alternative. But by not trying not to think about it, she's thinking about it, and it's making her feel panicky. "I was the only one who could walk, so I—" She gulps. Draws in a shaky breath.

Charlie dismounts his bike and squats down next to her. "Go on," he says. His voice is soft. His accent is southern. But not hillbilly southern. Deep South. He's not from around here either.

She can't believe her mind is wandering like this. She tries to focus.

"We found—Jonah found a trail, and I followed it to this road. They're at a campsite by the trail. I . . ." Hallelujah falters. "I don't know how far. I wasn't walking very fast. We haven't eaten in . . . a while. And Rachel—she's sick. She was throwing up. And Jonah cut his leg and it wouldn't stop bleeding. . . ."

"Jesus," the woman says.

Charlie has his cell phone out. He's waving it in the air, pointing it in different directions. "No reception," he says, frowning. He shakes his phone, like that will fix it.

"Why don't we just ride back to Cades Cove?" the woman asks. "It'll only take a couple minutes."

"Good idea, Nora." Charlie rises up out of his squat, groaning as his knees crack. He extends a hand to help Hallelujah up. She looks at it. Lifts one arm. She can barely grip him, much less use her own legs, so he really does have to pull her up. The momentum makes her stumble forward, landing hard against his chest.

"Steady there," he says. His brow is furrowed. His eyes are deep-set and sad. "You can ride with me. All you have to do is sit and hold on. Okay?"

Hallelujah nods. And then what he's saying actually sinks in. They'll be riding *away* from Jonah and Rachel. She can't do that. She can't. Her breath starts coming faster. "We have to go back," she says, her voice cracking. "I can't leave. I have to go get them. I promised." Breath in, out, in, out, in, out. "I promised!"

Charlie has her by both shoulders. "Hallelujah. Calm down. It's gonna be all right."

"We have to go back!" Hallelujah repeats, almost sobbing now. "Please!"

Charlie hesitates, then turns to Nora. "The trail she was on crosses this road. I can take her to the trail. She can point us toward her friends. You go get the rangers. Bring them to meet us. With medics. Ambulances. Equipment to carry the kids out. And food and water. We'll wait for you on the side of the road."

Nora nods. "I will be back *so fast*," she promises. She gets on her motorcycle and speeds away.

Hallelujah is suddenly so tired. It would be really nice to close her eyes right now.

*Jonah. Rachel. Jonah. Rachel.*

Charlie holds her up while he mounts his bike. He hoists her onto the seat. Wraps her arms around his waist. She rests her head against his back. She holds on with as much grip as she's got in her, and then they're moving.

He doesn't go too fast, but it still feels like she's flying. The wind whips her ponytail around, sends strands of hair dancing into her face and away from her head. The motorcycle kicks up gravel around her feet. She looks to one side, sees the trees rushing by in a blur. She looks up. The sky is the rich blue of late afternoon, on its way to twilight, with just a few white clouds. A bird passes overhead, racing them. The bird wins.

Hallelujah lets her eyes close, and then it's just the sensations: the worn leather of Charlie's jacket against one cheek, the wind against the other, the aching muscles in her arms wrapped around his waist, the bump of the motorcycle over the uneven gravel, the purring of the motor, the sharp smell of gasoline.

They stop too soon. They've only been riding for a few minutes.

She opens her eyes to see what's wrong, and is stunned to see the wooden trail marker by the side of the road. How slow was she walking?

"This the right place?" Charlie asks.

"Yes." She looks down the trail. "The campsite's that way."

"Good. I'm gonna try to call my wife." He pulls his phone out of his pocket and dials. The call drops, so he dials again. The third time, he gets through. "Nora? It's the Hannah Mountain Trail." He pauses. Repeats, slowly: "Hannah! Mountain! Trail! Okay. Love you." After he hangs up, he turns to Hallelujah. "They're on their way."

Charlie stands, and without him to lean on, Hallelujah slides off the bike into a heap on the ground.

"Oh God, I'm sorry, I didn't mean to—" He rushes

around to help her up, but she waves him away. She's done standing. Charlie seems to understand. He sits down next to her. "Do you know how far?" he asks.

"No. I was walking for hours, but like I said, I wasn't moving that fast." She thinks. "I left the campsite in the morning. I found the road after lunchtime."

"The campsite is right by the trail?"

She nods.

"Then the rangers will know. There aren't that many sites out there."

Hallelujah's stomach growls, loud and angry, and Charlie flushes like he's embarrassed.

"Oh God," he says again. "You need to eat. We've got energy bars and some apples and bananas and a can of tuna—what do you want?"

A bounty of riches. She stares at him, feeling like she might lose it again. "A banana?" she asks softly. Easy to eat. Easy on the stomach. "And some more water?"

"You got it." He hands everything over, even unscrewing the water-bottle cap and starting the banana peel for her. Then he leans back against the bike. "You were out there since Monday?" he asks, staring into the woods.

"Yeah." She takes a bite. She chews. It's heaven.

"Do you want me to try to call your parents?"

Her parents. She hadn't even thought about them. Yes. She wants him to call her parents. Despite everything that's wrong between them, she wants to hear their voices. She wants them to know that she's okay. She gives him the number, and then finishes the banana and sips at the water while he dials. She feels numb, but somewhere underneath all that numbness is screaming and crying and relief.

"Mrs. Calhoun?" Charlie says into the phone. "Sorry for the bad signal. I'm up on Parson Branch Road and—well, ma'am, I found your daughter. She's alive."

Hallelujah can hear the shout on the other end of the line, though she can't make out any words.

"My wife went for the rangers. The other two kids are still out there. Your daughter hiked out for help." A pause. "Yes. Of course." He hands the phone over.

She holds it to her ear. "Mom?" She can't keep her voice from wavering; that one word is maybe five syllables.

"Oh, Hallelujah! Oh, baby! We thought we'd lost you! We thought—" The phone cuts out. Then back in: "—okay?"

"I'm okay, Mom. I'm okay." Focusing on the phone is taking a lot of effort. "I love you. And Dad," she manages. She does. She loves them. Even though they've made it hard lately.

"We love you so, so much!" There's crying, and a clattering noise like her mom dropped the phone.

The next person to speak is her dad. "Hallelujah? Honey?" His voice sounds far away. Fuzzy.

"Hi, Dad. I'm okay."

"Oh, thank God. Thank the Lord. We'll be there soon. We're coming."

"Okay." The world is going black. Her fingers are losing their grip on the phone.

She feels Charlie take the phone from her hand. Hears him say something else to her parents, though she can't make out the words.

Her eyes close.

She did it. She's done.

# 8

After that, everything happens in flashes.

A motor. Tires crunching on gravel. More motors. More gravel sounds.

Feet on the ground around her.

Hands on her shoulders. Gentle shaking. "Wake up, Hallelujah."

She doesn't want to wake up.

Charlie's voice. Nora's voice. Other voices. Lots of them.

She opens her eyes to see neon-orange vests vanishing down the trail. Toward Jonah and Rachel. Rescue. Relieved, she closes her eyes again.

Water at her lips. A little makes it down her throat. More goes down her chin.

She's lifted. She's in the air. An arm under her shoulders. Another under her legs. She bounces with each step. Her head rocks back.

She's on her back. Stretched out. There's someone sitting

next to her. An unfamiliar voice. Unfamiliar hands holding her head.

A motor starts. She's in motion.

Bumping up and down. Swerving around curves. She feels like she's rolling downhill.

The banana she ate comes back up. She feels it on her face. On her arm.

A wipe. Antiseptic smell. Cold.

A prick in the crook of her elbow, like a bee sting.

A siren. Loud and long and wailing.

Only then does it occur to her that she's left Jonah and Rachel behind. She struggles to sit up. Hands force her down. And then she feels sleepy again. The world goes dim and fuzzy at the edges. She falls back and passes out before the word *Wait!* reaches her lips.

*She remembers the story her parents always tell. Same wording, every time.*

*She was born on Christmas Day, but that's not why they named her Hallelujah.*

*At least, not the only reason.*

*Her parents were in their forties. Her mom had had three miscarriages. And early on the afternoon of the twenty-fourth, the snow started. It buried East Tennessee and most of the Smoky Mountains under a soft, thick blanket. While everyone else celebrated a rare white Christmas, Hallelujah's mom went into labor. The roads weren't clear enough to drive. So Hallelujah was born at home. Small, but healthy. All toes and fingers accounted for. Screaming.*

*Their miracle. Hallelujah Joy Calhoun.*

the
**seventh**
day

# 1

Hallelujah wakes in a bed. It's a thin mattress; she can feel the bed frame beneath. But the pillow is plump and she's covered up by a blanket and she feels like she's sinking into softness. Her body is so tired, so heavy, that she almost feels like she has no body at all. She can't move. She wouldn't if she could.

Even her eyelids stay shut. She can see light through them. Bright, fluorescent light. Not the sun.

The smell hits her next: antiseptic and ammonia and detergent and . . . her mother's perfume. The notes waft toward her, carried on an air-conditioned breeze, and she breathes it in. It smells like fake flowers and sugar and safety.

Her mom is here.

She forces her eyes open. It feels like pulling apart sticky adhesive. But she needs to see.

A few blinks, and the hospital room comes into focus. A

table to her left. A bathroom beyond that. A TV mounted on the wall directly ahead of her, near the ceiling. It's showing an infomercial on mute. And to the right, folded awkwardly in a reclining chair, is her mom. Asleep. Head dropped down onto her chest, mouth open. She's wearing her old gardening sweatshirt and the high-waisted pleated jeans Hallelujah hates. Socks that don't match. Her house slippers. No makeup. Gray hair in a loose ponytail.

She looks like she got dressed in a hurry.

Hallelujah feels a surge of relief so strong it's like her heart stops for a second. "Mom," she croaks. It's barely more than an exhalation. It scrapes her raw throat. Still, she tries again: "Mom. Mom."

Her mother stirs in the chair. She yawns. Shifts position. And her eyes blink open and connect with Hallelujah's. She freezes. Then smiles. Then starts crying.

"Oh, Hallelujah! Oh, baby, you're awake!" She's out of the recliner and at the bedside in a second. She runs one hand along Hallelujah's cheek. Wipes her own wet cheeks with the other hand. "I am so glad to see those eyes! How are you feeling?"

"Tired," Hallelujah says. "And thirsty."

"Of course you are. The IV doesn't help with the dry mouth, does it?" Her mom picks up a cup of water with a pink bendy straw and holds it for Hallelujah to sip. It's harder than she expected. Not even her mouth muscles want to work. "When I was in the hospital all those times, before you," her mom goes on, looking out the window at the dark

270

outside, "all I wanted was water, water, water."

It gives Hallelujah a chill, this reminder that she was her parents' last hope for a child, the first joy after a string of sadnesses. "Am I okay?" she asks.

"You'll be just fine. They want to get lots of nutrients and fluids in you before we take you home. You sprained your ankle, too. Pretty bad."

That surprises Hallelujah. "My ankle doesn't hurt," she says. "Not anymore."

A wry smile from her mom. "Well, sweetheart, that'll be the pain meds."

"Oh." Hallelujah sits up a little higher in bed. "Where's Dad?"

"I sent him home to get you a change of clothes. He'll be back soon."

"Good." Something else is nagging at Hallelujah. But she's so tired, almost ready to go back to sleep again . . . And then it comes to her. "Jonah and Rachel—did they get them out? Are they okay? Are they here too?" The urgency hits her as a vise squeezing the air from her lungs.

"They got here last night. A couple hours after you, since the rangers and the paramedics had to hike in and find them and carry them back out to where the ambulances were. They took Jonah right to surgery to sew up his leg."

"And?" Hallelujah asks, still breathless.

"And they sewed him up and now he's doing the same thing you are: resting and getting IV liquids. He'll be fine too. I talked with Vera at the nurses' station. Can you believe

Vera still works here? She was old when I was a brand-new night nurse."

Hallelujah nods, impatient. The vise has let up a little, but it's still there. "And Rachel?"

"Vera said Rachel was real dehydrated. And still sick to her stomach, poor girl. They're testing her to see what's making her so sick."

That reminds Hallelujah of something. Something important. She frowns, waits, lets the thought bubble to the surface. "Creek water. Rachel drank creek water. You have to tell the doctors."

"I will," her mom says. She leans over to kiss Hallelujah on the forehead. "Oh, Hallelujah. I was so worried. We both were. When they said you were missing—and I thought of you all alone out there—" She breaks off, swallowing. Her eyes are full again.

"I know, Mom." Hallelujah smiles, trying to reassure her. "But I wasn't alone."

"Of course not. God was taking care of you that whole time."

The way she says it bugs Hallelujah. It's the certainty. How does she know? How can any of them know? Hallelujah may be on speaking terms with God again, but that doesn't mean she's ready to give him all the credit for something that she worked really, really hard to accomplish.

Was God with her during her epic hike yesterday? Maybe. But it was her feet on the ground. Her pain and her sweat and her determination.

When she first woke up and saw her mom there, Halle-lujah felt nothing but happiness and relief. She made it. She's going home. Now, she remembers the distance between her and her parents. Between what they believe and what she's struggling with. How much has been left unsaid for the last six months. And they don't even know there's a problem.

It's time to start changing that. She has to speak up. She has to be honest. "I didn't mean God," Hallelujah says. "I meant I wasn't alone because Jonah and Rachel were there. We took care of each other."

Her mom blinks. She looks surprised. "I'm sure you did. Of course you did."

Hallelujah repeats, firmly, "We saved each other."

They're both quiet for a second. Then, because she can't help it, Hallelujah yawns.

"You go on back to sleep now, baby," her mom says. "Just rest. We'll talk more later. And we'll take you home." She strokes Hallelujah's hair. The last thing Hallelujah hears before she dozes off is her mom murmuring, over and over, "Just rest. Just rest."

## 2

THE NEXT TIME HALLELUJAH WAKES UP, IT'S LIGHT OUT-side. Dawn has come and gone, leaving a bright, sunny day in its wake. Hallelujah's window looks out over a parking lot, but she can see the mountains in the distance. She wonders if they're her mountains. She thinks she might always wonder, when she looks off toward the Smokies, which one they spent the night on top of, and where Jonah caught the fish, and where she and Rachel hid from that last storm. She still doesn't know how far they walked.

"She's awake!" It's Hallelujah's dad. He's now occupying the armchair, watching ESPN at low volume. He swings around, throws the remote on the bed, and jumps up. "Your mother says she talked to you a little, around four a.m. You couldn't have waited for me to get back?"

"Sorry, Dad," Hallelujah says.

To her surprise, he's gone teary-eyed. He's blinking and clearing his throat like that will make the tears magically evaporate. He leans in and wraps her in a hug. "I was . . . I was real worried, Hallelujah," he says. "I won't lie. But God came through for us on this one. He really did."

She feels that flash of irritation again. The assumption that God did everything and she did nothing. Can't her parents at least say that God did something and she also did something? That she deserves some of the credit?

Her dad still has her hugged in close. Her face is pressed into his shirt. She's starting to feel suffocated, so she wriggles loose. "Sorry, Dad. I couldn't breathe."

He nods. She watches as he collects all the emotion that just welled up and buries it back where it usually lives. "Want me to find your mother? She went down the hall to talk to Jonah's mom. Jonah and Rachel are doing real well, by the way. Though they have to stay here a day or two longer."

Hallelujah's stomach rumbles. The only thing she remembers eating in almost forty-eight hours is that banana yesterday. And she puked that up. "Can you find out if I'm allowed to eat yet? I'm starving."

Her dad looks happy to have a job to do. "You got it. Don't get into any trouble while I'm gone." He says it like a joke, but she's heard those words meant completely seriously too many times to laugh, or even to respond. She lifts a hand in a small wave, and her dad leaves.

The room is quiet now except for the murmurs of the sportscasters on the TV. Hallelujah uses the remote attached to her bed to switch it off. She sits there for a second, staring out the window. It's not really quiet. Turning off the TV just highlighted all the other sounds: the hum of the hospital's air conditioner, the beeping of patient monitors, the wheels of a cart going by outside, the chatter from the nurses' station.

She misses the birds. And the breeze in the trees. The sound of rain on leaves.

Rain. She has to go to the bathroom. She wonders if she should wait for someone to help her. No; she hiked miles and miles by herself, with no food or water, which means she can totally make it the few feet to the bathroom and back. Besides, with the meds, she can't feel her sprained ankle at all. She throws back the blanket. Her bare legs look small and weak against the sheets, but she swings them around to hang off the side of the bed anyway. Her feet dangle.

They tingle as blood flows down into them. Her left ankle is wrapped tight, immobilized with metal strips on both sides. She balances her weight on her arms and slides down until her right foot hits the tile floor.

It's a shock. The cold. The weight. Being upright. Her knee almost buckles.

She stays up through sheer stubbornness.

She limps forward a step, and then another, using her IV pole for balance, holding her hospital gown closed behind her. Her legs feel like they belong to someone else. Like she's controlling them on puppet strings. But she's making progress toward the bathroom. Another three steps and she's at the doorway. She closes the door feeling almost as satisfied as when she found the road yesterday.

When she comes out of the bathroom, her mom is sitting on the bed. "You should've waited," she says.

"I wanted to do it myself."

Another long moment of silence between them. Her mom just looks at her. She studies her in a way she hasn't before. Like Hallelujah looks different, beyond being scratched up and bruised and thinner. After a second, her mom pats the bed beside her. Hallelujah hobbles over and climbs in.

"Your father went to see about getting you an early lunch."

Hallelujah's stomach growls again. "Great." She pauses. "As long as it's not fish. Or energy bars. Or bananas. Or dandelions."

"Dandelions?"

"Yeah. We ate a bunch on . . . one of the nights." She pauses, and her mom looks at her like she wants to hear more.

Hallelujah almost starts talking. The more she thinks about opening up to her parents, the more she wants to. Needs to. Every minute back with them is a reminder that they don't know anything about what she's been feeling. She never told them.

But at the same time, she knows that she needs to think about what to tell and how to tell it. So she changes the subject. "When can I see Jonah and Rachel?"

"I checked before I came back here. They're both still passed out. No visitors until this afternoon."

Hallelujah feels her face fall. "Oh."

"You'll see them before we go. And you'll have quite a few other people to talk to, in the next couple days. There's a bunch of reporters in the lobby. I told them you wouldn't be discharged until tonight or tomorrow, but they don't want to miss you leaving the hospital. And your father got a call from one of the morning shows. They want to have us on next week! All three of you, if Jonah and Rachel are healthy enough. And one of the park rangers said they'd be in touch to get your account of what happened out there, while it's still fresh. What did he call it—'debriefing,' that's right. Oh, and I need to call Rich and Jill, let them know you're doing fine. They were out with the search party every day. And some other people from church want to stop by this afternoon. . . ."

Hallelujah lets her mom talk. She leans back into her pillow, imagining all of the times she'll have to talk about what happened out there in the mountains. Not just to the people her mom is listing. At church. At school. She didn't think about it before, but she's going to be kind of famous. She and Jonah and Rachel are front-page news. Morning-show news.

A week ago, the thought of that much attention would've given her hives. Now, she knows she'll get through it, because she's been through worse. Sure, she's tired just listening to her mom, just thinking about what's ahead. But at the same time, she's okay.

And given how things used to be, okay is pretty great.

## 3

SHE EATS A LITTLE BIT OF LUNCH, WITH BOTH PARENTS AND A nurse watching her. It's weird, having three pairs of eyes staring while she tries to swallow just one more bite of mashed potatoes. And eventually, too soon, "just one more bite" threatens to bring everything else up, and she puts the fork down. "I'm done."

"Are you sure?" her mom asks.

"You should finish your plate," her dad says.

"I'm done," Hallelujah repeats. Her stomach feels packed. A swollen balloon. She barely ate a third of what was brought. "Thank you," she adds as the nurse takes the tray.

When they're alone, Hallelujah's mom helps her change into the pajamas her dad brought from home. They're ones she never wears—pink floral-print flannel pants and a matching top. A Christmas present from her great-aunt. They make her look about eight years old. But they're soft, and they're clean, and they beat a hospital gown any day.

Back in bed, Hallelujah looks from parent to parent. Her dad sits in the recliner. Flips on the TV. But he keeps glancing back toward her, as if to make sure she's still there. Her mom flutters around the room, straightening things that don't need straightening. Also with her eyes on Hallelujah.

The tiny room and the TV and the fluttering and the eyes are making Hallelujah feel claustrophobic. She looks out the window, toward the mountains, missing space and sky and air that didn't taste like chemicals. Then she feels guilty for missing all of that. She's lucky to be here. To be alive. And her parents have been through hell.

Still, she wants out of this room.

She's rescued by a head poking around the door. One of the younger nurses. A petite, pretty blonde. "I'm sorry to bother y'all," she says, "but Rachel Jackson is awake. She's asking to see you."

*Rachel's awake!* If she could, Hallelujah would leap out of bed. "Thanks," she says to the nurse. "I'll be right there."

"Room 353," the nurse says. "Just down the hall. Do you need help? I'll get a wheelchair."

"A chair would be great," Hallelujah's dad says, before Hallelujah can even open her mouth.

The blond nurse disappears and is back a minute later wheeling a chair in front of her. Hallelujah swings her legs over the side of the bed, slides down to land carefully on her good foot, and sits. "Thanks," she says, watching as the nurse transfers her IV bag to the pole sticking up from the back of the chair.

"I'll take you," Hallelujah's mom says. She's hovering. Her hands are already on the chair, ready to go.

Hallelujah says, gently but firmly, "I kind of want to go by myself. But thanks, Mom. I'll be back in a few minutes."

Her mom steps back. "Are you sure?"

"I can do it. Really."

Her dad looks over from his chair. "Hallelujah, let your mother take you—"

"No, it's okay. She can go by herself. It's just down the hall." Hallelujah's mom leans down, kisses the top of Hallelujah's head, and pats her on the back.

Hallelujah wheels to the door. She looks over her shoulder to see both parents watching her. And she feels compelled to take the next step in her opening up, her re-creation of herself. "Later—when we get home, when everything calms down—we need to talk," she says. "There's a lot I need to tell you." She wheels out of the room.

The blond nurse points her to the right. Hallelujah rolls down to room 353, near the end of the hall. There's a woman outside the door. Well dressed. Heels. Bobbed hair. She's having an angry, whispered phone conversation. As Hallelujah approaches, she puts her hand over the phone.

"Hallelujah?" she asks.

"Yes, ma'am."

The woman holds out a hand to shake. Hallelujah takes it. "I'm Jean Wright. Rachel's mom. I can't thank you enough for what you did for my daughter—" She breaks off, listening to an angry buzz from the other end of the phone line. "No, I'm not ignoring you! I'm *talking* to the girl who *saved* our daughter's *life*! So you can just . . ." She moves away. Keeps hissing into the phone.

Hallelujah hesitates, then enters Rachel's room.

It's exactly the same as her own, minus the parental bustling. The TV is on mute. The lights are dim. Rachel is propped up in bed, staring out the window. She looks pale and made of bones. But she turns when she hears Hallelujah's wheelchair.

"Hal," she says. A ghost of a smile.

"Rachel." Hallelujah wheels right up to the bedside. She stands and, with effort, hoists herself up onto the bed. "How are you feeling?"

"Tired. Foggy. Slow. Like my brain's not . . ." Rachel wavers, like she can't find the word. A blush hits her cheeks. Embarrassment. "Sorry," she says.

"You look great. You sound great."

"Liar." Rachel lifts an arm to give Hallelujah a weak punch in the arm. It's like being punched by a kitten. "I look like death," Rachel says, leaning back, closing her eyes. "And I sound like I'm drunk."

"You're alive." Hallelujah leans over to give Rachel a gentle hug. "We all are."

"Thanks to you. Rock star."

Out in the hall, Rachel's mom's voice rises to a shout, and then hushes abruptly.

Rachel grimaces, opening her eyes. "My dad just left," she says. "He had to go back to Nashville. Work thing."

"He left?"

"He said he's glad I'm safe, and he'll see me when his conference is done. On Tuesday. My mom's letting him have it."

Another shout. Then a murmur of another voice. Maybe a nurse.

"I'm sorry," Hallelujah says.

"Thanks. It's not just that he had to go. It's like . . ." Rachel searches again for the words. "I'm just a weapon. All over again. They're fighting about me, but it's not really about me. And she's out there . . ." Her eyes well up.

". . . and not in here," Hallelujah finishes. She hugs Rachel again. "She'll calm down."

"I know."

They're both quiet for a moment. Then Hallelujah asks, "How long do you have to stay in the hospital?"

"A couple days. They want to make sure whatever's making me sick is out of my system before they let me go."

"I'll visit. Cheer you up."

"You better." Rachel yawns.

"And we'll still see each other, after you go home. Bristol's not that far. We can meet in the middle."

"Right. In that one McDonald's that represents civilization between here and there." Rachel cracks a true smile for the first time since Hallelujah came into the room. "Maybe we can go on this hiking thing again next year. What do you say?"

"I am *never* going hiking again." Hallelujah laughs. Even as she shakes her head, she knows it's a lie. She'll be drawn back to those mountains, to the beauty and openness and lurking sense of danger. She'll just be smarter next time. Plan ahead. For every possibility.

"Or we can do another youth group retreat. I'd put up with the God stuff to see you and Jonah."

Hallelujah takes a second to think about her response. It isn't just the God comment. It's also that she's not sure when—or if—she'll want to go on another youth group trip. But maybe everything would be okay with Rachel and Jonah there. "It's a deal," she says.

They sit in silence for another few moments. Hallelujah doesn't know what Rachel's thinking, but for now she's happy to be lost in thought beside her. Even when she sees Rachel start to nod off, she's reluctant to leave.

But then Rachel's mom comes in. She looks exhausted, despite the makeup and the sleek hair and the put-together outfit, and Hallelujah suddenly sees that she went through every bit as much this past week as Hallelujah's own parents did.

"Hallelujah," Rachel's mom says. "I'm sorry, but Rachel needs to rest. Can you come back later?"

"Sure. Of course." Hallelujah slides off the bed and gets

back into her wheelchair. Then she reaches up and grabs Rachel's hand. "See you soon."

"Promise?" Rachel is already half-asleep.

"Promise," Hallelujah echoes, and lets go of Rachel's hand. She nods at Rachel's mom and wheels silently out the door.

# 4

HALLELUJAH IS HEADING BACK TO HER OWN ROOM WHEN SHE sees him. Exiting a room a few doors beyond hers. He's walking away from her down the hall.

Luke. Here. Now.

Seeing him freezes her in place. There's a part of her that wants to hide before he spots her. Duck into her room and have her parents close the door and pretend she's asleep. It's too soon to deal with Luke. She's not ready.

As soon as that part of her speaks up, Hallelujah knows what she has to do. She wheels down the hall to her door. "Mom, Dad," she says, barely slowing down. "I'll be back in a sec."

She doesn't wait for an answer.

She moves. Luke is standing by the elevators at the end of the hall. His back is to her. He's messing around with his phone while he waits.

Hallelujah stops next to the nurses' station. *You scared off a bear yesterday*, she reminds herself. *You scared a bear, and you*

*hiked out alone, and you got help. You saved Jonah's and Rachel's*
*lives. This is nothing compared to that. Luke is nothing.*

She pushes herself out of the wheelchair up to standing. Wobbles for a second, and then gently places her left foot down. She unhooks her IV bag from its pole and cradles it in one hand. She takes a halting step, her slippered feet shuffling on the cold tile floor. Her left ankle feels stiff and clunky in its splint, but the meds are doing their job: standing on it doesn't hurt. Much.

And she wants to be standing for this. She needs to be standing.

She doesn't say Luke's name until she's right behind him. "Hi, Luke."

He turns. His eyes widen. His signature smirk falls into place. "Well, look who it is. The hero of the hour." He looks her up and down. "Nice jammies. You trying to win me back, hot stuff?"

Hallelujah's mind goes blank. For an agonizing second, she just stands there, open-mouthed. She wants to dissolve into the floor.

"I was just in Jonah's room," Luke says. "Get this: He told me to leave. Said we weren't friends anymore. Did you brainwash him out there? Turn him to the loser side?" Underneath the joking tone, there's venom. Hallelujah can hear it, the threat in his words.

But he can't hurt her. She knows that now.

She finds her voice. "No," she says quietly. "I didn't brainwash him."

"Well, that's a relief." Sarcasm. Dripping from each word.

The elevator next to them dings. The doors open. Two doctors exit, comparing notes on a chart.

"That's my cue," Luke says. "Good chat. Let's do it again sometime. Or not." He steps into the elevator.

Hallelujah follows him. The doors close and then they're alone.

She hasn't been alone with Luke since that night six months ago. She presses herself against the wall across from him, heart beating faster. And she forces herself to speak.

"I wanted to tell you that this is over."

Luke laughs. "This"—he waves his hand between the two of them, then punches the button for the ground floor—"never started." He makes a face like something big just occurred to him. "You're not gonna try to jump me again, are you?"

Hallelujah ignores the dig. She presses on. "What you've been doing to me—I want it to stop." She takes in a deep breath. "It's going to stop."

"That so?"

"Yes." Hallelujah feels like she's facing that bear all over again. Trying to make herself into the alpha. Confronting fear head-on. She stands up straighter. Looks Luke right in the eyes. Says, in a voice that doesn't waver, not even a little, "I told Jonah and Rachel everything."

No response. But the mocking smile falters.

"Everything," Hallelujah repeats.

"You wouldn't," Luke says.

"I already did. And I'm going to keep on telling people."

They stare each other down, Hallelujah gripping the handrail on the wall behind her like it's the source of her newfound strength. Luke's eyes are narrow. His shoulders are stiff. His lips are pressed shut, an angry slash across his face.

They reach the ground floor. The elevator doors open. Luke stands completely still for a moment, and then turns on his heel and steps out into the hospital lobby.

And for once, Hallelujah has the last word. "Good chat," she says to his back. "Let's do it again sometime. Or not."

She knows he heard her. But he doesn't turn around. She watches him retreat until the elevator doors close between them.

Hallelujah slumps back against the wall, feeling lightheaded. A little dizzy. She closes her eyes. It takes her a moment to be able to reach out and press the button to go back to her floor. But even as she's trying to stay standing, shaking a little, she feels her lips curl up into a smile.

She did it.

5

SHE SITS, BACK IN HER WHEELCHAIR, OUTSIDE JONAH'S room. Her heart is still racing. Her skin still feels flushed. She keeps smiling; her mouth can't help it. Because she stood up to Luke. She told him off. And soon, more people will know her side of the story.

She wonders what Jonah will say. And whether he'll still want to be with her, now that they're home. There's only one way to find out.

She wheels inside.

It turns out that she doesn't even have to talk. Because when Jonah sees her, he smiles. And his smile is so open and genuine, so unmistakable, that it pulls the nerves right out of her chest.

"Hallie! I was hoping to see you." He beckons her over with one arm, his IV line dancing in the air. "How are you feeling?"

"I'm okay. How are *you* feeling?" She rolls her chair to sit next to his bed.

"Like my leg got eaten by a lawn mower," Jonah says, making a face. "And that's *with* the pain meds."

"I'm sorry."

"Don't be. The doctors say I'm gonna be fine. Slow recovery, but I should be ready for sports again in the fall. And I'll have one heck of a scar. And hey, if you hadn't pulled me out of the creek, and scared off that bear, and hiked out and got help . . ." He fades off. "You're like a superhero or something. You know that?"

"I'm not," she says. But it gives her a warm glow inside that he thinks so.

Then they both speak at once:

"I have to tell you—" Jonah.

"You won't believe what——" Hallelujah. She gulps down her words. "You first."

"Okay. I wanted you to know that I'm not friends with Luke anymore. He came in here earlier, and he started going on and on about how us getting lost and the retreat getting called off messed up his chances to hook up with that girl Brittany, and I was just——" Jonah shakes his head, looking disgusted. "I was done. So I made him leave."

"I know," Hallelujah murmurs.

"You know?"

"I——I saw Luke in the hallway. I followed him to the elevators. He accused me of brainwashing you."

Jonah lets out a snort of laughter.

"And then I——I——Jonah, I did it. Told him I'd told you and Rachel the truth about what happened that night, and that I was going to tell everyone else, too. I told him he wasn't going to mess with me anymore. And he just——he just shut up and walked away!" She shakes her head, still a little disbelieving.

"That's so great, Hallie." Jonah grabs Hallelujah's hand and gives it a squeeze.

"Luke's not off, I don't know, plotting his ultimate revenge or something. Is he?" In an instant, the knot is back in her stomach. Tightening. This might all be too good to be true. "Do you really think he'll leave me alone now?"

Jonah's grin drops away. "He better. But if he does start messing with you again, you'll make him stop. *We'll* make him stop. Right?"

"Right," Hallelujah echoes. "Right." And just like that, she doesn't want to talk about Luke anymore. If she could never talk about him or think about him again, that would be amazing. "Can we change the subject?"

"Sure. Do you want to, um, sit? Up here?"

The open bit of mattress next to him. Jonah smiling, now looking a little shy. His shyness makes her shy. "Okay," she says.

Jonah scoots over, wincing as he moves his right leg. When he's settled, resting back against his pillows, Hallelujah takes hold of the bedrail and climbs up to sit next to him. Her legs are surprisingly shaky, and she's happy to stretch them out next to Jonah's. She pulls her IV pole closer to give the line some slack, then leans into his pillows, too.

Jonah takes her hand again, giving her a look like, *Is this okay?* She nods. "How's Rachel?" he asks.

"She's okay. We talked for a few minutes. She has to stay here for a couple days."

"She was really bad, just before the rangers showed up. She couldn't stop puking, even though nothing much was coming up, and all I could do was sit there and bleed." He pauses. "How was yesterday for you?"

Hallelujah thinks back. Yesterday is a blur, from the bear until the two bikers and beyond. "I just remember walking and walking and feeling like I couldn't walk anymore and still walking," she says. "Thinking about everything. With Luke. And with you and Rachel. And then there was the road, and I knew I could make it. I sang for a while," she adds as an afterthought.

He nods. He gets it. They're both quiet for a few moments, listening to the dripping of their IVs and the beeping of an alarm down the hall and the voices of people at the nurses' station. A car honks in the parking lot outside. There's an announcement over the intercom. All these sounds of civilization, and again Hallelujah misses the birds. The morning birds and the afternoon birds and the night birds, swooping and calling.

"You sang," Jonah says, sounding thoughtful.

"Yeah."

"How'd it go?"

"It was . . . I mean, I was terrible." Hallelujah laughs, shaking her head. "But I guess that wasn't the point. It felt . . . good. It felt right."

He squeezes her hand again. "Think you'll come back to choir? In the fall, maybe?"

She knows he knows how hard it is, what he's asking. But she's happy he asked. "Maybe," she answers.

"For real?"

"Yeah."

"And you and me, we're . . . ?" He doesn't finish the question. He doesn't have to.

"Yeah," Hallelujah repeats. "You and me."

Jonah tilts his head so it meets hers on the pillow. They lie there, side by side, with him under the sheets and her on top of them, holding hands and touching foreheads. Jonah's eyes are closed. Just when she thinks he must have fallen asleep, he murmurs, "Stay."

"Okay."

Outside the window, clouds are rolling in over the mountains. A storm. But beyond the band of rain clouds, the sky is blue again. Bright, shining blue. The storm won't last long. And, Hallelujah realizes, sometimes you need the storm to really appreciate the sun and the blue sky.

Jonah is breathing evenly. She can feel each exhale on the side of her neck.

She smiles, and she stays.

# Acknowledgments

Thanks to my editor, Alexandra Cooper, for loving this book as much as I love it and for pushing me to make every scene, sentence, and word count. Your incisive, encouraging feedback made the revision process a joy and the final product everything I'd hoped it would be. Thanks also to Alyssa Miele for your thoughtful comments, and for helping to usher me through the debut-author whirlwind. And to the rest of the team at HarperCollins—designers Erin Fitzsimmons, Heather Daugherty, Laura DiSiena, and Cara Petrus; production editor Bethany Reis; production managers Allison Brown and Lillian Sun; marketing manager Jenna Lisanti; and publicist Olivia deLeon—thanks so much for all of your hard work!

Thanks to my agent, Alyssa Eisner Henkin, for your enthusiasm and for believing in me and in Hallelujah's story. From our first phone call, I knew my manuscript and I were in excellent hands. I'm so thankful I have you on my team.

To all of my writer friends who've been there during these last few crazy years: you are my community, my people, and I'm lucky to know you. Thanks to Michael Ann Dobbs, Elizabeth Dunn-Ruiz, Benjamin Andrew Moore, Ghenet Myrthil, Jodi Kendall, Gina Carey, Kristi Olson, Cassie Bednall, and Lauren Morrill for reading and critiquing early drafts and for cheering me on. Thanks also to Kim Liggett, Bridget Casey, Bess Cozby, Michelle Schusterman, Rebecca Behrens, and Gabriela Pereira for your friendship, support, and inspiration. Write Night forever! And to everyone else who, by asking how my book was coming along and being excited for me at each milestone, kept me excited and motivated—thank you. You're more important than you know.

A big thank-you to Clay Jordan, the chief ranger of the Great Smoky Mountains National Park, who was kind enough to answer my questions about the logistics of getting lost in the woods and about the GSMNP's search-and-rescue procedures. Special thanks to Kohli and Jimmy Calhoun and their daughter Clara, for Hallelujah's name—the germ of inspiration that became this book.

Some of my earliest forays into creative writing were guided by Aleta Ledendecker at New Horizon Montessori School. In Maryville High School's powerhouse English department, John Kerr, Gail Rhodes, Penny Ferguson, and Cynthia Freeman whipped my writing into shape. At Goucher College, Jonathan David Jackson nurtured my creative writing while urging me to venture outside my comfort zone. And at the New School, Hettie Jones, Tor Seidler, Sarah Weeks, David Levithan, and Honor Moore helped me discover what kind of writer I wanted to become. Thank you all.

I've been a bookworm since the day I learned to read. Thanks to my parents, Laurie and Greg Holmes, for encouraging my bookish tendencies, for backing my writing aspirations wholeheartedly, and for reading everything I write. Mom and Dad, I'm so proud and happy to be able to dedicate this book to you. Thanks to my sister, Mary-Owen, for being a cheerleader, a careful reader, and a sounding board during revisions. Thanks to my brother, Ben, and my sister-in-law, Kate, for supporting me every step of the way. Thanks to my husband's family—Sheila, Jack, Niki, and Ed—for celebrating with me. I've truly hit the family jackpot.

And on that note, to my husband, Justin: Thank you for taking a chance and going on a date with a graduate student who was struggling to write her first novel. Thank you for being by my side through the ups and downs, the queries and submissions and revisions and every other moment in this journey. Thank you for always making me smile. I love you and I couldn't have done this without you.

For a sneak peek at Kathryn Holmes's novel
*How It Feels to Fly*, turn the page.

# one

I FOCUS ON THE MOVEMENT. MY ARMS EXTENDING from my shoulders. My back curving and arcing. My knees bending and straightening. My feet pressing into the floor.

I focus on all that, and for just a moment, I'm able to forget that I'm in a cozy meeting room, not a dance studio. That my ballet slippers are brushing across carpet. That I'm holding the back of a folding chair instead of a barre. That I'm seeing my reflection in a dark window instead of a mirror.

In that window, I'm not much more than a shadow. Ghostly. You can see right through me to the trees outside.

*Even transparent, you're fat. Look at you. You're disgusting. You're—*

I flinch, turning away from the window. I rearrange my face into its usual pleasant mask. I try to let the choreography distract me.

In front of me, Jenna's doing the same series of movements. I watch her extend her leg into a high développé and then lower it, with control, back to the floor. Her legs are lean, her muscles streamlined. Her thin arms move through the port de bras like clockwork. She's a blade slicing the air, petite and precise.

She's a figure skater, but she clearly has ballet training. *Proper* training. Russian, maybe. As we turn to do the other side, I tell her, "You're really good."

"Thanks," Jenna answers coolly, giving me a brisk nod as she settles into fifth position. She doesn't say anything else. Just waits for the music to cue up.

I take my own preparatory position, right hand on my folding chair-barre. Then I unfold my left leg into the air in front of me, pointing my toes as hard as I can. I try to keep my port de bras soft and airy, even as my quad quivers with effort. I carry my leg to the side, then to arabesque. I drop my face toward the floor in a deep penché, my toe pointing straight up to the ceiling.

My muscles feel strong and limber. My form feels perfect. But then I look past my own standing leg at Jenna, behind me.

*She's judging you. Your bubble butt and your thunder thighs and your C cups and the way your stomach pooches out. That's why she didn't say anything back when you complimented her earlier. That's why—*

My knee buckles a little as I pull myself upright. I move from arabesque to a back attitude, lifting onto demi-pointe. I bring my arms to fifth position overhead. I balance, and I breathe, and I smile.

Because that's what I do. I don't let anyone see what's happening inside my head. Not my friends, not my classmates, not my mom. It's a performance that never ends.

Jenna and I move on to battements. I kick my legs up and up and up, punctuating each downbeat in the music with my pointed toe. I try to bring my focus back to the movement. The movement is what matters.

But just as I'm getting into the zone, the door swings open, slams hard against the wall, and bounces back. Zoe, my roommate for the next three weeks, catches it in one hand. "What are you two losers doing?" She walks over to the stereo and switches it off, midcrescendo.

"We're exercising," Jenna says, sounding annoyed. "You might want to try it while you're here. Twenty-one days is a long time without a consistent training regimen."

I ask Zoe, "Do you want to join us?"

Zoe barks out a laugh. "Um, no. *This*"—she rises onto her tiptoes and flutters around, mocking us—"is not exercise. And who says I want to stay in shape while I'm here, anyway?"

"Suit yourself." Jenna slides into a split on the floor, forehead touching her knee.

I give it one more shot. "Seriously," I say, "you're more than welcome to—"

"Whoa, Ballerina Barbie. What part of 'no' do you not understand?" Zoe saunters over to the sofa on the other side of the room and grabs the TV remote. She flips channels, stopping when she comes to a horror film. There's a skinny blond girl in a torn T-shirt and underwear running from a guy with an axe. The camera cuts in close on the girl's tear-streaked face as she screams. Zoe turns the volume up. "This won't mess up your concentration, will it?" she asks, grinning.

I turn around, wanting backup, but Jenna is already standing to leave. "I'll stretch in my room," she says, picking up her folding chair and leaning it against the wall.

"Oh. Um, okay." I'm surprised that she's giving in so easily.

And now I'm torn. I don't want to tick Zoe off—she looks like she could break me in half and would enjoy doing it, never mind the whole we-have-to-share-a-bedroom thing. But I'd planned on getting in at least another hour of strength training and light cardio tonight. It's really important that I stay in shape while I'm here.

*In shape. Ha! No such thing.*

The panic swirls up. It's like there's a tornado brewing in my belly. But I don't let it show on my face.

I say, "Stay, Jenna, please."

Jenna looks at me over her shoulder. "Sam, no offense—you seem nice and all—but I'm not really here to make friends." She pauses. "If you want, we can do barre again tomorrow. Good night." She glides from the room, leaving me standing there.

"Burn," Zoe says from the couch. "And props to her

for pulling out *that* line. Welcome to America's Next Top Neurotic Teenager, the group therapy camp where we are absolutely not here to make friends." She laughs to herself as, on-screen, the axe murderer finally catches up with his victim.

I consider staying to work out alone, with screeching violins and screams as my soundtrack, but the magic is gone. I used to be able to completely lose myself in dance, no matter where I was or what was happening around me. Ballet was my safest space. Then my body changed. I got curvy, and I got self-conscious. I couldn't stop thinking about everyone looking at me—what they were seeing. When the comments started coming—both painfully kind and sweetly cruel—I heard them echo inside my head. Before long, my nasty inner voice had more to say about me, and worse, than anyone else ever could.

*You're fat. You're weak. You're worthless.*

*You might as well——*

I can do my conditioning exercises upstairs, in the thin strip of space between my bed and Zoe's. That'll have to work, despite the storm in my stomach. The only way to kill the panic is to dance through it.

Even that barely helps these days.

But I'm coping. I am.

And Perform at Your Peak, a summer camp/treatment facility for elite teen artists and athletes with anxiety issues, is supposed to give me even more coping mechanisms. That's what the website says. It's what Dr. Debra Lancaster, the director here, talked about earlier this evening, at orientation. When she was telling the six of us campers about all the different types of activities we'll be doing—one-on-one therapy sessions with her, group discussions, simulations of real-life situations we might face—she sounded so confident. She's sure we'll get something positive out of this experience.

I want to believe her. It's just so hard to ignore the voice in my head.

*Everything about you is wrong. Nothing can make it better. Nothing except—*

I look at Zoe, who's lounging on the sofa with her feet propped up on the wooden coffee table. She's drumming on her thigh with the remote, eyes narrowed at the screen. When a guy jumps out from behind a shed and tackles the axe murderer to the ground, only to get immediately axe murdered, she throws her arms in the air and cheers. "Way to die, idiot!"

"So, um, see you upstairs?" My voice comes out more like a squawk than I want it to.

Zoe doesn't even glance my way. "You're still here?"

The other thing Dr. Lancaster kept mentioning at orientation earlier was group cohesion. She wants us to bond with one another, so we feel comfortable discussing our feelings. She made us do all these getting-to-know-you exercises. We had to toss a beanbag around the circle, shouting a random fact about ourselves each time we caught it. And we played a version of Simon Says where we took turns giving instructions, going faster and faster. It might've all been okay—if we were anywhere else. And clearly, the bonding didn't take. Not with sarcastic Zoe, and not with frosty Jenna, and not with the other three campers—Katie, Dominic, and Omar—who vanished to their rooms the moment we were released.

Not that I blame them. The games felt so forced. Like a distraction from why we're really here, or a trick to get us to let down our guard. A bait and switch. That doesn't mean it wouldn't be nice to have someone to talk to for the next three weeks.

I walk out into the hallway. It's empty. I'm alone.

I let my face relax. My cheeks are sore from smiling. I massage them with my fingers. I dance more than twenty hours a week, but lately it's been the muscles in my face that hurt the most.

I pass the stairs to the second floor and head for the kitchen. I'm thirsty. I'll need to stay hydrated if I'm going to keep exercising. Plus, filling my stomach with water will distract me from the hunger that's creeping in. I don't eat after eight p.m., as a rule, so water will have to do until morning.

When I enter the kitchen, the fridge door is open. I can see a guy's legs sticking out underneath. At the sound of my footsteps on the tile, the door moves. A head pokes around it. It's the guy counselor—I mean "peer adviser." Andrew. He and our other peer adviser, Yasmin, are former campers at Perform at Your Peak. Success stories, according to Dr.

Lancaster, who looked like a proud mom when she introduced them earlier.

"Hey there," Andrew says.

*Suck that gut in. Now!*

"Hi," I say, my smile snapping into place as I adjust my posture.

"You hungry?" Andrew steps away from the fridge, letting the door swing closed. He's holding a loaf of bread, a pack of cold cuts, a hunk of cheese, a tomato, a jar of pickles, and mustard and mayo. All crooked in one arm.

"No, thanks. I just wanted a glass of water." At the sight of all that food, my stomach rumbles. I can't look at it, not for too long, so I look at him instead. He's cute, in a wholesome way. Like he should be on a farm milking cows or something. He has warm brown eyes. A nice smile.

He dumps his bounty on the counter, grabbing the pickle jar before it rolls off the edge. "Well, the first thing you need to know about me is I'm always hungry. I think it's a football-player thing."

"I think it's a guy thing," I say, moving past him to get a glass from the cabinet. "My boyf—my ex," I correct myself quickly. "He basically never stopped eating." I keep my voice light. Like thinking about Marcus, what he said to me a few days ago, doesn't hurt a bit.

Andrew laughs. "As a guy *and* a former football player, I eat twice as much as anyone else I know."

I barely register that he said *former* football player—if that's true, how can he be a Perform at Your Peak success story?——before my nasty inner voice kicks in:

*Imagine if you ate twice as much as anyone you know.*

*You look bad enough as it is——*

I fill my glass with tap water and sit on one of the stools at the kitchen island.

"So, Sam-short-for-Samantha," Andrew says, quoting my stammered-out intro from orientation. He takes two slices of bread and waves them at me. "Prepare yourself. You're about to see something pretty special."

I raise my eyebrows and lean forward, resting my elbows on the gray marble countertop. "Oh yeah?" I make eye contact, smile, and then look down. Which is when I see how slouching like this is making my stomach stick out.

*Ugh. You're disgusting——*

Slowly, casually, I lean back and cross my arms in front of my midsection.

Better. I don't think he saw.

Andrew assembles his sandwich, stacking ingredients like he's building a Jenga tower. Pull out the wrong pickle and the whole thing falls down. When the sandwich is done, it looks too big to possibly bite. But he lifts it up, grins at me, opens his mouth wide, and shoves what looks like a third of it inside.

"Mmm." He chews and swallows. "It's good. Sure you don't want one?" He makes the cold cuts and bread do a little shimmy dance on the countertop.

"I'm okay. But thanks."

"How are you settling in?" he asks, before taking another

giant bite. Chew, swallow. "Orientation is always kind of awkward. Icebreakers are the worst." He gives me a knowing smile. "But do you feel like you'll get along with everyone?"

I don't know whether I should tell him about "I'm not here to make friends" Jenna or "what are you losers doing" Zoe. As a peer adviser, he's basically a camp counselor—not a trained therapist, but not one of the campers, either. I don't know whose side he's on. "Dr. Lancaster seems nice," I finally say. It seems like a safe statement.

"Dr. Lancaster's great. She really helped me when I was a camper here." Andrew finishes his sandwich and brushes the crumbs from his hands. "I think you're going to get a lot out of this program."

*Yeah, right*, my inner voice cuts in. *Like anything will make a difference for you at this point. Unless Perform at Your Peak is a front for Dr. Frankenstein's lab and you're about to get a total body transplant, you're out of luck.*

"I hope so," I answer, raising my voice so it drowns out the noise in my head. "I have a ballet intensive to go to when this is done. I'm really looking forward to it."

*As long as they don't see how much weight you've put on since the audition and send you packing.*

"That's great," Andrew says. "When does it start?"

"It actually overlaps with this place by a week. But my mom—she used to be a ballerina, before I was born—she and my teacher got permission for me to start the intensive a week late."

It's the only reason I agreed to come here. My best

friend, Bianca, got into four ballet intensives this summer, including her top choice. I was accepted to one program. I only have one shot.

"Since I can't do the whole program, they bumped me to the wait list, but my mom's not worried. Spots always open up. People pick other schools, or get injured. I'm definitely going." And I'm definitely babbling. Andrew's been looking at me long enough that it's making me uncomfortable. I don't really like it when people look at me. Not while I'm dancing, not while I'm sitting still—not ever.

"Well, I'm glad they could make the schedule work for you." He turns to put his plate in the sink, and I'm able to exhale.

"I guess. But I'd rather be dancing than . . ."

He finishes my sentence when I can't. "Going to therapy camp? I'm not surprised. But if you can't become a professional dancer—"

I'm on edge again immediately. "What do you mean, if I can't?"

"What you learn here should help you in any career—"

"I don't *want* any career. I want to dance. That's all I want." The panic is back. Rising from my swirling stomach, wrapping itself around my lungs, making it hard to breathe. I try to steady my voice. "This place is supposed to help me do that, right?"

My mask is slipping. Any second now, Andrew is going to see *me*. The real me. Messed up and broken and flailing. I can't let him.

# READ MORE STORIES OF COURAGE, FAITH, AND FINDING YOURSELF FROM KATHRYN HOLMES

# JOIN THE

## Epic Reads
### COMMUNITY

**THE ULTIMATE YA DESTINATION**

◀ **DISCOVER** ▶
your next favorite read

◀ **MEET** ▶
new authors to love

◀ **WIN** ▶
free books

◀ **SHARE** ▶
infographics, playlists, quizzes, and more

◀ **WATCH** ▶
the latest videos

◀ **TUNE IN** ▶
to Tea Time with Team Epic Reads

   Find us at www.epicreads.com
and @epicreads